The wind [across th]e [...]
sound re[...]
she was a[...].

She combed the stairs, but found nothing. No sign of the ghost of the child she'd thought she'd seen. The noise must have been the wind blowing debris on the roof.

Still shaken, she pushed back the heavy drape and stared into the darkness, searching for signs that someone was nearby. A light burned from the big stone house at the top of the hill.

Rex Falcon.

Her body grew hot just thinking about his dark eyes.

He was big. Strong. A towering specimen of a man with a muscular body that emanated strength and power. The kind of man who could protect a woman.

The kind who could hurt her with those big hands.

She didn't intend to get involved with him. Men were trouble.

Especially one as dangerous looking as Rex Falcon.

Available in October 2005 from Silhouette Intrigue

The Cowgirl in Question
By bJ Daniels
(McCalls' Montana 1/5)

Not-So-Secret Baby
by Jo Leigh
(Top Secret Babies)

Protector S.O.S
by Susan Kearney
(Heroes, Inc.)

The Man from Falcon Ridge
by Rita Herron
(Eclipse)

The Man from Falcon Ridge

RITA HERRON

SILHOUETTE®

INTRIGUE™

First published in Great Britain 2005
Silhouette Books, Eton House, 18-24 Paradise Road,
Richmond, Surrey TW9 1SR

© Rita B. Herron 2004

ISBN 0 373 22810 4

46-1005

Printed and bound in Spain
by Litografía Rosés S.A., Barcelona

RITA HERRON

Award-winning author Rita Herron wrote her first book when she was twelve, but didn't think real people grew up to be writers. Now she writes so she doesn't have to get a real job. A former nursery teacher and workshop leader, she traded her storytelling for kids for romance, and writes romantic comedies and romantic suspense. She lives in Georgia with her own romance hero and three kids. She loves to hear from readers, so please write to her at PO Box 921225, Norcross, GA 30092-1225, USA, or visit her website at www.ritaherron.com

CAST OF CHARACTERS

Hailey Hitchcock—A woman running from a past she doesn't remember into a future just as terrifying as the nightmares that plague her.

Rex Falcon—A man determined to find the real killer behind the Hatchet Murders.

Randolph Falcon—Rex's father. He's spent the past twenty years of his life in jail for killing the Lyle family—but is he really guilty?

Deke and Brack Falcon—Rex's brothers are determined to free their father from prison.

Thad Jordan—A man obsessed with Hailey. Will he kill to keep her his?

Lawrence Lyle—The man and his family were brutally murdered twenty years ago. Did he carry the secrets of his family's murder to his grave?

Sheriff Andy Cohen—He arrested Rex's father for murder, but did he have ulterior motives?

Bentley McDaver—The prosecutor put Rex's father in jail for life. Did he have reason to rush the trial?

Carl Pursley—Rex's father's defence attorney. Did he help frame him for the murder?

Lindy Lou Lyle—She died in the Hatchet Murders, but now her ghost is haunting Hailey.

Ava Riderton—She was Lyle's secretary. Does she know more than she's telling?

To Kim Nadelson:
Thanks for all your enthusiasm and
support with my first gothic!

Prologue

Ten-year-old Rex Falcon stared in horror at the yellow crime-scene tape wrapped around the Lyle house. It was dark now, the night sounds adding to the eeriness. When he'd gotten here, he'd peeked inside the window and seen the gory murders. Then the sheriff and his deputies had pushed him and his brothers and mother into the yard with the other neighbors and refused to let them talk to Rex's father.

Just because his daddy had found the bodies, they were treating him as if he'd killed the people inside.

His mother hugged the boys close to her. "You boys go on home. You shouldn't be seeing all this."

"I'm not going anywhere till they let Daddy go," Rex said, hands fisted.

"Me neither," his middle brother Deke said.

His youngest brother Brack jutted up his chin, his eyes wide. "I'm staying, too."

An image of the dead people flashed into Rex's head. There was so much blood. It looked like a river on the kitchen floor. The mother lay in it. The boy cuddled beside her. The father, too. It covered his hands and face, and his head….

"Little girl's dead, too," a neighbor murmured behind him. "Found her blood near the river."

"Randolph Falcon." Sheriff Cohen jerked Rex's daddy to a standing position and handcuffed him. "You're under arrest for the murders of the Lyle family."

"No!" His mother collapsed into a neighbor's arms, sobbing.

His father's hawklike eyes pierced Rex as the sheriff yanked him down the steps toward his squad car. "Take care of your mama and brothers for me, son."

Rex shook his head in denial. His father's words had sounded so odd, as if he wasn't coming back. But they couldn't take his father away and lock him up.

He was innocent.

"Daddy!" His brothers chased after the sheriff, and Rex ran after them.

A bald eagle that had been perched on top of the porch swooped down and soared toward the car, its talons bared. Rex's father nodded toward the bird. The animal knew what it was like to be caged. He was a bird of prey. He needed freedom.

Just like the Falcon men.

The blue light flicked on, the siren screeched and a cloud of dust rose behind the police car. Rex gathered his brothers and mother and walked them home, but it was dark inside and cold and so quiet the house echoed like a tomb. It was as if his father had just died.

Fear and anger and sadness knotted Rex's throat. He wanted to do something to get his daddy out of jail. He wanted to make his mother stop crying. And his brothers…they were heartbroken.

But he felt so helpless. He was only ten. A stupid ten-year-old boy. What could he do? He didn't know anything about lawyers or courts or anything else.

Tears pushed against his eyelids, but he blinked them back. Big boys didn't cry.

But he had to be alone and think, so he fled into the mountains, silently venting his pain in the midst of the snow-laden pines.

Chapter One

Twenty years later

"You can never escape me, Hailey."

Hailey Hitchcock inhaled to stifle a cry as Thad Jordan's hands tightened around her jaw. She desperately wanted to scream, but it was useless. No one would hear.

An icy breeze swirled around her, sending her skirt flapping about her legs. Thad had been so angry with her on the way home from the Christmas dinner party that he'd pulled over on this deserted stretch of highway outside Denver, then half dragged, half carried her down a path in the woods. "It's freezing out here, Thad, please take me home."

"You're bound to me forever," he murmured.

A shudder rippled through her. His voice was as brittle as the winter wind. Why hadn't she seen through his charismatic act to the devil that lay beneath? How could she have been such a bad judge of character?

Because he was an attorney. A well-respected, handsome man she'd thought she could trust. And he'd been so charming at first.

Until she'd told him she didn't want to see him anymore, that she'd quit her job, bought a house and was moving. Then he'd revealed his hidden side.

He lowered his mouth to kiss her, the stench of bourbon on his breath. His other hand slid clumsily to her blouse, and he jerked a button loose.

Cold air assaulted her breasts. Her stomach convulsed.

"Please, Thad, stop. Go home. Sleep it off."

"No. Nobody humiliates Thad Jordan." His eyes darkened with an evil flare she'd never seen before. He looked menacing. Brutal. As if he meant to punish.

Then his fingers closed around the ruby necklace he'd given her, the cold stone dangling against her bare skin. "You accepted my gift, now accept that we're together."

"You can have the necklace back," Hailey said, wishing she'd never let him put it on her in the first place. But he had insisted.

His fingers slid to her neck, and she swallowed, her heart racing. What was he going to do? Choke her? "Please, Thad," Hailey whispered. "Take the necklace, then drive me home."

His jaw snapped tight, then he backed her up against the tree. "I'll never let you leave me, Hailey. You're mine forever."

Fear spiked her adrenaline, and she swung her knee into his groin. He released her with a bellow. "You'll pay for that."

Panic surged through her. She ran, jumping over the rotting tree stumps and bramble. He yelled and ran after her. She clawed her way through the forest, her breathing erratic. Leaves crunched behind her. He was chasing her. Closing the distance.

Briars stabbed her thighs, and she tripped over a tree stump. Her hands hit the dirt, and she struggled to regain her balance. Suddenly he was there. He latched on to her hair and jerked her so hard her neck nearly snapped. Dead brush and pine needles pricked her knees. She swept her hands blindly across the ground for a weapon. Just as he lowered his head, she clutched a branch, then jabbed it upward with all her might. He howled in pain, then fell backward cursing. Blood gushed from his cheek and eye.

Shaking, she jumped up and ran through the forest opening. He screeched her name like a wild animal, once again on her trail. She spotted the car and dashed toward it.

Thank God he'd left the keys inside.

She flung herself into the driver's side, hit the locks and turned the key. The ignition chugged, then died. He burst through the opening in a thunderous roar, one hand covering his bloody eye, the other fist flailing. "Stop it, Hailey. Come back here!"

She cried out and patted the gas. The car had to start. She couldn't be trapped here with that monster.

He closed the distance, then banged on the door. "Open the door, Hailey. Dammit, open it!"

His eyes wild with rage, he threw himself on the front window. The car rocked sideways.

His bloody hand streaked the glass as she twisted the key again. She pressed the gas one more time. The car roared to life. Panting, she accelerated, and spun forward. The jolt sent him sailing into the air. She screamed, then steered the opposite way and sped off. She couldn't look back now. And she couldn't stop.

If he caught her, he'd kill her…

HIS FATHER WAS NOT A KILLER. He was *innocent*.

On the long ride home from the Colorado state prison, Rex Falcon's stomach churned with the certainty that his dad had spent the last twenty years in jail for a crime he hadn't committed. Shame and sorrow mingled with anger. All his life, Rex had questioned his father's innocence.

And now with new criminology techniques and the airing of a recent show on *The Innocents,* more cold cases were being reopened and solved. With his father's upcoming parole hearing and Rex and his brothers experience in their private investigative business, they'd reviewed the police reports and trial transcripts and found discrepancies that cast doubt on the original case.

The Hatchet Murderer.

The press had given his dad the name because of the vicious slayings of the Lyle family. That was the reason his mother had dragged him and his two brothers to Arizona to live. But now Rex had returned to their childhood home at Falcon Ridge to learn the truth.

Rex shifted his SUV into Park beneath the towering pines next to his family's stone manor, got out and went to the backyard, to the wildlife sanctuary for the hawks he and his brother rescued and trained for flight. A kestrel sat on its perch, its wings spread in an arc. Although it was dark, and snowflakes drifted down to pelt him in the face, Rex homed in on the animal's watchful movements. He and his brothers had inherited an affinity for the creatures of the wild from their father. And just as the birds had special sensory skills to stalk and track their prey, so did Rex and Deke and Brack.

At one time, Rex had wondered if his father had given in to that primitive need to prey on the weak and had killed the Lyles. Now he knew differently, and was ashamed he'd ever doubted him.

He'd also wondered if he'd inherited that dangerous, uncontrollable side.

He glanced down the hill at the house where their father had supposedly butchered the family. The Hatchet House had been closed up since the murder. The fading, chipped paint and latticework of the Victorian structure testified to its disrepair. The angles and attic window seemed macabre in the murky light. It was tucked on the side of a cliff, isolated but closer to the main road and town than Falcon Ridge, but the way it jutted out over the mountain made it look as if it might slide into the canyon any second. The location, coupled with its gruesome history and the fact that locals claimed it was haunted had kept buyers away. He'd already conducted a preliminary sweep of the downstairs. Tomorrow he'd search every inch of it and the grounds for evidence the police might have missed in their hasty, slipshod investigation.

And he'd run off anyone who got in his way.

HAILEY HAD BEEN DRIVING for hours, battling the snowstorm. Putting the miles between her and Thad. Between her and her past.

A mountain road twisted to the side, and she veered onto it. Darkness bathed the graveled road, shadows from the trees flickering like fingers reaching for her, crystals of frozen ice pelting her windshield. For a brief second when she'd left Thad, she'd considered going to the police. But he had too many friends in the police department, too many important people to protect him. Just like her fifth foster father had. She'd traveled that rocky road before and managed to survive.

Her foster mother hadn't been so lucky.

So, she'd left Thad's car at his house, taken her own and left for good. Just to be on the safe side in case he'd followed, she'd traded her Civic for a VW. She'd also traded her golden hair for a brownish-red and had layered it into a shoulder-length bob.

Thank goodness she'd already bought a place in the mountains, so she wasn't running without a plan.

The majestic view of aging trees, their boughs heavy with icicles, and wildlife roaming free stirred her awe. She'd always wanted to come to this area, had been saving for the right place for months. Here she'd find a sanctuary from the dark shadows that had dogged her all her life.

Here, she would have a new beginning. A future.

She made another turn, then spotted the house in her headlights. The Victorian mansion sat at the top of a cliff overlooking the densely populated woods beyond. She hit the brakes. The For Sale sign dangled precariously over the edge of the cliff as if it had been there a long time and had barely managed to withstand the last storm.

Her gaze swung to the house. Just like in the pictures the real estate agent had shown her, it was weathered-looking and had fallen into disrepair. Boards on the front porch needed replacing, the shutters were loose and the paint peeling. But the price was right, and fixing it up would be cathartic.

Although it was slightly isolated, it was also near enough the supposedly haunted mining town of Tin City to entice visitors. She envisioned her Internet antiques business being housed on the bottom floor, her private quarters on the top. And if she researched the house's history, the tale of its ghosts would draw customers to her showroom. She'd always been fascinated with history, especially local legends of small towns. Her fascination with storytelling coupled with her degree in history had been an asset when she'd worked at the auction house.

Thad had thought her interests spooky, even boring. But somehow learning about others' past seemed to help compensate for the fact that she'd forgotten so much of her own.

The hair on the back of her neck prickled as she climbed from the car. Wind howled through the snow-tipped treetops, ruffling the bare branches. A whisper of danger coasted on its tail.

She glanced back down the mountain road. Had Thad found her?

No, she was safe.

Her destiny awaited her. Her future. She felt it in her bones.

Renewed determination filling her, she walked up to the front porch, ready to start over. Towering pines cast spiny shadows around the property like bony fingers hovering over the roof. Spiderwebs and dirt clung to the yellowed wood, and the dark window of the attic seemed sinister in the gray light. She could almost see the ghost of a child's face peering out through the blackness, her cry of loneliness echoing through the eaves. The house had spoken to her.

And she was unable to escape the lure of its call.

SOMEONE WAS AT the Hatchet House.

Rex couldn't wait until the next day. He barreled down the curvy mountain road, gravel and ice spewing as he slowed to a stop. A VW sat in the clearing, and a woman stood in front of the picture window, staring up at the sagging latticework. She jerked around at the sound of his Jeep, her startled expression reminding him of a baby eagle cornered in the forest by a hunter.

He killed the engine and climbed out, his pulse accelerating. Even though night had fallen and darkness engulfed her features, he could tell she was small with choppy auburn hair that almost looked unnatural. A baggy denim shirt and jeans covered her frame, revealing nothing about the curves he sensed lay beneath. He zeroed in on her eyes, though. He'd never seen any that color. His body reacted involuntarily, heat spread through his limbs and his sex hardened. Stunning was the only word to describe her.

No, add cold and scared to stunning.

"Who are you?" She hunched deeper inside her coat, backing toward the porch awning as if it might offer safety. But the lights were out and shadows closed around her, fresh snow crystals clinging to her hair.

"Rex Falcon. I live on top of the mountain at Falcon Ridge." He dragged his eyes from hers and skimmed down her face. Primal instincts overtook him. Even in the shadows, the rose-petal color of her lips made his mouth water for a taste.

But the trembling of her lower lip warned him that his gut instinct had been right.

She was running from something.

No other woman in her right mind would have traveled up this mountain alone. Not at night in this storm when the roads became almost impassable. Not to look at the Hatchet House. That is, unless she was some kind of reporter. Or maybe one of those nuts who chased ghosts and tried to prove they were real.

"What's your name?" he asked.

"Hailey Hitchcock."

"What are you doing here?"

"Studying the house." She squared her shoulders in a show of bravado, but the purple bruise on her chin negated the effect.

Their gazes locked. A tension-filled moment passed between them, fraught with questions and an undeniable awareness of their isolation. His body began to throb, the call of the wild inside him drawing him to her.

But that could only mean trouble. And he would not give in to those instincts.

Maybe he could scare her off. "You must be a tourist, stopping by to gawk at the house because of all the rumors."

Her eyebrows drew together. "You mean about the ghosts?"

"Yes, and the murders." His voice rumbled out hard. Cold. "They say the house is haunted."

She swallowed, the pale skin of her neck glowing in the twilight. "I know, the real estate agent told me about the ghosts when I bought the place."

His pulse kicked up with surprise. "A family was killed here twenty years ago. They say their spirits are waiting around for revenge. That doesn't bother you?"

"I'm not afraid of ghosts."

Just of real men. He saw it in her eyes and the hands-off look she shot him.

"You seem to know a lot about this house," she said. "Tell me more."

Her low voice sounded sultry beneath the whistle of the wind. Slightly shaken, he struggled for a reply, not ready to share the truth about his own family's involvement in the murders. If she stayed, she'd find out soon enough.

But her presence would complicate everything. How could he search the property with her inside?

"What are you planning to do with the house?" he asked, ignoring her comment.

She pulled the coat tighter around her throat, her breath a puff of white in front of her. "Live here. And I'm starting an antiques business."

He frowned. "Why antiques?"

"I like the stories behind them," she said. "The antiques once belonged to people, they were important to them at one time."

Did she belong to anyone? A man maybe? How about a family? It was none of his business, he reminded himself. "This house isn't in good enough shape to live in, much less house a business."

"I'm going to renovate it."

Dammit. She'd tear up the inside, get rid of things, any evidence that might still be around. "If you're looking for someone to do repairs, my brother and I happen to be in the business." At least they were now.

Her mouth parted in surprise, but her eyes flashed with wariness. Now he knew why they mesmerized him. They were the deepest reddish-brown he'd ever seen, like the earthy tones of a red-tailed hawk.

Her sweet scent invaded his nostrils, too, stirring urges that warred with his better sense. But old ghosts echoed around the house, reviving memories of the blood bath that had taken place within the rotting walls.

She studied him for another long moment, then nodded. "Thanks, although I'm not sure how much I can pay."

"No problem." He shrugged, blinking away fresh snowflakes. "We live simple lives in the mountains, our materialistic needs are few." But his need for the truth and revenge was strong.

She offered a tentative smile that twisted his gut.

He steeled himself against her beauty. He was interested in this place for one reason and one reason only. For the answers it offered about his father.

And he'd be damned if he'd let Hailey Hitchcock interfere with his plans.

HUNCHING HIS STOOPED shoulders inside his cloak, he watched from the shadows of the forest as the frail-looking woman opened the door and went inside the house. Who was she? And why had she bought a run-down house that was supposedly haunted?

She obviously didn't know its history.

A chuckle reverberated in his chest as he pictured her finding out.

The house had once been beautiful, painted blue with white shutters, the outside postcard perfect. The ultimate dream for the happy couple who'd moved inside. Laughter and dreams had abounded within the walls, the patter of small feet and children's voices filling the empty rooms with life and joy.

Then everything had changed.

Dreams had been shattered. Lives had been destroyed. The world had crumbled down just as the house looked as if it might crumble now.

The pain of the woman's cries still echoed in his head, the sadness in her eyes, the whisper of death as she'd clawed her way toward the boy....

It had been all her fault.

And now this...this other woman had come.

He had to get rid of her.

The Hatchet House held secrets. Secrets that would ruin his life if exposed. Secrets that would stay behind closed doors.

Secrets that he would kill to keep hidden...

Chapter Two

A whisper of unease tickled Hailey's spine, mingling with the icy cold temperature, as she entered the house. Rex Falcon's words about the ghosts echoed in her mind.

But ghosts weren't real. No, danger came from real, live men who wanted to control the women they were involved with. Not ones who were buried and long gone. Besides, the real estate agent assured her the killer was serving a life sentence in prison.

It was time to stop running and build her own life. She'd held her ground with Rex Falcon, refusing to let his gruff, mysterious demeanor intimidate her. His dark, sexy eyes had trapped her, though, and a spark of awareness had passed between them. A sexual spark that she had no intention of exploring.

The low hum of the snowstorm outside echoed through the house, reminding her she was alone. Rex Falcon's predatory expression flashed back. He hadn't wanted her here. She'd sensed that was the reason he'd mentioned the ghosts.

But she refused to let anything chase her away.

And she was not here to get entangled with a man.

The wood floor creaked as she closed the front door and fumbled for the light switch. But the power company had yet to turn on the electricity. The realtor claimed the furniture had been left in place. Maybe there were some candles around, also.

The stale smell of a house having been closed up filled the chilly air as she moved into the parlor. Twilight settled over the interior, painting the sheet-draped furniture with gray, but on the mantel she spotted a silver candelabra. She hurried over, blew the top layer of dust away, then found a pack of matches on the hearth of the brick fireplace. The pack was so old it took three times before she finally lit the slender tapered candlesticks, but she was grateful for the soft glow.

Then she studied the room. Heavy velvety drapes covered the windows and hung to the floor, obliterating the outside, and creating an ominous, claustrophobic feeling. Hailey shivered, her uneasiness mounting. But those curtains shielded her from the outside and any strangers who might be roaming in the woods. And they were thick enough to help ward off the cold, as well.

She'd replace the windows with Thermopane ones, trade the drapes for blinds so the natural light could spill in during the daytime, and she could shut them at night.

The walls were dingy and needed paint, too, and dust motes swirled in the halo of candlelight. Cobwebs clung to the ceiling and a spider retreated into a corner to spin its web. Clutching the candelabra in her hand, she decided to check out the rest of the house.

Her footsteps echoed in the empty rooms as she walked through the hallway to the kitchen. The counters and woodwork were faded and chipped, but the old-fashioned oven and stove supposedly still worked. The refrigerator was an ancient model with no ice maker, but was functional, and there was no dishwasher. Dust covered the dingy beige countertops, and she spotted droppings near the bottom of the wood cupboard door that had probably come from mice. A set of old-fashioned café curtains in faded orange hung over the bay window, but she nudged them aside to look out at a majestic view of the Colorado mountains. The valley below would be green in summer, but now brown dotted the trees, along with an increasing layer of snow.

She imagined the white-topped mountain peaks at sunset, and a smile tugged at her lips.

But the wind howled outside, the thin panes of glass crackling with the force. The floor was darker near the mudroom, too. She stepped closer to examine the deep brown of the planks, but a sense of horror immobilized her.

Was the dark area the bloodstain from the family who'd died inside the room twenty years ago?

TWENTY YEARS SINCE anyone had lived in the Hatchet House. And now this woman…

Rex couldn't shake his anxiety over her appearance. Hailey Hitchcock was beautiful. But she was in trouble. Running from something. Probably scared of her own shadow although she'd tried to appear unfazed by his appearance.

So why had she bought a supposedly haunted old house in the middle of nowhere in the dead of winter?

Because she didn't want to be found. But wasn't she afraid to live alone in a house where a brutal crime had occurred? And who was she running from? Her husband? A lover?

Or could she be in trouble with the law?

His father's haggard face materialized. Years ago, he'd been tall in stature, a mountain of a man with an animalistic nature and skin bronzed from the sun and outdoor work. Now, he was pale and drawn, the lack of ample light and time in his natural environment killing him. Just as it would kill Rex and his brothers to be locked away, deprived of the very essence of their being.

And his mother...she had suffered so much over the years. She'd loved their father unconditionally, had stood beside him at the trial, had endured the tauntings of the neighbors. Even after his father's conviction, she'd tried to hold her head up in the town, but some people were cruel. So, she'd finally taken her boys to Arizona, far away from the hateful gossip and condemning eyes.

Just returning to Falcon Ridge, Rex felt those damning eyes as if the past twenty years hadn't passed, as if he was that same child who'd been ostracized as a killer's child.

Telling himself Hailey Hitchcock was not his concern, that his job here was to find the man who'd framed his father, he strode through the ten-foot-tall stone walls that shaped his homestead on Falcon Ridge. The icy, cavernous rooms echoed with age, like a fortress that had stood the test of time against the bitter Colorado elements.

Although his mother had hated the monastery-like house and stone walls, the fact that they'd been virtually cut off from civilization during the long winter months, the house resurrected happy memories of his childhood. Of running through the mammoth structure, hiding in the labyrinth of rooms in the basement. Hiking with his dad into the woods to watch the birds of prey.

He went to his basement office, the space he had set up for his P.I. business, booted up his computer and pulled up the old case files on his father's arrest. The Lyles' son, eight-year-old Steven, had been the apple of his father's eye. Mrs. Lyle had become a recluse, though, and kept the little girl, who was supposedly autistic, at home. According to the locals, Lyle, an attorney, had been charismatic, covering for his wife with excuses.

Rex's father had been the caretaker of the grounds. He'd claimed Mrs. Lyle was afraid of her husband, that he was abusing his wife and daughter. But no one else could corroborate his story. And Rex's father's long trek alone into the woods that day had robbed him of an alibi.

Rex skimmed further, trying to figure out the motive they'd attached to his father's alleged crimes. If he'd had an affair with Mrs. Lyle, why murder her and the children? Why not kill the abusive husband?

Frustrated, he rammed a hand through his hair. In fact, they'd never found the hatchet itself or any bloody clothes or fingerprints. Were they somewhere in the house or on the grounds?

He stood and paced, thinking about Hailey Hitchcock in that house alone. She hadn't brought much with her, just a suitcase or two he'd seen in the back seat and whatever had fit in her trunk. Was she having her other things shipped, or did her lack of belongings suggest she'd left in a hurry?

He pictured those reddish-brown eyes and his body hardened, a surge of lust burning through him.

Was she sleeping in that house tonight? Thinking of the people who'd lived there before her?

SHE WAS LOCKED IN A ROOM.

Alone. Frightened. Only a child.

She curled within the darkness, listening for footsteps, but the house was silent. The air felt heavy around her. Sickening. Stale. Deathly quiet.

Was he coming back for her?

She opened one eye and scanned the interior of her

prison, the whisper of a breath cascading through the dust-filled room.

"I'll be back for you," he'd said.

She shivered. She wanted out. But she didn't want him to come. No, not him. He scared her so bad she'd wet her pants once. And that had made him madder.

A sob welled in her throat, and she rubbed her arms, fighting panic. Then footsteps pounded up the steps. The shuffling sounded familiar. It was him.

One. Two. Three. Four. He was getting closer.

A scream locked in her throat. The shadow below the doorway moved, blocking the tiny sliver of light she'd latched on to.

Her safety net. It was gone.

Then the doorknob rattled, and he opened the door. She shrank back against the closet door as he stalked toward her…

Hailey jerked awake, sweat-soaked from her nightmare. Her breathing erratic, she searched the darkness for intruders, trying to orient herself in the predawn light. Where was she?

She had been dreaming, hadn't she? Or had she been remembering one of her foster homes?

The floor creaked in the old house. Was that a footstep?

She hugged the sheets, listening carefully. Another squeak. It was coming from the attic. Chipmunks or mice maybe?

Struggling for calm, she pulled on a robe, rose and peeked into the hall. Shadows claimed the corners, then something moved at the opposite end. A shadow. Almost ghostlike, it floated into one of the extra bedrooms, the ones where the children had slept.

Her throat muscles worked to swallow. She had to have imagined it.

But another creaking sound broke the quiet. A footstep maybe. The distinct sensation of air moving around her caused her to pause, the scent of lilacs drifting nearer. She wasn't alone, the smell, the sound of someone walking—this time it was real.

As USUAL, REX WOKE with the dawn. He slid on the protective gloves he used to work with the hawks, lifted the cloth from the cage and looked inside. Sutter, he called him, a ferruginous hawk who'd been hit by a pellet gun, stared up at him with caution. After the pellets had been removed the bird needed rest, but soon he'd be able to hunt again. A few quiet moments passed as they assessed one another. Rex felt the connection, the bond of trust forming between himself and the animal.

Sutter's wings fluttered slightly, revealing his dark brown underbelly, and the whitish comma at the wrist, a good sign. Rex reassured the hawk that he was a friend, then eased open the cage and left him some food. The bird wasn't ready to come out just yet, maybe the next day.

Finally, he went inside and gathered his work tools. He'd start at the Hatchet House this morning. His suspicions over the young woman who'd bought the place rose again, so he'd run a background check on her. The more information he had, the better equipped he'd be to handle her.

His phone jangled. "Falcon here."

"Are you settled in?" Brack asked.

"Pretty much. I've got the computer system up and running, and installed a fireproof safe for backup files. The security system was a bitch, but it's in, too." He paused. "How's Mom?"

"She's fine, just worried about you. She's afraid reopening Dad's case might be dangerous."

It probably would be. He drummed his fingers on the desk. "Remind her that her boys are grown now."

"Yeah, like that'll pacify her." Brack barked a laugh. "Be careful, Rex."

Rex sighed. "Listen, there's a slight complication. This woman named Hailey Hitchcock moved into the Hatchet House." Rex explained his offer to work for her. "I pulled up some information on her. She was living in Denver, where she worked at an antiques auction house. Apparently there's a missing person's report out on her. It was filed by a local attorney."

He couldn't stop wondering why exactly the man had been looking for her. Had the two been involved or was their relationship work related?

"You want me to check into it?"

"Yeah, it seems too damn coincidental that she showed up right after I moved back."

"You think someone might have hired her to come there?"

"I don't know. But I don't like her being in that house."

It was too dangerous for one thing. Not that he cared about the woman…

Brack promised to investigate Hailey, and Rex hung up, his thoughts jumbled. If she was in trouble, he needed to know exactly what kind.

THE WIND HURLED a branch against the window, the scraping sound reminding Hailey that she was alone. But she was in Colorado, inside her new house on top of the mountain. No one could find her here. She was safe. Starting over.

Putting the past behind her.

Thankfully, the sound of footsteps had died. She combed the upstairs, but found nothing. No sign of the ghost of the child she thought she'd seen. The noise must have been the wind blowing debris on the roof.

Still shaken, though, she pushed back the heavy

drapes and stared into the darkness, searching for signs that someone had been nearby. A light snow had fallen overnight, with promises of more to come. If she managed any renovations to the house, it needed to be within the next few weeks before winter seized the land and immobilized everything. A light burned from the big stone house at the top of the hill.

Rex Falcon.

Her body grew hot just thinking about his dark eyes.

He was big. Strong. A towering specimen of a male with a muscular body that emanated strength and power. The kind of man who could protect a woman.

The kind who could hurt her with those big hands.

She didn't intend to get involved with him. Men were trouble. Especially one as dangerous looking as Rex Falcon.

After dressing in jeans, a sweatshirt and jacket, she carried her morning coffee into the woods. Inhaling the crisp cool December air, she savored the solitude. Except for the forest creatures, she was alone. Blissfully, peacefully alone.

A beautiful eagle flew above. She watched it glide across the sky. It was free, content, soaring through the azure sky as if it didn't have a care in the world.

Maybe she'd find that peace and tranquility, too.

"Miss Hitchcock?"

Hailey startled and jumped backward, then realized the voice belonged to Rex Falcon. She glanced up into his piercing dark eyes and fought a shiver of anxiety. His gaze seemed probing, as if he was trying to see into her soul. Her defenses rose.

He wouldn't like what he found there, she was sure.

"What are you doing here?" she asked.

His dark eyebrow slid up a fraction at her tone. "I'm ready to get started." He stood ramrod straight, his massive shoulders powerful inside his work shirt. Early-morning sunlight glinted off his black hair, a few water droplets clinging to the overly long ends as if he'd just stepped from the shower.

She dragged her gaze downward, grateful to see the toolbox in his hand. He'd said he was a carpenter. He'd come here to work, not socialize. That she could deal with.

"Have you decided where you want to begin?"

Rattled by his gruff voice and the magnitude of his masculinity, she shook her head. "There's so much to do, I'm not sure where to start."

"I'd suggest the bathrooms, plumbing probably needs checking."

She sipped her coffee. "Right. They just restored the power in time for coffee."

He nodded. "Do you always get out this early?"

She tensed, then realized he was simply making conversation. "I couldn't resist a morning walk. It's so beautiful here."

"Yes, it is." His gaze roved over her, and she hugged her coffee mug, trying to ignore the tingling sensation his heated gaze evoked.

As if he sensed the heat, and didn't like it, either, he cut his gaze to the sky where a hawk swooped low. His expression changed, grew more intense, yet more peaceful at the same time.

Hailey swallowed, wondering at his thoughts. Then Rex's gaze met hers, and another unnerving ripple of desire spread through her. She wanted him to touch her. To hold her. To make her nightmares go away.

Crazy. No man could do that.

Completely baffled by her reaction, she turned abruptly. "All right, start with the plumbing. I'll tackle cleaning up the rooms. Then we'll talk about where we go from there."

He gave her a clipped nod, then followed. Hailey snuggled inside her coat, reminding herself to keep her distance. She had no idea what Rex would want with a woman like her. But they were alone in the woods, and he was stronger than her.

No one knew better than she did what a deadly combination the two could be.

HE SHOULD HAVE KNOWN Hailey was dangerous.

Thad Jordan examined the stitches around his eye, frowning at the discolored skin. He was going to have a scar. And all because of that damn woman.

Hailey would pay for what she'd done to him.

"Sir, are you all right?"

His secretary's voice drifted from the doorway. As usual, she sounded meek and mild, irritating him. The opposite of Hailey. She had looked small and fragile, but he'd sensed an untapped passion below the surface. She'd proven herself to be tough and spunky.

Too spunky for her own good it had turned out.

"Yes, I'm fine. Just bring me my coffee. And make it hot this time."

She nodded and slithered away to fetch it for him, bringing a grin to his face. At least she rushed to his beck and call when he barked—the way a woman should.

Before he finished with Hailey, she'd learn that lesson, too.

He picked up the phone and dialed the private investigator he kept on retainer.

"Carl Wormer here."

"Wormer, this is Jordan. I need your help."

"What is it this time? A case you want me to work on?"

"No." Thad ran his finger over the emblem on his signet ring. "This one is personal."

"Personal?"

"Yes. I need you to find Hailey Hitchcock."

"And then what?"

"Just let me know where she is." A chuckle built in his throat as he envisioned what he'd do to her. That pretty pale neck, those big brown eyes—he'd see her on her knees begging for her life before it was over.

And then, only then, would he decide her final punishment.

Chapter Three

The next two days as Hailey cleaned the house, she discovered a few nice antiques in the parlor, an iron bed in the master bedroom and a Chippendale sofa in the sitting room. The claw-foot dining-room table also added an ambience to the dreary interior. Painting the rooms would definitely spark new life to the inside.

But painting would keep Rex Falcon around longer, which was both a blessing and a curse. Rex distracted her from the fact that Thad might be looking for her, and kept her from dwelling on the fact that people had died in the house.

But his presence also unnerved her on a sexual level.

Not that he'd made any kind of advance toward her. But occasionally she sensed him watching her from a distance. Studying her as if he possessed a keen sight that could see inside her.

Another reason she'd maintained her distance. Her secrets would stay safely hidden.

Unless Thad decided to look for her.

His parting words echoed in her head, *I'll never let you go, Hailey. You're mine forever.*

Fighting the fear threatening to consume her, she headed up to shower before she drove to town for supplies. Then she'd meet the owners of the bed-and-breakfast and ask them to post an advertisement for her business on their bulletin board.

As soon as she undressed, the cool air inside the house brushed her nerve endings. It was almost as if someone was in the room with her. A ghost maybe?

No, that was ridiculous. Shaking off her foolishness, she climbed into the shower. The warm water soothed her, but when she closed her eyes, fingers of tension coiled inside her. She could almost feel Rex's heated gaze linger over her naked body. His hands trailing down her damp breasts. His lips pressing along her sensitive skin, loving her.

She jerked her eyes open. She'd never lusted for a man before, especially like this. Not even Thad, who she'd actually considered sleeping with, and he'd appeared to be charming, educated and a professional. So why was she fantasizing about Rex Falcon, a mysterious, dangerous man she'd only met?

The isolation—that was the only explanation.

The floor squeaked above her and she froze. The attic. Were there squirrels or raccoons inside? Or could someone have climbed in there to hide? A homeless person or stranded hiker might want refuge from the elements in the dead of winter. But she hadn't seen signs of anyone in the house when she'd first arrived.

She slipped on her terry-cloth robe and padded to the door, eased it open and listened. Another squeak. Rex?

No, Rex was working in the first-floor bathroom.

Taking a deep breath, she tiptoed down the hall, then unlocked the door to the staircase. The old-fashioned house had very poor lighting, and darkness shrouded the narrow spiral stairway, the scent of musk and some pungent odor she didn't recognize stifling. Maybe an animal had gotten inside. A hawk or vulture or even a bat.

Holding her breath, she started up the stairs, but darkness trapped her. She clutched the stair rail, unable to make her feet move. Panic overtook her, and her vision clouded.

She was a little girl. Alone. Scared.

Someone pushed her, shoved her forward. She was terrified, clutching her stomach. A harsh hand gripped hers and dragged her anyway. Her knees hit the steps, and she cried, but he jerked her on, blood trickling down her legs. A sob welled in her throat. Her throat clogged. A screeching sound echoed from above.

He flung her inside the room and shut the door, pitching her into the cavern.

DAMMIT. REX HAD TRIED to search the attic while Hailey showered, but now she was coming upstairs to find him. He fumbled for an excuse as he closed the trunk of memorabilia he'd been scrounging through. So far, he'd found nothing.

Deciding on his story, he headed down the steps.

A pang of concern hit him when he saw Hailey. She was frozen on the staircase, her hand clutching the rail in a white-knuckled grip, her face deathly pale.

His brain ordered him not to get involved, but instincts forced reason aside. "Hailey?" He lowered his voice to the soft, crooning pitch he used with the hawks. "What's wrong?"

She startled, her eyes drifting back into focus. "Rex?"

He nodded. "Are you all right? Did something happen?"

"I...I don't know."

He pried her icy hand from the rail and led her away from the entry. Her frightened eyes trapped him in their clutches. "What's wrong?"

She tugged at the top of her robe, looking confused. His gaze fell to the opening, tempting him, but purple bruises marred the creamy skin of her neck. Anger bolted through him, along with protective instincts. She reminded him of one of the injured birds that had been battered by the hypocrisies of mankind.

"Did something happen?"

"I…I thought someone was up there."

"It was me," he said. "I finished with the bathroom cabinets, and I was going to replace the hardware. I thought the owners might have left some of the original pieces in the attic."

She nodded, her lower lip trembling. A needy part of him that hadn't seen daylight in years surged to life.

But he'd never shaken the fear that he had violent tendencies, that he could prey on the weaker like the raptors. Or that he belonged alone, that no woman would understand him, much less overcome the fact that his father was a convicted murderer.

She ran a hand through her hair, drawing him to the damp strands and the way they cupped her delicate face. There were scratches on her palms that he hadn't noticed earlier. Had she gotten them cleaning, or had they been there before?

"I'd better get dressed," she said. Suddenly looking panicky, she fled to her bedroom.

His chest squeezed with anger and other emotions he didn't want to acknowledge. He couldn't let his guard down around this woman, worry about her problems or give in to this wild urge to be with her. He had too much work to do on his father's case.

Still, he wondered who had hurt her.

WHAT HAD HAPPENED back there in the attic stairwell?
Hailey hurriedly dressed, trying to warm herself.

Even though the rusty furnace rumbled, she was cold all the way to her bones. Why had she been afraid to climb those stairs?

It wasn't as if she'd been in that attic before.

She massaged her temple, trying to remember her childhood. When she was five and she'd misbehaved, her foster father had locked her in a closet. Maybe he'd shut her in an attic, too, and she'd forgotten. She had developed an uncanny way of taking herself out of her body when situations had gotten too bad….

Shaking off the disturbing memory, she grabbed her purse. She'd drive to town, forget the past and steer herself back on track.

Rex met her at the bottom of the steps. "Are you all right?"

"Yes. I'm going to town for supplies."

"Why don't I drive you?" Rex offered. "I need to pick up some things, too. You can buy paint for the interior walls while we're there. If we get snowed in, I can work on the inside."

Hailey frowned, but reminded herself she'd hired him to do a job. She could take care of herself. Besides, if Rex Falcon had intended her harm, he'd had ample opportunity to hurt her. In this remote area, he could have killed her and no one would ever know.

A chill engulfed her at the thought. How long had the Lyles lay dead in the house before their bodies had been discovered? Had Rex lived nearby when the family was slaughtered?

REX SILENTLY CURSED HIMSELF for insisting on driving Hailey. Her trip into town would have been the perfect opportunity for him to search the premises. But she'd looked so vulnerable and alone, his mouth had betrayed his brain.

Besides, he had to face the town sooner or later. Word of his return had most likely already spread. He needed to question the locals, too, especially the sheriff.

Should he tell Hailey who he was before someone else did?

Probably.

But her rose-scented shampoo swirled around him, and the tender skin of her throat made him itch to touch her. Sleet slashed the windshield, the defroster working overtime to clear the fog, adding to the tension as he steered his Jeep down the mountain road. The minute Hailey realized his father was imprisoned for the hatchet murders, she'd look at him differently. As if he was evil. Just like the kids had when he was younger. And just like Sharon, the woman he'd dated in Arizona, had a few years back.

Another reason he avoided relationships.

"Where are you from?" he asked, determined to learn more about her.

She fidgeted, clasping her hands together. "Denver."

"What brought you to Tin City?"

She burrowed deeper inside her coat. "I wanted a fresh start. I've always been drawn to the mountains."

"You mentioned opening an antiques business? Won't that be hard in the mountains?"

She shrugged. "Tourists like to browse in small shops. With some advertising, the Internet auction houses and the ghost stories to add to the flavor, I think I can make it work. Besides, I worked at an auction house before."

She was going to use the tragedy and his family's pain to promote her business. "How about your family?"

"I don't have any." She fidgeted with her hair, as if

she wasn't quite used to the cut, then turned to stare out the window. He wanted to ask more, but again her scent enticed him to forget. Made him ache to reach out and comfort her.

But her body language indicated she wouldn't welcome his touch. Better he keep his distance. He couldn't afford to care for her, and he had to remember it.

REX HAD ASKED so many questions. Did he have an ulterior motive? Could he possibly be working for Thad?

The piercing cold seeped through her as she studied him. His jaw was covered with beard stubble, his mouth set in a tight line, his dark eyes focused on the road. And his big hands…they were wrapped around the steering wheel now. But earlier they'd stroked her with a tenderness that had surprised her. Would he understand if she confided her past to him? If she told him about Thad?

No…she couldn't allow herself to open up to anyone. Much less a dark man like Rex.

The rest of the ride passed in a strained silence, the sleet and wind adding to the tension. Hailey grocery shopped in the small supermarket, stocking up on basics. The paint selection in the hardware store went quickly, although people stared and whispered behind their backs just as they had in the grocery store. Did they think she was crazy for buying a house where a family had been murdered?

Painful childhood memories surfaced. How many times had she attended a new school and been the center of gossip? She'd been the little orphan girl nobody wanted.

Rex frowned as they stepped up to the cash register. Hailey paid the elderly man behind the register in cash.

"You the lady who bought the Hatchet House?"

Hailey shifted on her heels. "Yes."

The old man cut his gaze toward Rex. "You're one of the Falcon boys, ain't you?"

Rex stiffened beside her and offered a curt nod. "Rex."

"I thought you boys were gone." He leaned back in his cane-back chair, his eyes bulging. Several customers turned and stared. A white-haired woman in a purple knit pantsuit pressed a hankie to her mouth, and another lady ushered her kids out the door, not even bothering to button their coats before braving the elements.

"No, I'm back at Falcon Ridge." Rex's boots clicked on the floor as he strode out the door. Hailey followed, wondering at the hostile atmosphere between the men.

Granted she had her reasons for being wary of Rex, but the townspeople had almost seemed afraid of him....

REX'S RESOLVE to exonerate his father grew stronger as he left the hardware store. This time he wouldn't let the locals run him and his brothers off. Not until he knew the truth.

He drove back up the mountain road, his body tight with tension, the Jeep occasionally skidding on the icy pavement. Though fog and snow enveloped them in the vehicle together, thankfully, Hailey remained quiet. She seemed lost in her own world, oblivious to his problems.

"Thanks for driving," Hailey said as they parked in front of her house.

"No problem." He killed the engine, then jumped out and carried the paint and hardware supplies to the storage room while Hailey unloaded the grocery bags onto the front porch.

Late-afternoon sunlight splintered through the forest, flickering off her reddish-brown hair, reminding him again of a red-tailed hawk. But the owl's incessant cry for a mate echoed in his mind, and the wind whipped those long strands around her face, tempting him to touch her. They were alone here together. Inside, they could light a fire. It would be cozy.

Jeez, he was only feeling this way because of the town's reaction. That and the natural attraction of man to woman. Not because Hailey was special or could be anything important in his life.

Rattled, he suddenly felt a desperate need to escape her for a while, and an even more desperate need to focus on his reason for returning to Falcon Ridge.

"I'm going to the house to pick up some tools to repair the kitchen sink," he said curtly. "And I need to check on this injured hawk I found in the woods. I'll be back later."

Her cheeks glowed with the cold as she nodded, her body relaxing slightly as if she was relieved to see him leave.

He jumped in the Jeep and started the engine, then ripped across the icy dirt drive, eager to put Hailey out of his mind.

He'd hike in the woods, clear his head, talk to the only creatures in life who understood him—the birds of prey.

Then he'd drive back to town and question the sheriff to see what he remembered about the murders.

AN ODD ODOR PERMEATED the house. It smelled like gardenias… A pile of dead ones lay on the table.

Hailey's breath caught.

What in the world? How… Who had put dead flowers on her table?

Was the person still inside?

She paused and listened, her breath wheezing in the tense silence. Nothing. Except another scent—cigarette smoke…and aftershave. Old Spice?

The smell turned her stomach, reminded her of her third foster father.

A creaking sound jerked her head toward the stairs.

Maybe there was a vagrant nearby who wanted her to leave? Or a ghost? Or had Thad found her already?

Perhaps she should call the police, or Rex. But then she'd have to tell them about Thad. For all she knew, he'd spread the word that she'd stabbed him in the eye, and the cops were looking for her. They might even arrest her. With Thad's connections, she'd end up rotting in a jail cell for assault and battery when she'd only been defending herself.

Grabbing her cell phone from her purse and a kitchen knife for protection, she slowly moved through the parlor. The floor squeaked again as she walked, a sharp wind whistling off the thin windowpanes. Nothing downstairs, so she slowly climbed the staircase. An ominous foreboding tickled her neck as if she wasn't alone.

Then she spotted the attic door. A note had been stuck on the wooden frame. "Leave the Hatchet House or you'll end up like the Lyles."

She swallowed hard, then inched closer to study the photograph taped below the note. In the picture, the family was lying in a river of blood, gashes from the hatchet exposing bare bones, their eyes bulging in horror.

Her stomach convulsed as she staggered down the steps to escape. The sound of footsteps creaked again.

Whoever had put the picture on her wall was still inside and they were right behind her....

Chapter Four

Hailey's heart pounded as she ran down the stairs. She had to escape. Get help. The gruesome murder scene flashed into her mind again. So much blood. Raw bones exposed. Gaping slashes on the woman's chest, scratches and stab wounds on her hands. The man was the same, his right hand nearly severed, his bloody injuries beyond ghastly.

And the child…

A sob welled in her throat. The little boy…he had died so young. It wasn't fair.…

Tears filled her eyes, grief for the family welling in her throat. What kind of crazy person could do that to another human?

She swayed, her stomach lurching, and gripped the banister in an effort to hold herself upright. The floor creaked behind her, and she skipped a step, lost her footing and fell. Shrieking, she grappled for control, but her bottom hit the corner of the step with a painful thud. Flailing, she bounced down the last two steps and fell on her hands and knees. She tasted blood and realized she'd bitten her tongue. The furnace rumbled. The floor creaked again.

She shoved herself up, and darted toward the front door. Shadows rose behind her. Her vision blurred. The dim light in the hallway flickered, then went off, cloaking the house in darkness. She screamed and jiggled the door to open it, but the knob wouldn't turn. He'd locked her inside.

He was going to kill her.

Panicked, she yanked at the knob again, then flung open the door. Cold air nipped at her cheeks as she ran across the porch and down the steps to her car. Her palms stung as she pulled at the door. But the car was locked, and she didn't have her keys.

No! He was going to get her.

She had to think.

The screen door screeched behind her, flapping in the wind. No. No time to think. Pivoting, she tried to decide where to go. But the screen door hit the casing with a whack, and she took off running again, this time into the bowels of the forest. Maybe she could outrun him. Lose him. Hide behind a rock or in an old mine.

Or maybe she could make it to Rex's house, and he'd help her.

She shoved through the bramble, forcing herself not to turn around. Every second counted. Steep, jagged red rocks coated in snow and ice rose around her. Massive pines and aspens stood like giant boulders, creating a maze. She turned to the right, sprinting through layers of icy slush and dead leaves, then veered to the left, reminding herself that Rex's house was on the northern slope only a mile away.

It seemed like hundreds, though, as she forced her rubbery legs forward. A gunshot rang out, and she shrieked, picking up her pace. Was the man firing at her?

A bullet *pinged* past her head, and she ducked, losing her breath. Yes, he was going to kill her. And if he buried her in the snow, no one would ever know.

THE SOUND OF a gunshot blast from the forest sent a jolt through Rex. A hunter maybe? He parked and rushed to the edge of the woods, searching the depths. He had enough damn problems without some loose cannon of a shot coming this close to his property.

His trip into town with Hailey returned to haunt him. Facing the town who'd labeled his father the Hatchet Murderer had resurrected painful memories. He didn't want Hailey to think of him as a cold-blooded killer's son.

Although God knows why he cared. She certainly hadn't looked at him with interest. Just a wariness that spoke volumes about the past she was running from.

Through the trees, he glanced at the property down the hill, the hairs on the back of his neck standing on end. He could still see the blood-soaked floor, the listless eyes, could smell the foul stench of body odors and death inside that kitchen.

Shadows and ghosts lurched all around him.

Just as he had twenty years ago, he strode deeper into the forest to purge his emotions. He had to free his father, get revenge against the person who'd butchered the Lyles and stolen his father's life by letting him take the rap.

He couldn't worry about Hailey and her secrets.

Inhaling the fresh cold air, the tension from his body dissipated slightly as the earthy scents and sounds of the forest engulfed him. Becoming one with the untamed wilderness, with the hawks soaring above, had become his solace. The only place he felt free, at peace.

The endless long nights of hearing his mother cry whispered from the snow-laden bellies of the aspens and fir trees. And then there were his little brothers. Deke had cloaked himself in anger and Brack had withdrawn into a shell made of human mortar that still kept him prisoner, barring anyone from getting too close. And both of them had had trouble with the law.

His father's parting words, "Take care of your mother and brothers," echoed in Rex's mind.

He'd tried. But he'd failed so many times.

A squirrel scampered up a nearby pine, snow swirling from the branches in a white cloud as a gust of wind whistled through the spiny needles. Fresh blood marked the white, and he frowned, squinting at the spatters, trying to decide their origin. Human or animal? Another gunshot shattered the tranquility, bouncing off the rocks. He froze, senses honed to detect its source. He didn't want to be mistaken for a deer or elk.

Another shot echoed from the hills and he turned, searching the distance. It was coming from the southern slope near the Hatchet House. What if Hailey decided to take a walk? It could be dangerous.

His boots crunched as he hiked toward her place. He'd have to warn her to be careful of hunters and their stray bullets.

There were other dangers for a woman living alone in the wilderness, too. Some of the men who liked to comb the hills were more predatory than the animals they hunted. They would take advantage of a woman in a second.

The scent of death floated toward him, fresh blood marking the icy path. Through the bed of trees, he spotted a buck sprawled near the creek, its tan flanks covered in blood, its once agile body deathly still. The hunter would be back to collect his kill any minute.

Trees rustled up ahead. He called out a warning, but Hailey burst through the brush, her face pale, her eyes wide in terror.

Worse, she was running straight toward the ravine.

SUDDENLY A MAN'S HANDS grabbed Hailey from behind. Panic zinged through her. She screamed and swung her arms back, struggling to free herself, but they fell to the ground in a tangle. Icy snow seeped through her clothes as she bucked upward, trying to throw his weight off of her. But his hands gripped her tightly, pinning her to the spot.

"Hailey, stop it, dammit, it's me."

She dug her elbows into his chest, trying to force him to loosen his grip. Instead, his fingers tightened around her wrists, pushing them into her back. The rest of his body was on top of her, his thighs rubbing hers as he lifted his head.

"Hailey, be still," the voice growled. "It's Rex. I was just trying to keep you from falling over the cliff."

Hailey froze, her breath rasping out as the husky voice registered. Was Rex following her? Had he been inside her house?

No…that was impossible. She'd heard him drive away.

Rational thoughts returning, she slowly relaxed, spitting out snow. But his body was still pressed firmly on top of hers. He stiffened, and his hard sex pressed into her hip. Fear crawled up her spine, the need to escape him mounting. "You can let me go now," she said through clenched teeth.

"All right." His grip loosened. "But be careful. The cliff drops off to the creek about fifty yards in front of you."

She nodded. She'd been running so fast she could have sailed over the edge. A shudder gripped her at the thought. Only the possibility of being murdered like the Lyles wasn't any better.

Uncertain whether she'd imagined Rex's physical reaction to her, she brushed snow and debris from her jeans, the cold seeping through the wet denim, chilling her inside and out. He helped her stand, then cradled her elbows in his hands as he turned her to face him. His breath whooshed out as he reached up and traced a finger over her lip. Uneasiness spread through her limbs. They were alone in the woods, just like she'd been with Thad. Would this man try to use force on her as her former boyfriend had? Would he turn on her in a second?

Then she realized he was wiping away blood.

His brown eyes searched her face, a frown pulling at his mouth. "What the hell were you running from?"

"S-someone was shooting at me." She inhaled, shivering again. Beard stubble darkened his tightly held jaw, the wind ruffling the black strands of his hair and sweeping it across his forehead. He looked ominous, like a big black bear ready to tear apart anyone that stood in his way.

Then she remembered the feel of his arousal pressing into her and another feeling splintered through her—a tingle that felt like attraction.

Good heavens, no. Not now. Not to this man. Not when she was trying to put her life together. Trying to escape her past.

Remembering Thad's control issues, she melted backward, pulling away. "Did you see him?"

"A hunter," Rex said in a gruff voice. "He probably thought you were a deer or elk running through the forest."

Another gunshot blasted, and she startled so badly he pulled her into his arms. "Shh, it's all right now."

Her breath quivered out. "No…he shot at me, he was trying to kill me."

His black eyebrows rose, his hand automatically playing along her neck and shoulders, soothing her. "I saw a deer he killed," Rex said. "I'm sure he mistook you for an animal."

"But the bullet nearly hit my head, and s-someone was in the house when I went inside," Hailey said, stiffening. "He…left a note. He threatened me."

"What?" He pulled her closer against him, but Hailey backed away again, hands fisted, her survival instincts roaring to life.

"When I went inside," Hailey said, struggling for a steady breath, "someone was upstairs. They left dead gardenias on the table and a picture of the Lyles' murder…" Her voice broke as images of the carnage flooded her.

Another shot rang out, echoing in the distance. Thankfully it sounded farther away this time. Hailey's gaze found the cliff. A vulture soared above, swooping downward in a wide arc, its black feathers stark against the aquamarine sky, its talons bared as it zeroed in on its target. Just seeing the bird reminded her all too much that if Rex hadn't grabbed her, she might have plunged to her death below.

REX STUDIED HAILEY, his mind battling his body's natural reaction. He'd only meant to keep her from running off the cliff, but the moment he brushed against her, his sexual instincts had stirred to life, strong and more alive than they had been in months. Hell, maybe years.

Physical arousal, he told himself. A basic human reaction, a natural animal one. But this time his senses had become skewed with the need to fold her in his arms and hold her for the night, to protect her and make promises that he couldn't keep.

But these urges went against the free man he needed to be. Free like the falcons…

Some birds of prey are monogamous, a voice whispered.

But not him. He had no room for a woman in his life. Especially this troubled one.

Had someone really been in her house threatening her? Maybe it had been a prank…

"There was a note, too," Hailey whispered.

The wind swirled the strands of her reddish-brown hair around her face. Her cheeks were red from exertion and cold, her lips parched from the sun and wind. She looked so damn beautiful another twinge of desire spurted through him.

"And they tacked pictures of the Lyle family's murder on the wall," she said, knotting her hands together. "It was awful."

He nodded. He'd seen the photos, had imprinted them in his brain since he was a kid.

"Come on." He coaxed her forward, back through the thick pines and aspens, up the rocky hills toward Falcon Ridge. "You're freezing, we need to get you inside."

She stiffened. "Where are we going?"

"To my place." He grabbed her arm again and hauled her close to him, lowering his voice. "If that hunter returns, we don't want to be here."

"But…"

"You're not going back to the Hatchet House alone," he growled. "I'll go with you and check it out, but I need my gun."

"You have a gun?"

He nodded, wondering at the streak of fear that darted into her eyes. "It's for protection. You should get one, too."

Her breath glowed white in the air as she nodded and stumbled forward, trying to keep up with him. He slowed his pace to accommodate her, pushing the loose branches and bramble out of the way so they wouldn't scratch her delicate face as they threaded their way back up the mountain.

He'd never brought a woman to Falcon Ridge before, never shown one his home. He wondered what she'd think of it.

A few minutes later, they stepped onto the portico of the stone structure, and he opened the massive front door and ushered her inside. She was trembling, the temperature outside having dropped ten degrees in the last hour. The frightening ordeal had obviously drained her, because her shoulders were beginning to slump, and her flushed face paled with exhaustion.

"Come on, let's go to the kitchen. I'll fix you something hot to drink."

She scanned the inside of the foyer, the ten-foot ceilings and dusty old paintings. He tried to see the monastery-type house through her eyes. His mother had hated the desolate location, had claimed the stone walls and dark paneled interior shrouded any light and warmth that might filter through the mass of trees surrounding the five-thousand-foot structure. He opened his mouth to explain that his parents had inherited the place, but he refrained, avoiding the subject of his family.

He reached for her arm to guide her to the kitchen's woodstove, but she squared her shoulders and resisted.

"I'm not going to attack you," he said, irritated that she was afraid of him. She'd felt his erection, knew he wanted her.

The realization put him on the defensive. He didn't like this craving that happened when he was around her. And he especially didn't like the fact that she didn't reciprocate the feeling.

Was she afraid of all men or just him?

Had another man taken advantage of her?

He swallowed hard, the mere idea making his blood run hot. But he realized it was true. The bruises on her cheek and neck the first time he'd seen her had come from a man's hands.

A man she had probably trusted.

HAILEY DIDN'T TRUST THIS MAN, although she had no idea why. He had saved her life. If he'd wanted to kill her or hurt her, he could have done so by now.

But he hadn't. He'd offered to help her renovate her house. He'd escorted her into town. And now he'd rescued her from an attacker, and saved her from plunging over a cliff.

Who had been in the house? Thad maybe? Or someone who didn't want her living in the Lyle house?

Rex moved through the doorway, obviously giving her space. Keeping her distance, she followed. The finely woven, handmade dream catchers dangling in the window seemed at odds with the masculine stone structure.

"Coffee, hot chocolate or tea?" he asked once they were in the rustic kitchen. Copper pots hung above a center work island, the stove encased in a brick arch. Natural light bled through a bay window that overlooked the woods and mountains above, looking majestic and giving the room an airier feel than the foyer. A small garden area surrounded a terrace, and beyond it, she noticed several large birdcages. She counted three that were empty. The fourth one was draped in a cloth.

"Hailey?"

She tensed, her mind in a tailspin, distrusting everything. "Whatever you're making."

He reached for the coffeepot, filled it with water and added coffee, then pressed the on button. The slow drip splintered the awkward silence.

"You can heat your hands by the woodstove." He retrieved two thick ceramic mugs from the cabinet, found the sugar and cream set and put it on the scarred plank table.

She moved slowly to the stove, thrusting her hands above the steel frame, relief echoing in her sigh as heat drew the sting from her numb fingers. He filled the mugs, then gestured toward the sugar. She nodded.

He added sugar, then handed her the cup, their fingers brushing. His hot look unnerved her, enticed her to forget the reasons she needed to keep her distance. For once, she ached to bury herself in a man's arms and let him take care of her.

"I like the dream catchers," Hailey said. "Did you get them around here?"

"My mother collects them," Rex said. "She thinks they bring good luck and ward off bad dreams."

Hailey gave a self-deprecating laugh. "I understand. Bad dreams, sometimes they seem so real."

"Want to talk about it?"

She shook her head. Her dreams were her own demons. "What are the cages for?"

He glanced out the window, then turned to her, his expression wary. "I rescue injured birds of prey. My brothers and I train them."

"You release them back into the wild?"

He nodded. "When we can."

She relaxed slightly. Any man who rescued injured animals had to be more human than Thad. Then again, she'd been wrong before.

"Maybe I should call the police about the threat?" he suggested.

She immediately stiffened, her fleeting moment of safety shattered. Thad had power, influential friends. "No."

His black eyebrow shot up. "You don't want to report an intruder and the threatening note?"

She shook her head. "No, not yet." She sipped the coffee, grateful he'd made it strong. "What if it was just a prank? Maybe kids…"

Although her gut instincts whispered that the threat had been real.

Someone had snuck into her house while she was gone and planted the picture to frighten her off. Someone who'd chased her into the woods and wanted her out of the Lyle house.

What would he do if she didn't heed his warning?

Chapter Five

Hailey's show of courage contrasted sharply with the fear in her big brown eyes. Why didn't she want him to call the police? Was he right in wondering if she was in trouble with the law?

Or could a police officer have something to do with her fear of men?

God knows, they'd done a number on his father when he'd first been convicted. Going into jail as a child killer had trigged the worst in guards and other prisoners. Of course, some of them just enjoyed wielding their power on the weaker.

And Hailey was much more vulnerable than his dad. She'd obviously encountered violence before and still wore the bruises.

"Thanks for the coffee, Rex." She placed the empty cup in the sink. "I should go back now. Do you mind driving me?"

He squared his shoulders, his libido stirring again as his gaze zeroed in on the rose-petal sweetness of her parted lips. Struggling for control, he dragged his eyes from her mouth, but they fell to the soft swell of her breasts and a hot streak of desire surged inside him. Worse, her chest rose with uneven breaths, her bravado drumming up admiration. A few minutes earlier she'd fled in terror, yet now she was ready to face whatever had frightened her.

Because she didn't want to be alone with him?

Was he that damn scary?

"Sure." He strode to the corner, removed his SIG Sauer from the cabinet and tucked it into his belt. He wanted to check out the items, too, see if they might help him find the real killer. "Let's go."

She bit down on her lip, then nodded, hugging her arms around her to ward off the cold as he led her back through the foyer. He stopped at the door, yanked his bomber jacket from the closet and handed it to her. "Put this on. It'll keep you warm."

Hailey hesitated, then shrugged into the worn, warm leather. The jacket nearly swallowed her whole, making her appear small and so damn sensual he nearly reached out to tug the coat around her. An image of her alone at the Hatchet House rose to taunt him, his desires mingling with protective instincts again. Another vision coasted on its tail—Hailey in his king-size four-poster bed, his down comforter brushing her nakedness while he trailed kisses along the pale skin of her neck.

"Maybe you should stay here or in town tonight."

Her eyes flashed with wariness, and he realized his gruff voice had sounded suggestive.

"I saved for a long time to buy a house," she said, her tone stronger now. "I refuse to let anyone run me off."

He read fear in her eyes, but determination and strength darkened her irises, too. Damn, he didn't want to like her. Even more unsettling, he sensed his own loneliness mirrored in her words. She'd run here to find solace and now someone had messed with her security, so she was fighting back.

His mother had let the locals run them off from Falcon Ridge years ago. It had taken growing up for him to have the courage to confront the people who'd shunned his family.

What had shaped Hailey into the strong woman she was now? And who the hell was she running from?

ALTHOUGH REX'S BIG STONE KITCHEN was intimidating and austere, the woodburning stove and smell of freshly brewed coffee wrapped her in warmth, tempting Hailey to accept his offer and forget about the dangers haunting her—at least for a night.

But Rex's dark raking eyes and towering presence posed another danger. One she wasn't prepared to tangle with now. Maybe never.

An intoxicating aura shimmered off the man in rays that heated her blood and created an illusion of false security. Sexual attraction did not mean caring or safety.

It usually meant trouble.

Hadn't she learned that from experience? Or was she forever going to be lured into trusting a man just because he hadn't yet hit her?

This man could turn on her in a second....

"What kind of bird do you have in back now?" she asked, changing the subject as they walked to his Jeep.

"A ferruginous hawk." His grim expression indicated he hadn't liked the way he'd found the animal. "It was hit by a pellet gun. The pellet damaged soft tissue in its right wing."

"So it'll recover enough to be returned to the wild?"

He nodded. "He's grown, he should do fine. But sometimes the juveniles get too dependent and have trouble adapting, especially if they're kept in captivity too long."

"What sparked your interest in birds?"

He shrugged, his expression guarded as they drove to her house. "There was a local wildlife center nearby when I was growing up. I used to volunteer there." He gestured out the window, across the rocky terrain, his look pensive. "Just look at the space, the freedom the birds have. They're lucky."

He obviously identified with the birds of prey on an instinctual level, maybe even envied their freedom. She wanted to hear more, but they arrived at her house, and Rex parked. Even through the haze of snow flurries clogging her vision she noticed the screen door was still flapping in the wind. Another gust sent debris swirling across the porch. Hailey clutched the door handle, a shiver chasing up her spine.

"Wait here," Rex said in a low, commanding voice. "I'll check it out."

Tempted again to accept his offer, Hailey hesitated. It would be easy to relinquish control to this man. But this house belonged to her, and she'd never asked anyone to fight her battles for her. She couldn't start now.

"I'm going with you," she said, surprised at her calmness when an edginess tightened every cell in her body.

"Hailey—"

"Whoever was in there is probably long gone," she argued.

"All the more reason we should call the police and let them dust for fingerprints."

"No." Hailey opened the Jeep door. "Let's look inside first."

Dark clouds obliterated the dwindling afternoon sunlight as she followed Rex to the front door. He held his gun in front of him as he slowly stepped inside the entrance. He kept her behind him, his footsteps slow and steady, his eyes scanning the interior with caution. Shadows hovered in every corner, the dim lighting of the house adding to Hailey's anxiety, each footstep bringing another creak and groan to the old house. They searched the downstairs room by room but found nothing amiss.

Hailey sighed with relief, but a screeching noise above shattered the momentary peace. Rex pressed a finger to his lips to indicate for her to keep quiet, then inched up the steps. Hailey followed, holding her breath until they reached the landing, then her gaze flew to the attic door.

Her pulse pounded. "The note, it's gone."

Rex frowned and glanced at the doorway, then back to her.

"The picture, it was there, I swear it."

He pressed a finger to her lips, then motioned that he'd check out the rooms. Hailey followed, cringing when they entered the children's empty bedrooms.

Although the paint had faded in the boy's room, and someone had obviously removed most of the toys, wooden bunk beds still sat in the corner. Simple navy bedspreads, dusty and faded, were draped over the tops. Hailey froze, imagining the young boy at play, a train set winding around the room on the floor.

Grief for the poor child followed, her throat swelling.

The next room was painted pale yellow, the room bare except for a twin Jenny Lind bed and antique dresser. Oddly, there was no comforter or spread on the bed, but she pictured a frilly pink spread on top with lacy pillows scattered at the headboard and rag dolls and stuffed animals overflowing the now bare shelves.

"There's no one here," Rex said, jarring her back to reality.

"I told you he probably already left." Hailey's shoulders fell in relief. But the thought of the young lives lost so senselessly still troubled her. She had to talk to the locals and learn more about the people who'd lived here. More than ever, she wanted to honor their memory.

Rex studied her as they walked back to the attic door. "You're sure someone was inside?"

Hailey hesitated. Had there been someone inside or had she imagined it? "Yes. How else would the note and picture get there, and then disappear?" She pointed to the door, the image of the bloody massacre stark in her mind. "The article described the murders, and the picture was so stark. The father was lying on the floor a few feet away from the mother. Mrs. Lyle had her arm curled protectively around her son. And the man had his hand extended, as if he was trying to touch them."

"I've seen the photo." His mouth twisted into a grimace. "But I don't see any signs of an intruder here. No footprints, nothing."

"You don't believe me?" Hailey asked.

"I don't know. Maybe you heard a noise, the furnace squawking or the boards creaking with the wind and you just—"

"Maybe he was in the attic."

His eyebrows arched. "All right, I'll check." He reached for the door and Hailey froze, her sense of claustrophobia growing.

He yanked it open anyway, and suddenly a flurry of wings wrestled through the air, flapping in their faces. Hailey screamed and ducked. Rex grabbed her arm and pulled her to the floor while the bird flew in a circle, then soared down the steps and out the open screen door.

"A brown bat," Rex said, standing. "That's odd, bats are nocturnal. You rarely see one this time of day."

"How did it get in?" Hailey asked, wondering if there were more upstairs.

"Probably a hole in the attic. Bats hibernate in the

winter, so he might have been looking for a warm place to nest."

Hailey wiped at her forehead. "Do you think he'll be back?"

"I don't know. Usually they nest in caves or the mines around here and return to the same place each winter. But the bat is probably the noise you heard."

Hailey licked her dry lips. "Maybe, but that bat didn't leave the gardenias, and put the note and picture on the door."

His look turned skeptical. "Hailey, it's understandable that you heard a noise and got spooked, maybe you—"

"Maybe I imagined the picture of those dead people?" Hailey backed away from him. "What do you think I am, some kind of lunatic that invented this story just to get your attention?"

He hesitated, and her chest squeezed. "Staying in this house would freak out anyone," he finally said in a gruff voice. "The ghost stories especially."

"I didn't invent the note." Anger replacing her fear, Hailey guided him down the steps. "Thanks for coming, though. I won't bother you again, Rex."

Rex paused at the door, his dark eyes troubled. "Hailey—"

"Just go. I'm fine now." She pushed him out the door and locked it behind him, then glanced at the staircase warily. She hadn't imagined the flowers, the threat or the note.

But she wouldn't call Rex again and be treated like a crazy person.

No, in town, she'd ask about the Lyle murders herself. If someone wanted her to leave, she had to find out who in order to protect herself.

Thad's face flashed into her mind again. *You'll never escape me, Hailey.*

Had Thad found her already? He had been ruthless in competing with a business opponent, a virtual shark in the corporate world.

Could he have heard about the local ghost legends and put the note and picture on the door to terrorize her?

REX STOOD OUTSIDE the Hatchet House, the icy wind and cold beating at him as he contemplated what had just happened. Hailey seemed so certain that someone had been inside, that they'd threatened her, yet he'd seen for himself there was no note or flowers. Was she just imagining things? Could she be delusional?

Earlier, when he'd looked for tools to repair the bathroom, he'd noticed the odd collection of books she had in an unpacked box in the laundry area. Books on folklore, short stories of ghost towns, witches, tales of ancient rituals and century-old weapons.

Maybe she was one of those kooks interested in documenting haunted houses. She'd admitted she wanted to play up the house's history to draw interest when she opened her business.

Still, the truth about the murder years before lay somewhere in the house and town, and he had to find it. Besides, the fear in Hailey's eyes had been very real. And so had the bruises on her face and the scratches on her hands. Someone had hurt her recently.

Take care of your mother and your brothers.

He had failed them because he couldn't replace his father. He couldn't fail this vulnerable woman.

A flutter of wings above drew his eye, and he frowned at the thought of the bat nesting in Hailey's attic when earlier the attic had been empty. Granted, the mammal had probably slipped in through a hole in the attic, but what if someone else had sneaked inside the house, someone who'd been in the attic and had opened a window?

His instincts alert, he scoped out the house. If something happened to Hailey tonight, and he'd written off her story, he'd never forgive himself.

Dusk was setting, so he squinted, allowing his eyes to adjust. Grateful for his keen night vision, he moved slowly around the house, searching the snow-covered ground for footprints and checking all the windows to see if they'd been tampered with.

Tomorrow he'd suggest Hailey install a security system. That is, if she was still speaking to him and intended for him to continue the renovations.

Although a paw print here and there attested to the fact that a wild animal might be combing the area, the wind hurled dry snow across the ground, quickly obliterating his own footprints. He should warn Hailey about the woods, insist she buy a shotgun to carry with her on her walks.

His gaze drifted to the lattice around the back corner. A tiny piece of something black fluttered from a nearby branch of a fir tree. His pulse accelerated as he moved closer and plucked it from the branch. Bringing the sliver of fabric closer to his face, he studied the jagged square. It was a small piece of a wool scarf that had caught on the limb.

Someone *had* been snooping around the back of the house.

Had the piece of fabric belonged to Hailey's intruder?

Dammit. If someone wanted Hailey out of the house and didn't like her asking questions, it could only mean one thing—That someone in town knew the truth about the murder. Someone who wanted to keep it buried.

He scanned the woods again, searching the darkness, then headed back to his SUV and started down the mountain. He'd talk to the sheriff, find out his version of the story.

If Hailey was in danger, the only way to keep her safe was to find out who really murdered the Lyle family.

DISAPPOINTMENT FILLED Hailey as Rex Falcon left, surprising her. She'd never expected him to doubt her story, to think she'd fabricated it to get his attention.

As dusk fell outside, the shadows grew larger, more ominous. But she'd dealt with shadows all her life and survived, and she would now. In fact, she'd visited other supposedly haunted houses before, had even participated in a séance once. But none of those places had ever given her this eerie feeling.

Wind whistled through the windowpanes, rattling glass, and a branch scraped at the wood frame. Her clothes were still damp from the snow, so she changed into warm sweats, then built a fire and unloaded her books. Her propensity toward local legends and the supernatural had been a turnoff to most of the men she'd encountered. Thad had even insinuated it was weird.

But history shaped a town and the people in it.

How had her own troubled past changed her? Had it made her paranoid? Distrustful of all men?

She finished the task, then decided to clean out the antique rolltop desk in the corner of the room. Newspaper clippings of the Lyle murder were scattered inside, the photos similar to the one she'd found taped on the wall upstairs.

Her stomach twisted. Someone wanted to scare her away.

The phone trilled, cutting into the silence. Hailey glanced at the caller ID. Unavailable.

Had Thad found her?

No. He couldn't have located her already. Rex had probably copied down the number. Maybe he was calling to check on her, to apologize…. "Hello."

But the sound of breathing echoed over the line.

Hailey's fingers tightened around the phone, perspiration trickling down her neck. "Who is this?"

The whisper of silence that followed sounded ominous in the stillness of the room. The fire crackled, a log splintering. Then the breathy sound filled the air again. Someone was listening, taunting her.

Was the person who'd been inside the house before calling to make sure she was home so he could return and kill her?

THAD HOOKED HIS CELL PHONE to his belt, a smile curving his mouth. Learning Hailey's whereabouts had soothed his frazzled nerves. Nerves strung tight from waiting on that damn P.I. to locate her. From praying he didn't wreck his Mercedes on the black ice as he'd driven to this godforsaken hole-in-the-wall town.

She'd thought she could disappear into the untamed land, and he wouldn't find her. But she was wrong. So wrong.

She'd underestimated him. He'd told her she could never escape him. Thad Jordan didn't make promises he didn't keep.

Hailey Hitchcock was his forever.

No other man would ever touch her.

Bile caught in his throat at the sharp pain that splintered his cheek. His eye was healing, but that scar…without plastic surgery he'd look like a misfit. The women's lusty gazes would stop…

And it was all her fault.

The sudden fury that overcame him made him press the accelerator. He wanted to wrap his hands around that dainty throat, take what was his and make her suffer.

But the sound of her frightened voice drifted through the haze of anger. He knew where she was now. Knew her hiding spot.

Her isolation would only play into his favor.

And living in that damn old house with its ghost stories gave him plenty of opportunity. Oddly, her eccentric interest had intrigued him at first. It had set her apart from the snotty, debutante-type ladies he'd always dated. And when he'd investigated her past, he'd wanted to slay her demons and be her hero.

But Hailey had been too stubborn to succumb to his will.

He stroked the bandage on his cheek, another grin sliding onto his mouth. But the simple movement brought more pain slicing through his face.

He'd bide his time. Play a few games with her first. Watch her sweat as her courage and stubbornness slowly disintegrated.

Then she'd finally bend to him and beg for forgiveness.

Chapter Six

As night fell around the mountains, the temperature dropped to the teens, but the cold invigorated Rex just as it had when he was a child following his father's foot-tracks across the snow. His dad had taught him early on how to judge directions by the sun and wind, how to distinguish the difference in animals by the impressions their paws created in the snow and mud.

But then his father's guidance had been taken away—the day the sheriff had arrested him. The first few months, Rex had begged his mother to let him visit his father, but she'd flatly denied his pleas, too heart-broken and confused herself over the town's reactions to chance a trip to the penitentiary. And when he'd gotten older and tried to contact his father, his dad had refused visitors. He didn't want his sons to witness him being caged like an animal.

Rex understood that kind of pride. He intended to get justice and set his father free.

Battling the potholes in the road, he veered onto the main street running through Tin City. Once the area had thrived on mining, but with time most of the mines had closed, many buildings were deserted, others had been turned into tourist traps and businesses that catered to travelers wanting to experience the rugged mountains and to ski. Two bed-and-breakfasts had cropped up, a general store remodeled as a replica of the 1800s version had been built, and a shop catering to collectors of Native American memorabilia occupied one corner. Buster's Butcher Shop, Nancy's Curl & Style, Gus's Gun Shop and the Craft Hut sat adjacent to the general store while Hamburger Heaven, a new steak house, bowling alley, outdoor skating rink, movie theater and a Western saloon/dance hall offered food and recreation.

He found the sheriff's department, parked, climbed out of the SUV and stalked up the snow-crusted walkway to the sheriff's office, a small adobe structure that hadn't changed on the outside since he was a kid.

He'd been surprised to discover Cohen still held office as sheriff, but then again, the man had been young and cocky when the Lyles had been murdered. Cohen had made his claim to fame through Rex's father's incarceration.

A wooden desk sat front-and-center, a woman most likely in her midthirties with brownish hair behind it. She glanced up, then checked her watch, an annoyed look on her face.

"What can I do for you?"

"I'd like to speak to the sheriff."

"You got a complaint?"

He chewed the inside of his cheek. Oh, yeah, he had plenty. "It's private business, ma'am. Can you tell him I'm here?"

She raked her gaze over him one time, obviously unimpressed. "What's your name, sir?"

"I know who he is."

Rex jerked his head up at the sound of Cohen's grating voice.

"I heard you were back in town, boy. Figured you'd

stop by sooner or later." Cold gray eyes met Rex's, anger churning in Rex's stomach at Cohen's condescending tone.

He squared his shoulders, raising himself to his full six-three. "As you can see, I'm no longer a boy." Meaning he didn't intend to let this bully of a man push him around.

Age had settled on Cohen's face, giving him jowls, and the paunch that now protruded over his belt softened his hard demeanor. But the same cocky, smart-ass expression stared back.

"You're not welcome here, Falcon. This is my town. I don't want trouble." Cohen hitched up his pants with his thumbs, then signaled the receptionist to leave. Relieved, she grabbed her purse and practically trotted out the door.

"I'm here to find out the truth about who killed the Lyle family." Rex folded his arms across his chest, knowing his declaration would bring trouble. But he bit his tongue to keep from finishing his sentence with a threat— *And then I'll make you pay for putting the wrong man in jail and ruining his life.*

HAILEY TREMBLED as she skimmed the newspaper clippings of the Lyle murders.

Joyce Lyle, her husband, Lawrence, and seven-year-old son, Stephen, were found butchered in their home last night in what is being called the most brutal killing of the decade. Blood and torn clothing from the Lyles's four-year-old autistic daughter was found at the edge of Chicowaw Creek. Apparently the little girl died and was tossed into the water. Police are calling the killer the Hatchet Murderer. The funeral will be held at three o'clock at Langley's Funeral Parlor.

Why wasn't there more information?

She found the phone book, skimmed the listings and dialed the library to see if they'd archived the newspapers.

"Tin City Library, Mrs. Rogers, information."

Hailey identified herself. "I bought the Lyle house and am renovating it."

"My goodness, I heard someone moved in there. You know they say that house is haunted."

"Yes, I've heard."

"Have you seen any ghosts yet?"

"Not exactly," Hailey said, remembering the sounds in the attic, and the image of the little girl.

"I don't think I could sleep out there," Mrs. Rogers said. "Not knowing that poor family died in the house. I heard it was the bloodiest thing this part of the country had seen in years."

"I heard something similar," Hailey said. "Actually, I'm planning to start an antiques business in the house. I majored in history, and I'm interested in documenting the story of the house in case visitors are interested."

"Oh, my. You're not going to show pictures and glorify the murder, are you? I mean, what happened to that family was an awful tragedy. I don't think it's right to sensationalize their murders."

Hailey bit her lip. "No, ma'am, I don't plan to sensationalize anyone's death. I want to preserve the family's memory."

"Oh, well, then I guess it's all right."

Hailey sighed. "Do you have articles on the murders archived?"

A pencil thumped up and down on the desk. "Yes. If you want to come in, I'll show you."

"Good. I'll probably stop by in the morning."

"That's fine. We're closing in a few minutes anyway."

"Right. Were you living in Tin City at the time of the murders, Mrs. Rogers?"

The woman hesitated. "Sorry. I'd just moved to town. But thankfully they arrested the killer and locked him away. Our town historian, Faye Burton, would be the best one to talk with." She paused again. "Oh, and the sheriff and Bentley McDaver, he was the prosecuting attorney."

"Great. Thanks."

"Listen, you be careful," Mrs. Rogers lowered her voice. "The man who was arrested for the Lyle murders, well, he had some sons, and I've heard rumors that one of them is back."

Hailey froze. "Back in Tin City?"

"Yes, he moved into his daddy's house. It's near your place."

The hair on the back of Hailey's neck bristled.

"Some people think he's here for revenge. Other folks say he's strange like his father."

"How do you mean strange?"

"Randolph and the boys used to talk to the birds. Kept wild hawks and eagles right in their backyard. They say the boys are mean, too. Dangerous like their dad." She hesitated, then continued in a muffled whisper. "I believe it's the oldest boy that's back. Rex Falcon. Scary big guy with menacing eyes."

Hailey gripped the phone. Rex Falcon was the son of the Hatchet Murderer. He'd spent time with her. And he'd been up in the attic the day she thought she'd heard sounds. He'd also found her running through the woods and had grabbed her to save her. Or had he tacked the note on the attic door to scare her away? Was he trying to win her trust just so he could…do what? Use her? Hurt her like his father had the Lyles?

And if he didn't have foul intentions, why hadn't he told her who he was?

"YOUR FATHER KILLED the Lyles," Sheriff Cohen said in a deadpan voice. "End of story."

"He's innocent," Rex stated. "And I was hoping you had information you'd share about the case."

Cohen barked a sardonic laugh. "You're kidding, right?"

Rex raised an eyebrow, his expression stoic. "Do I look like I'm kidding?"

Cohen released an expletive. "Listen, Falcon, I know you didn't want to believe it back then, but a jury of twelve of your daddy's peers tried the case. Based on the evidence, they convicted him."

"I'm reopening the investigation," Rex said. "I'd like your cooperation, sheriff, but if not, it won't stop me."

Cohen frowned. "I don't know what you expect me to tell you. We went by the book, Falcon. Your father was the only one who could have killed the Lyles. He had motive, opportunity—"

"My father never would have hurt those children," Rex argued.

"Some people said otherwise."

Because they thought his falconer ways strange. "Did you ever find the weapon?"

Cohen's jaw snapped tight. "No, but your father's bloody fingerprints were at the scene. Hell, boy, they were everywhere."

"Because he discovered the massacre," Rex ground out. "He thought Mrs. Lyle might still be alive, so he felt for a pulse. He wanted to save her."

"Everyone knows Lyle had been attacked by your father, that he had a thing for Mrs. Lyle."

"Gossip and circumstantial evidence," Rex said. "You had no witnesses, no confession, no weapon, no concrete proof. Cold cases are being reopened across the country on a lot less."

Cohen glared at him, his hand stroking the butt of his gun holster as if he might draw it any second. "Go back to where you were, Falcon. The only thing you'll accomplish by reopening the case is to dredge up bad memories for the people of this town."

"And the real murderer," Rex said.

"No, the real murderer is in jail where he belongs."

Anger tore at Rex's patience. "No, he's still roaming the streets, Cohen. For all we know, he's living right here in town. He's probably sitting back laughing at you for not looking past your nose to find out the truth."

"Get out," Cohen snarled. "And don't come back."

Rex shot him a cold look. "I don't scare off as easily as my mother did," Rex said. "And don't bother threatening me again, Sheriff. I'll find out the truth about what happened twenty years ago, then I'll be back to make you pay for convicting the wrong man and robbing him of his life."

REX FALCON WAS DANGEROUS.

Sheriff Cohen cradled the phone to his ear and paced his office as he inhaled an antacid tablet. Sweat rolled down his neck and into his collar. Dammit. He needed his blood-pressure medicine bad, but he'd left it at home.

He had to put a stop to Rex Falcon. Protect the past. Keep his reputation intact.

Even if it meant guarding old secrets.

The phone trilled over and over. "Answer it, you confounded fool."

The machine clicked on instead, a familiar voice echoing in reply. "You've reached Bentley McDaver at the district attorney's office. I'm currently unavailable, but please leave your name, number and a brief message, and I'll return your call as soon as possible."

"Hellfire and damnation, McDaver," Cohen shouted. "This is Cohen. We've got trouble. Randolph Falcon's son is back asking questions. You better get your ass in gear and call me ASAP."

He left the office number, his home number and cell phone, then hung up and massaged his belly, the acid burning a path up his esophagus as he strode toward the door. Seconds later, he tore out of the lot, spewing ice and sludge in his wake.

He had made his career twenty years ago when he'd solved the hatchet murder. And he'd kept the town safe since. Nobody was going to interfere now, not when he'd decided to run for mayor next year. Not when he'd finally won over Ava Riderton.

He sped toward Ava's house, determined to convince her that they had done the right thing by keeping quiet years ago. If she'd come forward with her speculations, her testimony might have shed a different light on the case. But Falcon had been guilty and Cohen hadn't wanted the man to escape. Neither had McDaver nor Falcon's own attorney, Carl Pursley.

They'd all had their reasons.

He reached for his phone to call Pursley.

There was no damn way on earth Falcon's son was going to ruin their reputations by proving the case wasn't legit.

Or that they'd lied.

AS REX DROVE BACK to Falcon Ridge, he slowed slightly to check out the Hatchet House. Although woods bathed the house in shadows, lights still glowed inside the house, illuminating the interior through the sheers. Hailey must still be up. What was she doing? Getting ready for bed? Taking a long hot bath?

The mere thought of her naked body heated his own,

resurrecting desires that hadn't surfaced with any other woman recently. The sultry curves hidden beneath those big sweaters and jeans begged for a man's touch. He imagined the seductive softness of her breasts, the tips glistening with water, her nipples rosy and jutting, ready to be suckled. He would kiss her rose-petal lips first, then trail kisses over her breasts and down her stomach, then he'd follow the trail to heaven....

Dammit. His sex was throbbing, heat spreading through his body like a brushfire. Why Hailey? She was in trouble, a mystery woman who liked odd old stories and had books about ghosts. And she had backed away from him as if he was some kind of monster when he'd tried to comfort her.

His jaw tightened. Maybe he wanted her because he needed comfort right now himself. A few minutes of peace with a warm body to bury himself inside so he could momentarily forget the mission he'd come here to accomplish. But he wouldn't use her to sate his needs. He wasn't that selfish of a bastard.

Not unless she wanted him in return.

Still, the image of Hailey running into the woods, terrified and alone, floated back.

He'd insulted her when he'd suggested she might have imagined the threatening note. Hell, he couldn't rest tonight without checking on her, so he cut the engine and climbed out. A gusty wind shook the trees around him, raining snow and ice across the graveled drive and lawn. He hunched his shoulders inside his jacket and blew on his hands to warm them as he climbed the steps to her porch. Earlier, she'd been angry and had nearly slammed the door in his face. Would she react the same way now?

He raised his hand and knocked, bracing himself for a confrontation.

Inside, he heard rattling, then feet shuffling. "Who is it?"

"It's me, Rex. Falcon."

Silence.

Rex waited, kicking snow from his boots. "Can I come in?"

A long heartbeat of silence followed. "That's not necessary."

He cleared his throat. He couldn't leave without looking into her face one more time. "Please, Hailey."

The door slid open slightly, and Hailey's face appeared, her dark hawkish eyes wide and wary. "I'm fine. You can go home now."

Wild instincts overcame him. She looked so frightened. So small and vulnerable. As if she needed holding, the tension soothed from her face. He slid one hand in between the door to stop her from shutting it. "Let me come in. We can have some coffee. Talk."

She shook her head. "No, it's too late."

"Hailey, if you're angry about earlier, I'm sorry," he said in a low voice. "I didn't mean to insult you."

She bit down on her lower lip, sending a shard of desire rippling through him. "You lied to me."

He frowned. "What are you talking about?"

"About who you are," she said in a harsh voice. "Why didn't you tell me you're Randolph Falcon's son?"

Anger slammed into him, fresh with raw pain. The condemnation in her eyes ripped into him like a knife. "Because my father is innocent," he said in a gruff voice.

Fear flashed onto her face just as he'd expected, driving the knife deeper.

Suddenly, he couldn't stand it. He'd never wanted anyone to believe him the way he wanted Hailey to. And he felt compelled to prove to her that he hadn't come to harm her, that he wanted her.

He pushed open the door, captured her chin with his hand, lowered his mouth and drove his lips on top of hers. She stiffened at first as he claimed her, but slowly her lips moved beneath his, her fingers tentatively reaching up to grip his arms.

The kiss was hot, harsh, raw, tainted with pain and his own yearning. He thrust his tongue into her mouth, nipped at her lips, drove himself deep into her warmth. His entire body hardened and ignited with fire. She tasted like sweetness and coffee and desire. But something else lingered below the surface—fear.

Repercussions screamed in his head as he dragged himself away from her. Her cheeks were rosy with passion. Or was it terror?

"Why did you do that?" she murmured.

Guilt added to his confused emotions. She was afraid of him, that was obvious. Even more so now that she knew his identity. And kissing her hadn't helped at all…. "I wanted you to know that I wouldn't hurt you."

But he saw in her eyes that he had. His physical prowess frightened her. He'd overstepped his bounds.

"I'm sorry." Unable to tolerate the pained look in her eyes, he swallowed again, emotions tangling in his head. He wanted to stroke her hair, massage the tension from her shoulders, kiss her again and tease her senses until desire lit her eyes.

But she didn't want him.

He backed away and shoved his hands in his pockets so he wouldn't scare her any more than he already had.

Tears shimmered in her eyes, hitting him like a punch to the stomach. God, he'd screwed up good. "I won't touch you again," he said in a strained voice. "I promise. Not unless you ask."

He didn't wait for her answer. He didn't expect one. It was happening all over again, just like any time a woman learned who he was, who his father had been.

Why had he opened himself up to the hurt again?

Calling himself all kinds of a fool, he swung around and jogged to his car, berating himself the entire way home for his inability to control himself. Who was he kidding? He'd wanted Hailey, flat and simple. Wanted her to wash away the sting of the confrontation with the sheriff. Wash away his fear that he might not be able to prove his father's innocence.

He'd thought his desire would bring them closer. But it had been foolish. He'd only proven he was like the birds of prey who took what they wanted with no thought to their victim.

Self-recriminations dogged him as he sped up the mountain toward Falcon Ridge. But God help him, he still wanted her. Even worse, if he had the moment to do over again, he wasn't sure he would have handled himself any differently.

A TEAR TRICKLED down Hailey's cheek as she locked the door. Her insides were a quivering mass, her legs threatening to fold. No man had ever kissed her that way, or made her want to bow to his wishes and make love. She hadn't even thought it possible.

Thad's harsh overtures sliced through her memories. He had been patient at first, had thought it admirable that she'd saved herself for so long, that she had been untouched by another man.

But he'd grown impatient. He'd wanted to brand her, make her his, as if she were some head of cattle or piece of property that he owned. His brusque attitude had turned her off. His possessiveness had felt claustrophobic. She'd had to break free of him.

But Rex…

Rex had been bold and physical, yet the untamed passion beneath the surface had lit a flame inside her that still flickered with want. Only she'd been too stunned and frightened to admit it. Because playing with fire was dangerous. And Rex Falcon was a hot flame ready to eat up anything in his path.

Had he really wanted her, or had his kiss been meant to prove that he could control her as Thad had tried to do?

The photo of the Lyle murders flashed back in horrifying clarity. Was his father a murderer?

Rex claimed no. If he was innocent, what kind of life had Rex led with his father labeled the Hatchet Murderer? And why was he back here in Tin City, working on the very house where his father was convicted of slaughtering four innocent people?

A shadow loomed from the outside, shimmering through the window. Hailey froze, then moved to the window, hiding behind the sheers as she pulled the curtain back to peer out. There it was again. A dark figure sliding behind a tree.

Her heart raced. Was Rex lingering outside? Or was a wild animal roaming the forest? Or was someone else outside, watching her house? Watching her? Waiting to carry out the threat he'd left earlier?

THE FACT THAT THE WOMAN was inside the house now, sleeping in the bed where the Lyle woman had lain, using their furniture and plundering through cabinets and drawers and closets, disturbed him. Who was she? And why had she come? To stir up trouble?

And what if she discovered something in the house?

Something that would raise questions about the hatchet killings?

The issue had been put to rest two decades earlier. He had been a free man since.

Nothing was going to rob him of his freedom now.

Not some woman who had a penchant for haunted houses. Or the man who'd moved back to Falcon Ridge.

He was one of the Falcon kids grown up. And he'd come here asking questions, trying to clear his father. Yes, Falcon had to be dealt with immediately, before things got out of hand and someone in town decided to talk.

He hunched between the trees, accustomed to living in the darkness. Killing Falcon would be easy, a pleasure in fact. Or maybe he could kill the woman and frame the Falcon boy for it. Like his father, he'd spend the rest of his life in prison, defending his honor. Fighting off the other inmates.

A chuckle escaped him at the thought. Then he gazed at the miles and miles of forest, the deep ravines, the jagged rocky mountains, the dozens of deserted mines. So much snow and ice and rugged wilderness. So many wild animals ready to pounce and prey on human flesh. So many hiding places.

A perfect burial ground for Falcon and the woman.

Chapter Seven

Rex stared down the hill at the Hatchet House through his kitchen window, fighting the urge to go to Hailey's and apologize again. He had done enough damage for one night. If he frightened her any more, she might deny him access to the house. But he was certain there was evidence inside the Lyle homestead to help exonerate his father.

Besides, he knew himself too well. He couldn't return with lust still hot in his loins and his mouth burning with the taste of Hailey's lips. He'd take one look at her, drag her into his arms and kiss her again. Something happened to him when he was around her. It was as if his body sensed that hers lay in wait for him, like the monogamous birds that lay in wait for their mate.

He scrubbed a hand over his face. Maybe he'd been living in the wilderness with the animals too damn long. He was starting to think crazy thoughts. Him mating? A woman lying in wait for a loner like Rex Falcon?

That was ridiculous. Especially considering Hailey didn't even seem to like him. She certainly didn't want him touching her.

His hands fisted beside him. Who had hurt her and frightened her so badly? He had the sudden urge to find out. To rip out the man's throat, tear skin from bones, just as an eagle would shred its prey. Another reason he needed to avoid her. His basic animal nature was too strong.

He punched in the number for his brothers, tapping his foot impatiently while he waited. Maybe talking to them would ground him. The clock ticked in the background, sounding off the minutes, but finally Deke answered.

"What's up, man?"

"Nothing concrete yet," Rex said. "But I talked to Sheriff Cohen earlier. He's not going to cooperate."

"I'm not surprised. He was pretty damn cold back when we were kids."

"His attitude hasn't changed." Rex hesitated. "The woman in the Lyle house is a complication, too. She claimed someone left dead flowers, a picture of the murder scene and a threatening note inside."

Deke whistled. "Sounds like someone doesn't want the matter stirred up again."

"Which means we're on the right track," Rex said.

"I'm almost finished with this case," Deke said. "Hopefully Brack and I can be out there in a week."

Rex nodded, wishing it was sooner. "I have copies of the police investigation I plan to look at tonight, then I'll study the trial transcripts."

"Good. Keep us posted."

Rex gripped the phone, not ready to hang up, but he and his brothers hadn't exactly shared their private lives, and he wasn't ready to divulge his troubled emotions over Hailey quite yet.

"Don't let the woman mess with your head or the case," Deke warned, though, as if he'd read his mind.

"Right." He'd known his brother would set him straight. The Falcon men didn't need anyone but each other and the wilderness.

Rex said goodbye and hung up, vowing to find out the reason Hailey had run, but his father's case took precedence. Too wired to sleep or concentrate on the files yet, he yanked on sweats and running shoes and jogged into the woods. He needed space, the freedom of running through the wilderness and being one with the beasts that lived off the land.

His shoes crunched the ice and snow, the wind beat at his face and the scents of pine and fir trees mingled with other earthy scents of the forest. A large tree festooned with eagles vying for nesting rights drew his eye, the loud territorial call of the birds screeching into the dusky sky. One left a rebounding branch, the roaring of his wings sounding above the shattering of icicles, while a juvenile eagle flew more slowly behind, obviously wind-dependent. Their shadows tagged black over the barren stretch of snow ahead, the beauty of their flight patterns calming Rex as he pumped his legs and arms and darted through the maze of aspens and pines.

He ran for miles, uncaring of his destination or the lateness of the hour, simply allowing his tensions to drain as adrenaline pumped through his bloodstream. A low growling sound drifted toward him. He slowed. A mountain lion. He hid behind a boulder and watched, a sliver of moonlight illuminating the lion's actions. He was pawing at the ground.

Seconds later, the mountain lion cocked its head, and Rex noticed something lodged in his mouth. Then the animal darted the other way, gliding with agility and grace over the rocky incline.

He moved forward to investigate the site, then knelt and brushed dead leaves away. A bone was sticking out of the earth nearby.

A bone that looked like a human's.

HAILEY STARED at the flickering shadows in the woods until her vision blurred. She'd craved the solace of the mountains and wide-open spaces, had thought the quiet solitude would offer her the peace she needed from her nightmarish past, but she hadn't been prepared for the eeriness of being completely alone.

Except Rex Falcon was only a mile away.

She could pick up the phone—and do what? Ask him to come back? Admit that she was afraid of her own shadow? Beg him to hold her and shield her from the danger lurking around her?

Why was this house affecting her so badly? She'd researched others before and the grim stories of lost lives hadn't spooked her like the murder of the Lyle family. Of course, she'd never found threatening notes warning her that she might end up dead.

Finally satisfied that whatever had been roaming the woods had gone for the night, that she had only imagined it was a person, she crawled into the big iron bed in the master suite. The ancient furnace rumbled, but the room still held a chill that came with age and poor insulation. Thankfully, the snowstorm had lifted, but ice crystals clung to the tree branches and windows like long jagged knives against the fog-coated glass.

She forced herself to close her eyes, but Rex Falcon's face flashed unbidden in her mind. The rough coarseness of his beard stubble had scraped her cheek in an erotic dance of textures, his warm, passionate lips still imprinted on her own.

As she slowly drifted to sleep, she felt his hands lingering on her jaw, felt his fingers trail down her neck, then lower. One by one, in torturous slow motion, he unbuttoned her gown, slipping the fabric from her bare skin, sliding his fingers along her nakedness as his breath whispered over her breasts. She welcomed his touch, ached for him to tangle his body with hers and give her pleasure.

She moaned and reached for him…

BUT SUDDENLY his hands closed around her neck, choking her. His fingers pressed into her skin, the pressure so intense she gasped and tried to scream, but no sound came out.

Then she was a little girl again. Back in the nightmare.

The monster dragged her to the attic, shoving her up the steps, pushing her into the darkness. Her knees hit the hard wooden floor. She fell forward, bit her tongue and tasted blood. Grappling for control, she reached in front of her, searching for the door. But a thin stream of moonlight played on the shiny knob and she saw it turn. The sound of the lock clicking into place splintered the night.

She cried out and shrank back against the wall, despair filling her. The gray walls closed around her. The patter of mice skittering in the corner grated on her frayed nerves.

She couldn't stand it. Not again.

"No…please don't leave me," she whispered. "Please someone, come and save me."

A sound screeched behind her. A rat maybe? Or was someone else in the attic?

The air swirled around her, disorienting her. She couldn't breathe. She couldn't see. She couldn't move.

Then music drifted through the haze. A low melody that sounded familiar. The distant hum soothed her trembling slightly, and she inhaled, rocking herself back and forth. The melody grew louder. Closer.

What was the tune? It sounded so familiar…

Closing her eyes, she tried to concentrate, shutting out the darkness, the world, the fact that she would be a prisoner inside the room until morning. And then maybe even longer… unless he came for her first, but that could only mean one thing.

No…she'd rather stay here than face him again to-night. But she hated the blank emptiness. And it was so cold….

Tears streamed down her cheeks, but she brushed them away with the back of her hand, forcing herself to let the music calm her.

Her mommy was playing it for her. She pictured her face, saw her reaching out her arms to comfort her. The music from the snow globe, it was their little secret. Her mother's way of saving her when she could do nothing else for her.

She twisted, agitated. She was all alone. Forever.

No, her mommy was gone, too. And so was her daddy. He'd left her at the orphanage because he didn't want her. He didn't love her anymore. Maybe he never had….

Then she was running again. She wasn't in the attic but in the woods. Huge trees blocked her path, adding to the terror of the jagged mountain peaks that fell away to nothingness. A voice yelled for her to stop, but she kept running. He was chasing her, closing the distance. His feet drummed on the earth. His clothing rustled. He cursed as he pushed aside the bramble. Panting for air, she glanced over her shoulder and saw the big shiny blade of the hatchet glinting in the infernal black. He raised the hatchet above his shoulder, then swung it down toward her.

She screamed and ran faster. But her foot hit a bear trap and she fell down. Pain knifed through her ankle. Then he was above her, his teeth bared, the blade coming closer.

It was Rex Falcon and he was going to kill her….

HAILEY JERKED AWAKE, sweating and disoriented. She gasped and glanced around, certain her attacker was on top of her. She was in the woods….

No, she was on the floor of the master bedroom, crouched into the corner. Hugging her arms around her, she fought the trembling that had taken root deep inside her. Another nightmare.

Only this one had been more vivid. And this time the Hatchet Murderer had been after her. And it had been Rex.

But Rex wasn't a killer, was he? It had been his father….

She grabbed the bedpost to haul herself up, but a faint sound invaded her senses.

Music.

She froze again, hands clenched around the iron bed. The snow globe. Was it real?

She reached for a light, but when she hit the switch, it flickered on, then off again. No! Had someone tampered with the lights? An intruder maybe…

She couldn't panic. The house was old. A fuse had probably blown. She inched forward, listening for footsteps, then glanced out the window. Deep in the woods, she saw a beam of light. A flashlight maybe.

Someone was out there.

Another noise screeched through the walls. Then the soft melody that had played in her dreams floated toward her. Where was the music coming from?

Her hands shaking, she clutched the wall as she stumbled to the door. She felt for the hall light, flipped the switch, but the interior remained unlit. The tune grew louder. Closer.

She pivoted, praying it wasn't coming from the attic. Then she glanced at the door. It was closed. Still locked from the outside. Thank goodness.

Her chest tight, she inched her way toward the boy's room, then froze in the doorway searching the darkness. Barring the furniture, though, the room was empty.

Silently she moved to the little girl's room. The sound floated to her, soothing, yet rattling her nerves. As soon as she stepped inside the doorway, she knew she'd found it.

A beautiful white snow globe with a snowman twirling on the top sat on the dresser. Her lips mouthed the words to the tune, "I'm dreaming of a white Christmas…"

But where had the globe come from? And was the person who'd put it there still inside the house?

Hailey reached for the globe, but a shadow suddenly appeared, accentuated by the tiny stream of moonlight. Panic tightened her muscles. She tried to scream, but someone grabbed her around the neck and shoved a rag over her mouth, stifling the sound. She kicked and struggled, biting at the man's hand. He shook her violently, his hands tightening around her throat as he dragged her toward the hallway.

No! He was taking her to the attic. Except this time it wasn't a nightmare. It was real.

And he was going to kill her….

REX'S ANXIETY MOUNTED as the sheriff, his deputy and the coroner crowded around the area where he'd discovered the bone. The deputy, a younger guy in his twenties named Melvin Larkin, dug up the ground while Sheriff Cohen watched with a scowl.

"I can't believe you dragged us out in the woods this time of night," Sheriff Cohen growled. "This had better be good."

"I wouldn't call finding a body good," Rex shot back. "But it is interesting, and it was my duty to report it."

"Probably some hunter or a hiker got attacked by a bear or mountain lion, then got buried in one of the snowstorms."

"I don't think so."

The sheriff's eyes narrowed. "You know who it is?"

"No." Not ready to share his suspicions, he shoved his hands in the pockets of his coat as he stared at the recently turned snow-crusted ground. "But it's human, and I think younger than a hunter would have been. Just look at the bone size."

Cohen swallowed, a branch slapping back and forth in the wind beside his ruddy face. "You think it has something to do with the Lyle case, don't you?"

Rex shrugged. "It could be the little girl's body."

Cohen's blustery curse caught in the wind and echoed across the mountain. "I told you to leave town, not to start trouble."

"I'm supposed to stumble on a body and not call the police?"

"Who the hell jogs this time of night in this weather?"

A man running from something, like a woman. "Exercise is good for the body and soul," Rex said instead, glancing pointedly at Cohen's belly.

Cohen glared at him. "Listen, Falcon—"

"We've got something." Will Snyder, the M.E., knelt to examine the bones.

Rex frowned.

"How do I know you didn't plant these?" Cohen asked.

Rex's head jerked up. "Don't be ridiculous."

"If it is the Lyle girl, maybe you knew exactly where to find her because you saw your daddy bury her here." Cohen stuffed a cigarette in his mouth, lit the end and puffed, the ring of smoke spiraling upward, then evaporating into the frigid air. "Maybe you even helped your daddy." His beady eyes half closed. "What were you—about nine, ten at the time? Hell, maybe you were the one who killed the family, and your daddy covered up for you."

Rex jerked the sheriff's collar, his breath hissing out. "You're an SOB, Cohen, you always were."

Looking worried, the deputy slid one hand over his pistol.

Rex reined in his temper. "If that bull was true, why the hell would I show you the body? That would only make me look guilty."

"You thought it would throw suspicion off of you."

"That's ridiculous and you know it." Rex released him so quickly the sheriff stumbled backward. "Just do your job and examine the remains." Fed up with Cohen, he turned and addressed the medical examiner. "I want to know who the body belongs to, cause of death and any other evidence you find."

Snyder nodded although he didn't look happy. The deputy squatted to study the grave, a troubled expression on his face. "Looks like you might have been right, Falcon."

Rex's stomach churned as he spotted a rag doll in the dirt. Damn. He didn't want to be right. But he was more determined now to get to the truth. And he wouldn't stop until he did.

"If it is the Lyle girl," Cohen said, "all this proves is that your old man buried her instead of dumping her in the river."

Rex ground his teeth together. "You know, Sheriff, you're way too quick to jump to conclusions." He stepped closer, his breath hissing in the cold air between them. "Was there some reason you hurried up the trial twenty years ago? Something you wanted to hide or cover up?"

Cohen vaulted toward Rex, but the deputy caught his arm. "Come on, Sheriff. The body will speak for itself."

Cohen shook his deputy away and turned to the M.E. "Do whatever it takes to preserve the evidence."

Rex frowned. He'd hit a nerve with Cohen. The sheriff had arrested Rex's father within hours after the murder, had never considered another suspect, hadn't explored any other possibilities. There had to be a reason.

If he was covering something up, maybe that explained his agitation over Rex's appearance. He also wouldn't like Hailey staying in the house….

Worse, the killer might still be around. He'd be getting nervous now.

Rex's gaze shot down the hill toward the Hatchet House. He raised his binoculars and peered through the woods. His father had said he had the eyes of a hawk. The house was cloaked in total darkness. Odd, even the outside light by the road was off.

Something was wrong.

His gut instincts told him so, and he had to listen. What if the threat she'd mentioned had been real?

His heart began to race, the bad feeling in his gut intensifying. He had to make sure Hailey was all right.

Chapter Eight

After one last warning to the sheriff and medical examiner about preserving evidence, Rex raced through the woods toward the Hatchet House, his heart pounding as he imagined the killer having returned to murder Hailey.

He should have listened to her earlier. He shouldn't have dismissed her claims of a threat so readily.

Get a grip, Falcon. You're overreacting, letting your emotions override rationale. Something he normally didn't do.

The house was old. A fuse had probably blown or the electricity had gone out from damaged power lines. His calves ached as he jogged down the hill, the air charged around him as he approached Hailey's house. Darkness bathed the run-down exterior.

A foreboding feeling settled over Rex again.

His footsteps faltered as he remembered that fatal day years before when he'd heard there was trouble at this house, the day he'd seen the blood-splattered bodies of the Lyle family.

His lungs tightened, squeezing at the air. Dear God, he hoped he didn't find a repeat of the scene tonight.

He slowly edged up the steps, moving with the prowess of an animal. He had to focus, to zero in on the sounds around him. A bird squawked above. Squirrels scrounged in the snow nearby, foraging for food. A noise erupted from inside the house.

Scuffling. A woman's soft cry. Hailey.

His stomach knotted. He'd left his gun in his SUV. Fists clenched, he slipped inside. Another low cry echoed from above. The sound of footsteps. Then shoes scraping the floor.

Rex moved slowly inside, scanning the shadows, but the scuffling sound splintered the eerie silence again. It was coming from upstairs. He crept toward the staircase, but a loose board in the floor creaked, and the scuffling above stopped abruptly.

He froze, backing up against the wall, but the shadow shifted to the top of the staircase, then suddenly Hailey tumbled down the steps, screaming and flailing for control. Dammit. The bastard had seen him and shoved her.

He lunged forward and caught her in the landing, bracing her head in his hands as he searched her face. "Hailey, are you all right?"

Glazed eyes stared back as if she couldn't see him.

He shook her gently. "Hailey, answer me, sweetie. Are you all right?"

"Yes." Her whisper was so faint he barely heard it.

Relief whooshed out. "I'll be right back." Gently releasing her, he darted up the stairs and raced down the hall, but the man had disappeared. Where the hell had he gone? Heart pounding, he searched the rooms. The shades in the boy's room flapped back and forth. He ran to the open window, and scanned the darkness. A faint outline of a figure flickered against the trees. The man had somehow climbed down and fled into the woods.

Rex wanted to hunt him down and kill him like an animal.

But Hailey might be injured.

He turned and raced back to the steps. She was leaning against the wall, massaging her throat. He knelt and searched her face. Fresh bruises colored the pale skin of her neck, a tinge of blood dotting her lower lip.

"He t-tried to k-kill me."

"I know." He swallowed bile. "Are you hurt anywhere else?" He patted her arms, her legs, checking for injuries.

"No…I'm okay." The last word broke on a soft cry. Needing reassurance that she really was alive, he cradled her head against his chest, and wrapped his arms around her, holding her tight.

HAILEY HAD NEVER BEEN so frightened in her life. She had known she was going to die.

But now Rex was here. Holding her. Caressing her. Soothing her with quiet whispered utterances.

His breath brushed her neck, and her body sprang back to life, senses tingling with his touch. Burrowing deeper into his embrace, she savored the strength of his arms around her. She never wanted him to release her. The realization should have frightened her, but for some strange reason, it didn't. Maybe because he had saved her life.

But there was more.

Some deep connection she felt for this man. A connection she thought he sensed, as well. His breath against her cheek was tantalizing, his whisper sultry, his hands seductive. His body provided a tempting haven of male need and offering.

Or was it just the circumstances? The danger?

It didn't matter, at least not at the moment. He was warm and safe and all male, and she nestled closer, the tight-throat feeling she usually experienced with a man dissipating.

"Hailey." His gruff voice teased her nerve endings,

stirring hidden desires. He sounded worried, as if he really cared for her. That was a first, as well, and heightened the sensual arousal simmering within her.

"Did you see his face?" he asked in a gruff voice.

She shook her head, searching her memory banks. "No. He came at me from behind. Then he tried to choke me."

His jaw snapped tighter. "You should see a doctor."

"No." She reached for his arms, curled her fingers around his biceps, oddly soothed by the feel of his corded muscles bunching beneath her touch. "Please, I'm okay now."

He traced the tender skin where the other man's hands had gripped her, erasing the pain. Earlier she'd dreamed Rex had hurt her, but even with his size and fierce male prowess, his touch remained gentle, almost reverent.

"I should call the sheriff, report this."

Panic clawed at Hailey. "No...not yet."

"Why not?" His eyes narrowed, questions mounting. "Someone tried to kill you, Hailey. You can't let him get away with it. He might come back."

She dragged her eyes from his, but they fell to his chest. The force of his breathing made her aware how perfectly their bodies fit together, that his was reacting with hunger.

"Tell me what's going on," he said in a low voice. "I know you're running from something. That you're scared. Do you know who attacked you?"

Confusion clouded her brain. Her first instinct was to confide in him. But how could Thad have found her so quickly?

She shook her head. "No."

"Don't lie, Hailey. There's some reason you don't want me to call the cops. Are you in trouble with the law?"

His question cut too close to the truth. "No. I… Whoever was here, it must have to do with the Lyle murders. It had to be the same person who left the note earlier."

Rex studied her for a long moment, his question lingering between them. "Then we should tell the sheriff."

She chewed the inside of her cheek. Why was he asking her about her past? The timing of his appearance the first day she'd moved in seemed suddenly odd. Could he possibly be working for Thad?

That's crazy, Hailey. He grew up around here, he's the son of the man who killed the Lyles. He saved you.

She started to stand, but her legs wobbled, and he steadied her. If she explained about Thad, she might put Rex in danger. Thad had been so out of control he'd probably unleash his rage on anyone she became involved with. She couldn't take the chance.

"Maybe tomorrow." She sighed, calming herself. "But not now. Please, Rex, I can't deal with anything else tonight."

He stroked her cheek with his finger. His touch was so erotic that heat ignited within her.

Emotions rattled in her head. She wanted him as she'd never wanted another man. But she was still afraid.

He must have seen the fear in her eyes.

His hands dropped to his side, regret darkening his expression. "I'm sorry. I promised not to touch you again unless you asked."

She caught his arm, tentative but a step. "I… It felt good. Thank you for saving me."

The tiny tilt of his deep-set mouth forming a smile was his only reply. That and the smoldering look in his dark eyes.

HAILEY'S SIMPLE ADMISSION aroused emotions deep inside Rex that he wasn't ready to acknowledge. He still wanted to know the reason she'd run and who was after her, but details could wait.

Someone had just tried to kill her. Whether it was someone from her past or someone who wanted her out of the Lyle house because of the murders, he didn't know. But he would find out.

Only not tonight. She was right. They were both exhausted, adrenaline now waning, the heat rippling between them palpable. Besides the sheriff had been fighting him every inch of the way.

"Come on, pack some things," he said in a low voice. "You're going to stay at my house tonight."

The wariness returned to her eyes. "Rex, I can't."

"It's not up for debate," he stated bluntly. "It's either my house, or I phone the police."

She clasped the stair rail with a trembling hand. "Rex—"

"Trust me, Hailey." He wanted to reach for her, to shake some sense into her, but he'd promised not to touch her, so he refrained. "I'm not going to leave you here alone tonight, and it's not safe to stay in this house."

"But it's my home," she protested.

He could relate. He'd been torn from his home when he was young, too. "We'll come back tomorrow. I'll install a security system and safety latches on the windows and doors, then you can sleep here." He traced the purple bruises along her neck. "But tonight I want you close by, so I can make sure this madman doesn't get to you again."

Her gaze connected with his for a heartbeat of a second, then she seemed to accept his logic, nodded and disappeared up the steps. Having Hailey spend the night in his house would change things, even if she did sleep in the adjoining room instead of his bed. Once she warmed the big stone structure with her presence and her scent, it would linger there forever.

The ride to Falcon Ridge stretched into a tension-filled eternity, the air in the car steeped with sexual heat and the realization that they were going to share a house for the night. Afraid she'd slip on the icy stone walkway, he hurried to the passenger side to assist her, but she'd already climbed out. Her independence roused admiration. Or perhaps she was still running from him, just as she was from the person after her.

They entered Falcon Ridge in silence, the chill in the two-story foyer reminding him of his mother's distaste for the house. The drone of the furnace rumbled in the dim interior.

"How about some decaf coffee before we turn in?" The word "we" lingered on his tongue, suggestive, although he hadn't meant it that way.

She nodded, hugging her arms around herself to ward off the chill. "Thanks, it might help me sleep."

He set her bag near the stairs, then gestured for her to follow him to the kitchen. Out of the corner of his eye, he noticed the message light blinking while he made coffee. He punched the button.

"Falcon, it's McDaver. I got your message." Annoyance added a high-pitched quality to his voice. "I don't know what you think you'll dig up in the hatchet case, but your father was guilty. Leave the matter alone. The last thing this town wants or needs is to relive the trauma of that nightmarish case."

Rex clicked off the message, barely stifling a curse. Hailey was watching intently, her eyes softening with compassion. The old familiar shame washed over him. He turned and poured them some coffee. Hailey accepted hers, blowing on the hot liquid to cool it while he took a gulp, not caring if he scalded his tongue.

"Did the man who attacked you say anything?" he asked.

"No, nothing."

"Did you notice any unusual smells? Cigarettes, cologne, anything?"

"He smelled stale, sweaty, like he'd been outside…." She frowned. "There's something else, too."

"What?"

"I'd fallen asleep and was having a nightmare about being locked in the attic…." She hesitated, and he gave her time to compose herself. "When I woke up, I heard music playing."

"What kind of music?"

"The tune 'White Christmas.' I found a musical snow globe on the bedside table in the little girl's room. There was something familiar about the snow globe," Hailey admitted. "It was almost as if I'd seen it before."

He watched her over his mug. "Maybe you had one when you were a child."

"No." A frown pinched her face. "That's just it, I didn't. But it seemed so familiar."

Could she possibly have some kind of psychic ability?

No, he didn't believe in that nonsense.

"You could have seen one in a store. They're fairly common, especially at Christmastime."

"I suppose that's possible." She rubbed her forehead. "I'm tired. I think I'll go to bed now."

She looked so small and vulnerable he wanted to hold her again, to wipe away the worry on her face and erase the memory of the man hurting her. He'd replace those memories with new ones, with memories of gentle touches, of him making love to her….

He quickly jerked himself back to reality. He'd never thought of sex as making love before, just as pure raw animal release.

"Come on, I'll show you to one of the guest rooms."

She avoided his eyes as he escorted her to the second room on the left, a large suite in golds and creams filled with antiques.

"Was this one of your brothers' rooms?" she asked.

"No, just a spare room. My brothers and I shared a wing down the hall on the opposite end."

She nodded, then walked inside. He tried to see the room as she must. A stone structure with ten-foot walls that might appear cold. Yet she didn't react, simply thanked him and placed the coffee mug on the dresser. A soft wine-colored spread covered the bed. The antiques were classic, the room clean and elegant. Made for a lady just like Hailey. "It's lovely."

"There's a bathroom that adjoins the suite," he said. "You should find everything you need in there."

She glanced around the room, then toward the door that connected to his room. "What's on that side?"

"The master suite where I'll be." He'd purposely put them close together so he could hear her if she woke during the night. "I closed off the other wing to conserve heat and energy."

"Oh."

Her single word echoed with the realization of the intimacy of their sleeping arrangements. He barely resisted the urge to admit that he wanted them to be even closer, really intimate, at least on a physical level.

But then he'd always been a physical man.

The timing was wrong, though, and so was his choice in women. He sensed Hailey wouldn't accept a physical relationship, at least not without emotions, and he had nothing to offer except a night of uninhibited, feverish sex.

She needed a different kind of man than him. One who could offer tenderness and sweetness. Safety. Promises to stick around.

None of which described Rex Falcon.

He had to get the hell out. "Well, I'll let you go to bed."

She nodded, and he backed out of the room, hesitating at the doorway. An image of her naked lying on the bedspread with her hair fanned around her face came unbidden to him, tempting him to stay, to hold her all through the night.

But the cold facts of his father's case, of her attacker, of his life as a Falcon man stood between them as much a barrier as the great mountainous reefs that divided the continents.

"Thank you, Rex."

"Sure." He cleared his throat, trying to rid his voice of the lust and hunger warring with his common sense. "I'll be next door if you need me."

A ghost of a smile played on her mouth, although she whispered that she would be fine. Then she closed the door behind her.

Outside the room, his heart pounded. He placed his hand against the wooden panel and closed his eyes, imagining her reaching out to take his fingers and invite him into her bed. He could see her sliding her clothes off her shoulders, dropping them to the carpet below her bare feet, her nakedness welcoming him as she spread herself across the pillows and opened to him.

Frustrated, he groaned silently, willing himself to forget the tormenting image, to remember that the Falcon men needed nothing but the wilderness and their freedom. That sex with her might be exquisite but would compromise his very soul.

Rex Falcon needed no one. And it would remain that way until the day he died.

HAILEY LEANED AGAINST the door frame and closed her eyes, her heart fluttering. She'd almost died tonight. If Rex hadn't saved her…

His strong, angular face flashed into her mind. For

a second, she'd been tempted to ask him to stay. To pull down the covers, lie down beside her and hold her.

To erase the harsh memory of her attacker's intentions.

But staying would have meant intimacy. An intimacy she'd never shared with a man. An intimacy she wasn't certain she was ready to share with Rex Falcon.

He was an enigmatic man of few words who seemed driven by revenge. Unrestrained anger emanated from him in waves, holding him prisoner. His father's murder conviction had obviously left him with permanent scars, had made him tough, formidable. Dangerous.

Yes, dangerous was the only way to describe him.

So why was she fantasizing about offering her virginity to him? About allowing him to touch her in the secret places that craved him. About letting him tap into passions and hungers she hadn't realized she'd possessed until his dark eyes had unleashed this fierce need to feel his hands upon her, to bring her body to life.

Because you almost died tonight.

That had to be the only reason. That and the isolation of the snow-crusted, rocky mountains.

Shivering, she threw on a clean nightgown, then crawled into the plush queen-size bed. The sheets were soft, scented with a floral fragrance that soothed her nerves. Exhausted, she closed her eyes, shut out the world, and fell into a deep sleep.

In her dreams, Thad had returned to get her. This time she was running through the woods, then she crawled into one of the old mines where no one would ever find her.

THAD HUNCHED DEEPER into his suede coat, the wind whipping at his Mercedes as he stared at the monstrosity of a house. Falcon Ridge. Who the hell was Rex

Falcon? And how had he convinced Hailey to spend the night with him?

Fury and rage snowballed inside him, swirling with the intensity of a blizzard, shattering the last vestiges of admiration he'd felt for Hailey's innocence. She was supposed to be a virgin. Had stalled him countless times with excuses and coy phrases and that flutter of her eyelashes that had nearly driven him mad with want. But now, less than a week after she'd deserted him, she was crawling beneath the covers with a virtual stranger.

Or was he a stranger?

Had Hailey known this man before she'd met him? Was Falcon the reason she'd run off and left him bleeding, scarred and bellowing with pain in the woods like some freak of nature?

He gritted his teeth against the cold, the blustery wind seeping through the windows as he phoned Wormer. An animal's growl echoed from the woods, and he checked the locks on the doors, his other hand sliding to the pistol he always carried. He hated this godforsaken country. The freezing cold. The bitter elements and wild creatures.

He hated Hailey even more for making him chase her.

A groggy voice echoed over the line. "Wormer."

"Wormer, this is Jordan. Find out everything you can on a man named Rex Falcon." He recited the address. "If there's dirt in his background, I want it. And if not, hell, invent it."

Satisfied he'd started the ball rolling, he disconnected the call. No one messed with Thad Jordan and his woman. No one played him for a fool and got away with it. He'd find out everything he could on Falcon, and then he'd destroy him.

Even more gratifying, he'd make Hailey watch while he did it.

Chapter Nine

Unable to fall asleep, Rex headed back downstairs, gathered the files on his father's case and spread them on his desk in the study. Although he'd created a network of computer systems and links to resource agencies in the basement office, he didn't want to get that far away from Hailey in case she needed him.

Who are you kidding, Falcon? You just want to be near her.

Dismissing the disturbing thought, he examined the crime-scene photos, his chest constricting as it always did at the sight. He zeroed in on the clothing and position of the bodies, hoping the details could tell him the real story. The woman was curled protectively around her son, the father a few feet away on his back, his hand outstretched as if he'd been trying to touch them. Or had he been reaching for a weapon?

He studied the picture more thoroughly. Mrs. Lyle was a dark-haired woman with curly hair, about one hundred and thirty pounds, five foot three. Dressed in an old-fashioned housedress, the only jewelry she wore was a simple gold wedding band. He didn't remember ever seeing her in town. The autistic daughter had kept her home—the daughter the Lyles had been too ashamed to bring to town. Had the little girl been too out of control to interact in a social setting? Some people had said she was dangerous to herself, that she exhibited self-destructive behavior. But keeping her exiled from the rest of the world seemed extreme. Had Mrs. Lyle blamed herself for her daughter's condition?

The poor little girl. Everyone thought the killer had chased her into the woods, murdered her and pitched her into the creek.

But the bones Rex had found earlier would most likely tell another story.

Focusing on details again, he studied Lawrence Lyle. He'd been a well-respected attorney in town and a big man with an austere face. He'd supposedly been formidable in the courtroom. Odd though, in the photo Lyle was dressed in khakis and a denim shirt, not a suit as Rex would have expected.

Had he changed when he arrived home from work or had he not gone into the office that day? He made a mental note to check with Ava Riderton, Lyle's secretary back then.

Another detail caught his eye. Lyle wasn't wearing a wedding ring. Hmm. Had he ever worn a ring? Some men didn't….

He glanced down at his own hands, unable to imagine himself with one, because he'd never imagined himself giving up his freedom to commit to a woman.

He skimmed the report but found no notes on the ring. If he had worn one, what had happened to it? Had the killer stolen it as some kind of trophy? But if so, why take the man's ring and not the woman's?

Adding that question to his growing list, he skimmed the names and comments of the locals questioned and the ones who'd testified at his father's trial. Ava Riderton had worked as Lyle's secretary for five years. She testified that he was a hardworking, driven perfectionist who expected total dedication from everyone else, as well. He'd never met an adversary or problem he couldn't conquer. She'd foreseen a long career that was on the fast-track to recognition nationwide and had expected him to end up in politics.

She'd also been devastated by the man's death.

Had she and Lyle been involved in an inner-office romance? If so, and Lyle intended to leave his wife, he would have had motive to kill her. But Lyle had been brutally murdered, as well.

Unless, Lyle had scorned the woman and she'd wanted revenge…

A motive. That is, if Ava Riderton had been in love with Lyle. But was she strong enough to attack two adults and get away with it?

He doubted it.

On the other hand, Sheriff Cohen had been young, cocky, looking to make himself a name, the very reason he'd acted so quickly in the arrest. Could Cohen have murdered the family, then framed Rex's dad to win accolades from the community? In theory, that sounded feasible, but would Cohen have risked his life, jail time, and career just to make a name? He hadn't been that desperate, had he?

Who else in town might have wanted the Lyles dead?

Could Mrs. Lyle have had a lover?

He glanced at the photo again, remembered rumors about her being a recluse and decided it was doubtful. She'd pretty much holed up with the autistic child inside that house.

He checked for domestic disturbances but didn't see any charges filed. He also considered a murder-suicide theory but if Lyle had killed his wife and son, he wouldn't have killed himself the way he had. Lyle had owned a .38. If he'd wanted to commit suicide, he probably would have shot himself.

The neighbors who'd been questioned, Jolie and Howard Baits, claimed they hadn't heard the family fighting but then again, their houses were over two miles away. That real estate agent, Deanna Timmons, on the other hand, had suggested there was trouble in the marriage.

He skimmed further to see if Lyle had had some business investments that had gone bad, but found nothing mentioned. What about criminals he'd tried and convicted?

Lyle's practice seemed the obvious place to look. Had Cohen even investigated that possibility?

HAILEY ROLLED OVER IN BED, surprised she'd been able to sleep. She'd always been good at tuning out reality when circumstances became too difficult for her to handle.

The very reason she'd forgotten some of the experiences in her foster homes.

Early-morning sunshine splintered through the parted velvet drapes, the crisp stark white of the landscape nearly blinding as she looked out the window. The view was majestic, the rolling mountains and hills giving way to snow-blanketed canyons and valleys that would be green in springtime. She could almost see wild columbine dotting the mountainside. She imagined the house painted Wedgwood-blue, its wraparound porch and latticework welcoming guests and antiquers. Maybe even some small children.

Like a baby of your own.

She stiffened, her fingers worrying her nightshirt as she wondered where that thought had come from. She'd never even been with a man or even fantasized about a happily-ever-after. She certainly didn't know if she'd ever fall in love or trust one enough to commit to him.

Rex Falcon's intimidating face sprang to mind....

Baffled by her train of thought, she dressed quickly in jeans and a loose sweater. She planned to go to town and bone up on the Lyle case. If there were ghosts in her house, or if she was in danger because of the murders, she needed to know as much as she could about the past inhabitants.

Her interest had nothing to do with the fact that Rex Falcon's father had been imprisoned for the crime, and that Rex was obviously haunted by the conviction.

Although the towering stone walls created a daunting effect, as she descended the steps the boards didn't groan as the ones in her own house. And the large rooms felt airy; the massive pillars added a comforting flair that promised they'd last forever. Nothing could destroy this house.

Although the Lyle murder had destroyed the family who'd dwelled within it.

The scent of hot coffee and cinnamon rolls drew her into the tempting folds of the kitchen. She braced herself for Rex, but the room was empty, so she poured herself a cup of coffee and stepped outside to look at the bird sanctuary. Her mouth parted in awe at the sight before her.

Rex stood stock-still on the rock patio, his arm extended, his hand covered in a thick glove, an eagle spread across his forearm. His left hand anchored the bird's legs just above his ankles. The eagle's hunched feet lay inert, its toes arched forward.

She could almost feel the animal's tension, so she froze, aware that his startled dark chocolate eyes had snapped onto her figure as if to ask why she'd imposed on his private moment with his master.

The air smelled fragrant around her, the natural wooded setting painting a breathtaking ethereal view that invited relaxation. Rex slowly cut his eyes toward her, one thumb stroking the bird, his voice so low it was almost nonexistent as he spoke to the eagle.

The razor sharpness of the eagle's eyes glinted toward her. Rex stepped closer, his knuckles up, his fingers threaded between the eagle's legs as if to brace the bird should it decide to suddenly attack.

"Is he an adult?" she asked softly.

"No, a juvenile," Rex said. "He's about two. As he gets older, his beak will remain dark, but his head will become spattered with white. See how his big feet are yellow, they contrast with the dark brown plumage. Eagles molt toward their adult coloring. At six, he'll be as white as he's going to get."

"He's beautiful," Hailey whispered. Just like this man was. So calm and in control, so in sync with the natural terrain that it was almost as if he'd become one of the wild animals. His dark eyes were razor sharp, his intense gaze just as predator-like.

Those eyes darkened, heat flaring between them. She moved slowly toward him, watching the bird for signs of distress, aware with each passing second that Rex's breathing had grown more unsteady, that the sizzling hunger between them had become animal-like in nature. It was so alluring she felt as if she'd been trapped in a hypnotic spell that she couldn't break. Or maybe she just didn't want to break it.

"Would you like to touch him?"

Rex's low husky voice skated over raw nerve endings, sending ripples of desire spreading through her.

"Yes." She wanted to touch Rex, too. To have him stroke her as he did the animal.

Cradling the eagle on his arm like a baby, he gently

took her hand, then showed her how to touch the bird's wing. A sense of peace enveloped her as rich as the morning sun beating down from the sky. That warmth was melting the snow just as Rex's intense connection with her was beginning to melt her fear of him.

A slow smile curved Rex's mouth, the look he gave her so intimate she felt as if he'd physically touched her.

She answered with a smile of her own, her heartbeat accelerating as he lowered his head. His jaw was taut, his eyes blazing with passion, the force of his draw too heady to resist. She lifted her hand slowly from the bird's wing, slid it along Rex's jaw, and parted her lips. His beard-stubbled cheek rasped against her hand as he gazed at her. Then he lowered the bird into the cage, closed the door and turned to her, his need palpable.

In his eyes, she saw the question.

He'd promised not to touch her unless she asked.

She telegraphed a silent message that she was ready.

His lips touched hers with the same gentleness as his hands had the bird, although passion sizzled from his mouth to hers. He tasted like rich dark coffee and desire and raw passion, an intoxicating male combination that nearly drove her to her knees.

They finally pulled apart, but Hailey felt dazed, trapped by his need. By her own.

Then screeching sounds above them jerked her eyes to the sky. Birds circled her house in a manic swoop resurrecting memories of the night before in vivid clarity.

Rex hadn't brought her here to love her; he'd only kept her safe for the night because someone had tried to kill her. Because he wanted the truth about the hatchet murders to free his father.

"I'd better go home."

He simply stared at her, the hunger still flaming between them. But he didn't move to drag her back into his arms. "You can't run forever, Hailey. You said you liked antiques because the stories surrounding them told of their past, that they belonged to someone. So, what happened in your past?"

Hailey froze. "I…I don't remember very much about my childhood," she admitted.

"Maybe you should try harder. There might be some good memories in there, too."

A shiver chased up her spine, and she hugged her arms around her waist. "Then why am I so terrified of it?"

His expression softened, the compassion in his eyes so moving that Hailey backed away. She couldn't get any closer, couldn't allow him to. If she did, he'd only hurt her, just as…as everyone else in her life had.

"I…I really do need to go." She didn't wait for a reply this time. Instead, she rushed inside to call the librarian, away from Rex and the dangerous temptation he offered.

"YES, HAILEY, Mrs. Burton will be in the library around ten. I told her you want to talk to her."

"Good. I'll be there then."

"Oh, and I meant to tell you." Mrs. Rogers paused. "There was a man in here late yesterday asking about you. He didn't give a name, said not to mention he was here. He wanted it to be a surprise, but… I thought you might want to know."

A sliver of unease seeped through Hailey. "What did he look like?"

"Um…nice looking, well dressed. He was wearing one of those expensive suits, Italian loafers, really ridiculous for this weather, but a dead giveaway that he was from out of town."

Hailey closed her eyes, her heart pounding.

"He had dark hair, cut all sharp and neat, and he was nice-looking except for this nasty scar down the side of his face. When I asked him about it, he got all agitated."

Hailey dropped her head forward, drawing deep breaths so she wouldn't pass out. Thad had found her.

What would he do to her now?

REX HAD ALLOWED Hailey to get too close, to see him with his birds, to interrupt a session which might have been catastrophic for the animal or Hailey had the eagle reacted differently. Juveniles were unpredictable, especially injured ones.

But Hailey seemed to instinctively understand the caution and trust necessary to bond with the birds. It was as if she'd been drawn to nature herself.

Which was ridiculous. No one but a falconer could understand the true calling of the Falcon men's soul.

Except Rex's mother had, or at least she'd tolerated his father's differences. But his mother was rare. And Hailey had backed away because she was terrified.

Terrified of him.

That was the very reason she connected with the hawk—on an instinctual level, she understood its fear.

Ignoring the pain that realization brought was difficult as he drove her back to her house. Hailey acted distant, even more withdrawn and nervous than she had the day they'd met. Had his kiss frightened her so badly?

Rattled himself, he gave her space, and replaced the fuse, restoring the lights, then spent the next hour searching the house for evidence of the intruder the night before. Instinct cautioned him that the incident might be related to his father's case. But what if the intruder was someone from Hailey's troubled past? If only she'd trust him enough to confide in him.

He had to be patient, as patient as if he'd discovered an injured bird.

He discovered scuff marks on the floor upstairs, both from Hailey's shoes and a stranger's. Although the marks left no definitive imprints, they had to belong to the man who'd attacked her. There were no telltale traces of clothing or blood, though.

After exhausting the outside, he climbed on the roof. It needed repairs, shingles replaced. A hole big enough for a person to slip through drew his eye. It looked as if the shingles had been purposely removed, maybe several times.

Had someone used it as a way to break into Hailey's house? Disturbed at the thought, he climbed through the hole and once again searched for anything that might indicate the identity of her attacker, but came up with nothing.

Frustrated, he made a list of supplies he needed to repair the roof and phoned the company he'd used to install his security system about putting one in for Hailey. Then he went into the gardening shed. Most of the tools were old and rusted, paint brushes too hard and dried up to use, the few gardening supplies reminding him of his father and his love of landscaping. Ironic. He'd taken such good care of the Lyle estate only to end up being incarcerated for his dedication.

An old chest caught his attention, and he opened it, not surprised to see a few ragged old drop cloths, which would have to be discarded. He dug further, his pulse racing when he spotted some rags at the bottom, and a dirty dress shirt tucked in between them. Dark blackish-red stains covered the fabric. The stains might have been rust or some kind of chemical, but he'd seen old dried blood before, and he'd bet his last dollar this was blood. He slid it into a plastic bag he found on the top shelf. He'd take the shirt to town today, send it off to the state crime lab for DNA testing. If it was blood, and the shirt belonged to the real Hatchet Murderer, it might be the missing evidence that would exonerate his father.

Inside, he found Hailey hunched over her computer, studying something intently.

"I'm going to town for supplies," he said. "Your roof needs repairing. I think you should come with me. We can get you a shotgun or a rifle in town."

"Rex—"

"I don't intend to leave you here alone, Hailey. Isn't there something you need to do in town?"

She stared at him for a moment, then nodded. "You're right, I should buy a gun. And I want to go to the library and the bed-and-breakfasts. Let me get my coat."

He nodded. Of course, in town, she'd most likely hear horror stories of his evil father. She'd probably come back assuming he was the same.

He squashed his tumultuous feelings as they drove into Tin City, but as he parked, he saw the locals already gossiping, offering him a wide berth as if afraid of him.

Aware he'd never be able to escape the stigma of being a murderer's son, not in this town anyway, he rushed to the hardware store. Then he'd question the attorney who'd put his father behind bars and get some answers.

HAILEY'S FIRST ORDER of business was to visit the bed-and-breakfast inns in town. Both of the owners were friendly, although shocked that she'd bought the Lyle house. Still, they agreed to post fliers for her antiques business.

The owner of the first inn had only recently moved

to Tin City and knew nothing about the Lyle murders except for rumors. Minnie Atkins, on the other hand, had lived in Tin City all her life, and seemed to thrive on nurturing the gossip vine.

"That Falcon man was strange," Minnie said, bifocals perched on the tip of her nose as she sipped tea with Hailey. "Scary the way he talked to those birds up on the mountain. He had these dark eyes that would pierce right through you, never smiled, but they said he could grow roses to beat the band. That's the reason Mr. Lyle kept him on at his house to manage the gardens."

Except for the rose-growing part, she could have been describing Rex.

"His wife, she had her hands full with those three boys. Hellions they were, always getting in trouble, especially after their daddy got locked up. Fighting all the time. Sheriff even hauled the oldest one, Rex, in once for beating another boy to a bloody pulp."

"What were they fighting about?" Hailey asked.

The woman's teacup rattled as she placed it in the saucer. "Well, the way I heard it was a bunch who had taunted his brothers and called them ugly names—you know, kids' stuff."

Hailey imagined the ordeal the boys had endured, the cruel taunts that had precipitated the fights. "They ganged up on him because his father was in jail," Hailey said, compassion growing for Rex. How many times had she endured gossip and name-calling because she'd been a foster child? Every time she'd attended a new school, a new home, she'd been a target for the bullies.

"You can't blame folks for being scared of the Falcons. That was the most vicious massacre anyone's ever seen around these parts."

Hailey had heard enough. "Thanks for the tea, Mrs. Atkins. I need to go now."

"You be careful," Minnie said. "I hear tell that boy Rex is back. He's bound to be up to no good like his old man."

Hailey couldn't tolerate the scorn any longer. "I'm not sure he's the one who's dangerous," Hailey said. "In fact, someone broke into my house last night, and Rex rescued me."

The woman's eyes bulged. "Oh my goodness, are you all right?"

"Yes, but I might not have been if Rex hadn't come along."

Minnie snatched her hands to her face. "I can't believe it. We haven't had any trouble since those murders and the Falcon family left. Now that boy's back and you bought the Hatchet House, things are starting to turn scary again."

Hailey gritted her teeth, wishing she'd remained silent. The last thing she wanted was to create hysteria in the town and have the locals think she and Rex had brought trouble to them.   Except, if Thad was here, she had….

Minnie's warning echoed in her ears as she walked to the library, her eyes scanning the street for Thad.

"All the articles about the town's history are kept in here." Mrs. Rogers showed her to a small room where she could access microfiche. "I'll tell Faye to come in when she arrives."

Hailey thanked her and spent the next hour reading articles about the town's history. Apparently, Tin City had been a major mining town in the 1880s, and had had twenty saloons, numerous stores and four hotels. But in the early 1900s most of the mines had been exhausted, and the buildings fell into disrepair. Later, when the ghost stories became popular, a developer had turned the town into a summer resort.

Next, she moved on to the Lyle murder. Having found the photo of the murder scene in her house softened the shock of seeing it again, although a deep sorrow for the mother and children overwhelmed Hailey. It was easy to see why the town had turned their hatred on the Falcons. But Rex's declaration of his father's innocence disturbed her.

What if the wrong man had been imprisoned for the crime? What if the real killer was still in Tin City?

Maybe he didn't want her in the house because he was afraid she might find evidence to clear Rex's father.

She had to search the house, or at least allow Rex to do so.

Her heart fluttered. She'd defended Rex, and now she wanted to help him. Odd that the town was so afraid of Rex when she was beginning to trust him.

She flipped further, reading the articles on the arrest, but the third photo stopped her cold.

It showed Rex, his brothers and mother the day of the arrest. Randolph Falcon was being ushered to the police car in handcuffs. His wife was sobbing while Rex's brothers trailed after their father with anger and tears in their eyes.

But Hailey's gaze focused on Rex. He stood to the side, stone still just as he had this morning with the eagle, but the expression on his face hit her with the force of a punch. His horror and anguish were palpable, the sheer sorrow of his loss evident in his dark eyes.

She ached for him. Wanted to reach out and take that little boy into her arms. But that little boy was a man now.

He was still hurting, though.

She knotted her hands together, wishing he was there, that she could comfort him the way he had her.

"What are you doing?"

Hailey startled, then glanced up to see Rex staring at her, a murderous expression in his eyes.

"REX…I THOUGHT we were meeting for lunch—"

"You're researching the story about my family?"

The accusations in his gruff voice sent a shiver down her. "I…I just wanted to know the truth, the story about the murder."

"So you can use it to bring in tourists?"

Her defenses flared. "If someone is trying to run me out of the house because of those murders, I need to know to protect myself."

"And you think the paper is telling the truth?"

Sensing Rex's question was a test of their tenuous growing relationship, she weighed her answer. Did she trust Rex Falcon? Did she believe his father was innocent?

She had defended him, hadn't she? Yet now he was looking at her as if she was his enemy.

"I don't know," she said honestly. "But after reading this, I wondered if there might be some evidence in the house that the police missed."

He glanced away, an odd expression pulling at his mouth.

Then the truth dawned on her. "That's the reason you came to my house, isn't it? You wanted to search it, then you discovered I'd bought the property so you offered to help renovate it as an excuse to get inside." Good heavens, she felt like the biggest fool.

His gaze flashed with guilt, but he offered no apology, simply a clipped nod. "My brothers and I run a detective agency. My father's up for parole—we've reopened the case."

The breath left her in a rush. "I see." And she'd complicated matters by moving into the house. "So you befriended me in order to sneak around behind my back and search the house."

He didn't reply, just stared at her, his expression guarded.

Hurt flared inside her. He'd only been using her. Had he kissed her for the same reason?

GUILT ASSAULTED REX, but he shoved it away. He had only done what he had to do. If he'd first confessed to Hailey that he was the son of a convicted murderer, she never would have allowed him in her house.

She certainly wouldn't have let him get close enough to kiss her. Not that kissing her had been intentional or had anything to do with the case.

An explanation forged to the front of his mind, but his cell phone rang, halting their discussion. "I need to get this."

Hailey nodded, the librarian approaching, an elderly woman beside her.

Rex stepped outside into the hallway and answered the phone.

"Rex, it's Deke. Listen, we've got problems."

Had they ever had anything but? "What is it?"

"That chick who bought the Hatchet House. I did some checking. There's been an assault complaint filed against her by some bigwig attorney named Jordan in Denver."

Assault charges? Maybe he'd been wrong about Hailey. Maybe she wasn't quite so innocent.

"There's more. Dad called. Said his parole hearing has been postponed."

"Postponed. Why?"

Deke hissed his frustration. "I don't know, but he wants us to drop the case."

"What?"

"I was shocked, too," Deke said. "But he was adamant, said for you to leave Falcon Ridge and come back to Arizona."

Rex cursed again, his mind spinning. What the hell had happened to change his father's mind?

Chapter Ten

"Mrs. Burton, my name is Hailey Hitchcock." After greeting the town historian, Hailey explained about buying the Lyle's house, her idea for her business and her concern over the Lyle murders.

"You're mighty brave to move into that haunted place." Faye Burton fluttered a frail hand to her chest. "I swear, a couple of people looked at it before and got spooked. Said there were ghosts haunting it, that they heard creepy noises, like the house was talking." She leaned forward, fussing with her gray curls. "Probably that poor mama crying for her babies."

Hailey swallowed, the grisly image of the bloodbath returning. For a brief second, it almost seemed real, as if she was there seeing it firsthand.

Blinking away the morbid feeling, she patted the older woman's hand. "It was terrible. I want to preserve the family's memory, so I'd like to know more about them. From everything I've heard, Mrs. Lyle was a recluse."

"Holed up there to take care of that mentally sick daughter," Mrs. Burton said. "At least that's what everyone says. I thought it was odd myself."

Hailey frowned. "What do you mean?"

"Back then, people were ashamed when their children weren't quite right, but they could have brought the poor thing to church." The woman murmured several amens. "We could have prayed for her, bless her heart. God listens when we talk to Him."

Hailey nodded, although she had no real firsthand experience to compare to. None of her foster parents had been religious, nor had they taken her to church. Another thing she'd missed out on in her youth. If she ever had children of her own, she'd do things differently.

"Then there were rumors that Joyce had an affair, that Lawrence made her stay at home to keep her in line."

Hailey shifted, the idea of a controlling man trying to rule his wife reminding her of Thad and the reason she'd run. Had Mrs. Lyle given in to her controlling husband? "Do you think there was truth to those rumors?"

Mrs. Burton shrugged. "All I know was what I saw. Mr. Lyle was good-looking, charismatic and he knew how to get his way. If his wife had had an affair, I'm not sure why he didn't divorce her. He could have had his pick around town." She lowered her voice. "His secretary Ava Riderton, for one. She was always making eyes at him."

"Did something happen between them?"

"I don't rightly know. It wasn't like Ava didn't try. She practically flaunted her interest. Now she's got the sheriff wrapped around her little finger. Course he wanted her back then, too."

Hailey cataloged the information, jotting a mental note to talk to Ava. "Did you think Randolph Falcon killed the family?"

Mrs. Burton scrunched her face. "Well, he was at the Lyle house all the time, while Mr. Lyle worked day and night, so everyone assumed Randolph Falcon was Mrs. Lyle's lover."

"Everyone assumed it? Did anyone ever see them together?"

"The postman did when he dropped off packages—they were talking on the back porch. Then Mr. Lyle claimed Falcon attacked him in his own yard."

Hailey twisted her hands in her lap. From everything she'd heard so far, Rex's father sounded guilty. But Rex believed his father had been wrongly accused. Had the locals been unable to look past their small-minded assumptions to entertain the idea that Falcon might have been innocent?

REX HAD HEARD ENOUGH. He hadn't meant to eavesdrop, but after his conversation with his brother, he'd stepped back to get Hailey, and he'd heard the women discussing the Lyle murders.

"My father was innocent," Rex snapped. "He loved my mother. If he hit Lyle, he had good reason."

Mrs. Burton gasped, but quickly recovered. "There's never a good reason for murder, son."

"My father was framed," Rex said between clenched teeth.

Mrs. Burton backed up, her frail hand to her chest. "I…I'd better go now."

"Yes, I think you should. And don't spread any more rumors about my father, Mrs. Burton. If you're the town historian, you should verify the facts."

Her wrinkled skin paled. "I'm sorry for what happened to you and your mama, son. I understand folks weren't fair to you. In fact, I wondered myself why the sheriff was so quick to pin the murder on your daddy. It seems to me Lawrence Lyle made some enemies in town."

Rex's eyebrow shot up. "And who would that be?"

"Ted Trenton, for one. Lawrence sent him away for auto theft. And twice, he put Elvin Moon in jail for beating his wife. And Hooter Konan was always being hauled in for drunk and disorderly."

Petty crimes. There had to be someone else. "You said you thought Lyle had an affair. Anyone specific come to mind?"

"I believe you asked me not to gossip anymore," she said.

Rex gave the older woman credit. "I'm just looking for answers," he said. "My father's served twenty years for a crime he didn't commit. My brothers have grown up fatherless. My mother has…never gotten over it or remarried. If you know something, please tell me."

Compassion flitted into the woman's eyes. "Talk to Ava Riderton," she said. "She worked for Lyle. She knew more about him than anyone else."

Rex nodded. "Thank you, ma'am."

Her taut scowl softened into a smile. "You look just like him, you know. Same dark eyes. Same standoffish face."

Rex almost laughed out loud. But she was right. He was just like his father. Except that his father wanted him to close the case, to turn tail and run.

But Rex wasn't a quitter. No kind of threat was going to stop him now. If anything, it was becoming more and more obvious that he was on the right track.

He glanced at Hailey and wondered at her thoughts. Wondered if she'd stepped in the middle of something that was going to get her hurt. His chest squeezed at the thought. But he couldn't back down now. He'd just have to protect her until this whole mess was over.

Then he'd be able to tell her goodbye and get on with his life.

"I'M GOING TO TALK TO Bentley McDaver, the prosecutor for my father's case," Rex said in a clipped voice.

Hailey had watched his reaction with the town historian. He was on the verge of exploding. She wasn't sure she could help, but she ached to reach out and soothe his pain. "I'll go with you."

He hesitated, but nodded, not meeting her eyes as they stepped outside. She hugged her coat around her. Already the dark clouds had rolled in, obliterating the sun, casting an ominous feel to the skies.

"I thought you had business."

"I already finished," Hailey said. "I met with both of the owners of the bed-and-breakfasts in town."

"Then you had to read the newspaper clippings."

Even though he tried to mask it, she recognized the sting of humiliation in Rex's voice, so Hailey let the comment slide. She'd dealt with cruelty all her life.

Rex quickened his pace, his chin tucked into his coat to ward off the elements. She burrowed deeper in her own jacket, missing the closeness they'd shared earlier. But coming into town had changed Rex. He'd erected walls around himself as massive and stony as the ones that formed Falcon Ridge.

Five minutes later, they stood outside the attorney's office. Hailey's stomach knotted, déjà vu setting in as she remembered Thad's connections. Just how far did his power reach?

What if this lawyer knew Thad?

"Rex…maybe you were right. Maybe I should let you question the prosecutor alone."

His dark, probing eyes skated over her. Did he think she couldn't handle the truth about his father, that she blamed him for his father's actions? Ridiculous considering her past, but she couldn't admit the truth. Not now.

"All right." He gestured toward the small café across the town square. "I'll meet you there in a half hour. We'll eat, then I'll patch that roof before the storm sets back in and change your locks." He frowned. "I arranged for a security system, but it won't be installed for a few days."

She thanked him with a tentative smile, hating the distance between them, then rushed toward the diner. But she scanned the street as she crossed, praying the librarian had made a mistake, that Thad wasn't in town looking for her. But every shadowy corner held the threat of him.

What if he was hiding in the alley, or behind a storefront, watching for her, just waiting to catch her alone so he could finish what he'd started the night she'd left him?

REX HATED FEELING EXPOSED, and around Hailey he felt as if the old wounds of his youth were ripped open. The town had done this to him. Wary, he braced himself as he entered McDaver's office.

The austere district attorney stood behind a cherry desk. "Falcon, I'd welcome you back to town, but we both know that would be a joke."

Falcon simply stared at him. At age ten, this man had seemed menacing to him, the devil who had made horrible accusations against his father and convinced twelve otherwise sane people to lock him up for life. McDaver had aged since then, but still represented a formidable opponent.

"Then let's cut to the chase." Rex claimed one of the leather chairs, leaning forward to indicate he wouldn't be intimidated.

"There is no new evidence," McDaver said, lighting a cigar. "You're wasting your time."

"Why didn't you and the sheriff look at Lyle's enemies or the cases he'd prosecuted?"

"We did." McDaver's fingers curled around the cigar. "None of them panned out."

"How hard did you look?"

"We didn't have to kill ourselves. Your father was staring us in the face. He had means, opportunity, and a thing for Mrs. Lyle."

"That's bull," Rex said. "In fact, both the Lyles might have had affairs. Did you check into that possibility?"

"We didn't need to. We had your father's fingerprints all over the place. And the blood, geesh, he was covered in it."

"Because he tried to save Mrs. Lyle." Rex paused. "And if he was bloody when you found him, why didn't he have the weapon with him? Why would he have ditched it, then called the police without cleaning himself up first? That doesn't make sense."

"What doesn't make sense is you opening this case twenty years later. It's a dead issue."

"It's not dead until my father's name is cleared. Now, answer the question."

"Your father wasn't thinking clearly, he'd just murdered three people. That seemed reason enough for him to forget about cleaning up."

"What about Lyle? Did he go to work that day?"

"What does that have to do with anything?"

"In the crime-scene photos he was dressed casually. I wondered if he'd worked that day or if he'd been home."

McDaver scratched his chin. "I…I don't know. It's probably in the file somewhere, but it's been a long time…."

"It's not in the file." Rex frowned. "Did Lyle wear a wedding ring?"

McDaver again looked puzzled. "I don't know that, either."

"You really paid attention to detail, didn't you?"

McDaver stood, his mouth tightening with anger. "That's enough, Falcon. Get out."

Rex glared at him. He'd find more witnesses in town, someone who could answer his questions. Maybe his father's attorney would know. Unfortunately, he'd moved further north. Deke or Brack would have to pay him a visit.

"For the record, you don't have anything to hide, do you?" Rex asked. "Were you in Lyle's pocket?"

McDaver's nostrils flared. "I refuse to even acknowledge that question. Now, leave before I call the sheriff."

Rex smiled, sensing he'd hit on the truth. McDaver, Cohen and Pursley had all been young and driving for success when the Lyles were killed. The Falcon case had made their careers.

Maybe they'd glossed over the truth to build their own reputations. But they had no idea who they were dealing with now. Their reputations would be shot when he finished with them.

And if they'd kept secrets that had led to his father's conviction, if they'd broken the law in any way, he'd make sure they were sent to prison. Then they'd understand the ordeal his father had been forced to endure.

And he'd sit back and take great pleasure in watching them suffer.

As soon as she entered the diner, Hailey saw Deanna Timmons. The real estate agent raced over and hugged her. "Hailey, it's good to see you, dear."

"You, too, Deanna. How are you?"

Deanna pressed a hand self-consciously to her hair. "I'm all right. Business is slow this time of year, with the holidays coming up and all."

Slow and lonely. Hailey read the desperation in the woman's eyes. When Deanna had shown her the house, she'd confided that her husband had run off with her daughter years ago and that she hadn't seen either one since. The fact that Hailey and Deanna had both been alone so long seemed to have connected them, their shared bond of loneliness a common thread.

"I wish I could stay," Deanna said. "But I promised I'd help out at the church. I'm directing the children's choir. We're working on the upcoming Christmas musical."

"That sounds wonderful," Hailey said. For all Deanna had lost, she was an amazing woman, just the kind of friend Hailey wanted.

"Is everything all right with you, Hailey?" Deanna looked into her eyes as if probing for the truth.

Unaccustomed to sharing her problems, though, Hailey simply shrugged. "I'm fine."

"You're still happy with the house? Like I mentioned before, if you change your mind, I'll forgo the commission. I—"

"I'm fine with the house," Hailey said, hoping her face didn't flush from the lie. "Don't worry. Just come and visit."

Deanna stared at her for another long minute, the anguish in her eyes dissipating slightly when she smiled. Then she rushed away to make choir practice. Hailey ordered a cup of tea and asked the waitress about Ava Riderton.

The young girl with spiked red hair pointed her out. "She comes in almost every day. Usually meets the sheriff for lunch."

Hailey carried her tea to the neighboring table and introduced herself. "Do you mind if I sit down?"

"Sure. Welcome to town." Green eyes scrutinized her. "You're the woman who bought that old haunted house."

Hailey smiled. "I've always been a history buff and liked small towns." Actually she'd been drawn to this house in a morbid kind of way. Only now her interest had become personal. Her life might depend on the answers.

And so might Rex's.

She chatted for several minutes about Tin City, asking mundane questions to break the ice. Ava Riderton was an attractive woman, probably in her mid to late forties with dark brown hair and a nice figure. Her clothes weren't designer, but she possessed a flair for combining cold-weather attire that still looked fashionable.

"I heard you used to work for Mr. Lyle," Hailey said.

"That's right, that was a scary time." She angled her head, looking pensive. "So sad what happened to that family."

"Did you think Mr. Falcon killed the Lyle family?"

Ava twirled a strand of hair around her finger, contemplating how to answer the question. Because she had something to hide?

"You weren't sure, were you?"

She fiddled with her coffee cup. "I... Randolph Falcon was intimidating, but he was always polite in town. Now, Lawrence, he could charm the pants off anyone in a skirt."

Hailey read between the lines. Apparently he had charmed Ava Riderton. "I heard Mrs. Lyle might have had an affair. Was that true?"

More hair twirling. "I can't really say for sure, but their problems started after the little girl was born. He... I wondered if the baby was his."

Hailey's stomach fluttered. "Did he think it was Mr. Falcon's?"

She shrugged. "It seemed reasonable, what with Falcon always working in the garden. I heard he took fresh roses up to the house every day, sometimes even gardenias."

Gardenias? Remembering the crushed gardenias

she'd found in the house, Hailey nearly choked on her tea. "There was talk that Lyle forced his wife to stay at home, that he had control issues."

"He was controlling," Ava admitted. "A few times, Sheriff Cohen even went out to check on them because someone called in a domestic disturbance, but he never arrested Lawrence, and no one pressed charges."

Lawrence? So she had been on a first-name basis. Hailey frowned, more questions mounting. If the sheriff had been to the Lyles, was it possible he and Mrs. Lyle had been friends? Or more than friends? Or had the sheriff known something was wrong in the family, that Lyle was abusive and covered it up to protect Lyle?

But if Cohen wanted Ava, why cover for Lyle?

Perspiration beaded on her forehead, her hands trembling as memories of her own past fought their way to the surface.

"You sound like you were close to Mr. Lyle. Did you know Randolph Falcon?"

"Not well." She glanced around the café as if she was nervous. "But I saw them arguing a few times." Ava toyed with her napkin. "And Lawrence and I…we worked together, but nothing…ever happened."

"Come on, let's get out of here, Ava." The sheriff grabbed Ava's arm. "You've spread enough gossip already."

Ava gave Hailey an apologetic look, a moment of panic flaring in her eyes before she followed the sheriff meekly.

"What was that all about?" Rex swung around from the back of her chair and took the seat Ava had occupied. "Sheriff didn't look too happy."

"I was talking to Ava Riderton," Hailey said in a low voice. "He didn't care for our conversation."

Rex's eyes lit with interest, but the waitress appeared,

and he refrained from comment until she'd filled his coffee cup, taken their orders and left.

"What did she have to say?" Rex finally asked.

"She denied a past with Lawrence Lyle, but hinted he might have been abusive. Lyle didn't think the little girl was his."

Rex's expression turned to disgust. "He didn't think he'd have a mentally challenged kid, huh?"

Hailey leaned forward. "That's possible, but she suggested Mrs. Lyle had a lover. Rex, if that's true, it would change everything."

"You're thinking Mrs. Lyle's lover killed the family?"

Hailey shrugged, guilt assaulting her for speaking ill of the dead. What if the hint of Mrs. Lyle's affair was just gossip? Small-town rumors that had gotten out of hand? But if it were true… "What if Mr. Lyle came home and found another man at his house? They could have gotten into a fight, and it turned ugly."

Rex nodded. "It's possible. And of course, everyone assumed my father was the other man."

Hailey started to touch his hand to show her support, but pulled back, her own insecurities surfacing. "Who else could she have been seeing?"

Rex's jaw snapped taut. "I don't know. But both the sheriff and McDaver are upset that I'm here asking questions. Both were young and ambitious back then, making names for themselves in Tin City. And the sheriff went to the Lyles a few times. Maybe one of them has something to hide."

Like an old affair, Hailey thought. And an illegitimate child.

Two reasons for murder.

REX AND HAILEY ATE IN SILENCE, the tension in the diner thrumming through Rex. Word had definitely spread that he'd returned to avenge his father. He caught the frightened stares of women and children, the wary looks of the men warning him away from their families, heard the whispers and innuendoes that he'd listened to as a kid. He tried to let them roll off his back as he'd struggled so hard to do when he was ten, but the old saying that words could never harm you wasn't true.

They had stabbed him just as if they'd been carved into his soul with knives.

When Cohen had jerked Ava from the table, Rex had noted the menacing look he'd turned on Hailey. Had Cohen been the one who'd left that picture of the murder on her attic door along with the warning note? Would he hurt Hailey for asking questions?

"Hailey, maybe you should go someplace else for a while, at least until I figure out what's going on here."

A shuttered look crossed her face. "I'm not running from my new home, Rex. I told you, I'm here to stay."

"And you're willing to face whatever?" His tone sounded harsh, but he didn't care. "This is dangerous business. What if the person who threatened you decides to stop you from asking questions?" He leaned forward, hands balled. "In case you haven't noticed, I'm not too popular around town. My brother called and said my father wanted us to stop the investigation. His parole hearing has been postponed. Someone got to him. They might have even threatened the family." His dark eyes met hers. "Who knows? They might decide to hurt you just because you're hanging out with me."

Her look of bravado didn't fool him. She was scared.

"I can't run forever," she murmured.

Rex tensed. She was referring to her own past, to the missing person's report. To whomever she'd left behind. Most likely a man.

A man who might be looking for her….

He stifled his comment, waved for the waitress, then paid the bill. As he herded her to the gun shop, he barely kept his anger in check. Dammit, if she'd talk to him maybe he could help her.

Several people stared as they entered the shop, the news that he'd returned and was cavorting with the woman who'd bought the Hatchet House apparently creating some kind of hysteria.

Hailey surprised him by picking out a shotgun.

"Do you know how to use that?" Gus, the store-keeper asked.

Hailey nodded, although she averted her gaze from Rex. "Yes, one of my…my father taught me."

Rex's hands gripped the counter as she purchased shells. So she could handle a gun. What else was she keeping from him?

Seconds later, they walked to the SUV, but he saw her scanning the streets as if she was searching for someone. He had to find out the truth, had to know what he was up against.

She'd already pissed off Cohen. He sure as hell wouldn't help her. In fact, if Cohen was keeping up with the police database, he'd realize Hailey was wanted and probably turn her in.

Rex couldn't afford to get charged with aiding and abetting a criminal. Then he'd get locked up and he might never free his father. Besides, he didn't want Hailey in jail.

When they were safely inside the SUV, he turned to her. "Tell me what's going on with you."

She jerked her head up, a soft vulnerability shadow-ing her eyes. "What do you mean?"

"I want the truth, Hailey. You're running from some-one, and I want to know who it is."

She shook her head, pressing her lips together. "Just take me home, Rex."

"Not until you talk to me." He rammed a hand through his hair, tousling the ends.

"There's nothing to tell, Rex. I bought a house here, I want to settle—"

"Stop playing me for an idiot, Hailey. Why is there a missing persons report filed on you?" He gripped her arms and forced her to look into his eyes. "And why has some hotshot attorney filed assault charges against you?"

Hailey gasped. He read the truth in her eyes. She hadn't known about the charges, yet she wasn't totally surprised.

Because she was guilty?

SHERIFF COHEN'S HAND tightened around Ava's wrist as he pushed her into the back room at the police station. "What the hell were you doing talking to that crazy girl who bought the Hatchet House? I thought you were over Lyle long ago."

"I am." Ava's pale skin reddened beneath his scrutiny. Even with the years aging her face, she was beautiful. And she was his now. But he couldn't let her ruin their life. Their future. And he didn't want her thinking about Lyle again. Hell, he'd rushed the case years ago to impress her. Locking Lyle's killer behind bars had been the fastest way to earn her trust. Trust that eventually had turned to affection.

"I…I'm sorry, I didn't mean any harm," Ava said. "She wanted to know about the Lyle murders."

"And she's been carousing around with Rex Falcon, Randolph's oldest son." Cohen pulled her closer to him, the air between them fraught with the scent of arousal and fear. "That boy is trouble, Ava. What did you tell the woman?"

"Nothing…" Ava's gaze darted to the door as if she might escape.

He gripped her chin in his hands, forcing her to look at him. "From now on, keep your mouth shut. We put the murderer behind bars years ago. End of story."

"But…but what if you were wrong?" Ava whispered.

He raised his hand to slap her, then saw the terror in her face and reined in his temper. He loved Ava. He couldn't hurt her. He wouldn't be like his daddy. Or Lyle.

Instead, he stroked her jaw. "We weren't wrong. There haven't been any more killings in twenty years, have there?"

She shook her head no, her breath bathing his hand as she relaxed, exciting him more.

He'd hated that she'd had a thing for Lyle. He'd always wanted her for himself. And now he had her, he couldn't lose her.

"You know I take care of this town, don't you?"

"Yes, Andy. You've been a great sheriff."

His chest swelled with pride. "That's right. And I don't intend to let some boy hell-bent on revenge mess things up. I'm going to be mayor next year." He slid a finger over her throat, then lower to her breasts. She arched into him, and he cupped her plump mounds, his teeth nipping at her neck. "You're going to be by my side, aren't you, sweetheart?"

She nodded and melted into him as he slipped the buttons on her blouse free. Her breasts fell into his waiting hands. She was his. Just as it should have been years ago.

Just as it would continue to be forever.

And he'd be damned if anyone would ruin it for him.

Chapter Eleven

Hailey's first instinct was to run from Rex's probing eyes. Instead of worrying about him endangering her, she was concerned about the opposite. What if someone had gotten to his father and threatened his mother?

What if it was Thad?

If he'd seen her with Rex, it wouldn't have been difficult for him to find out about Rex's father. Thad might have retaliated by phoning in a favor to postpone the parole hearing. It was exactly the kind of power play he'd use to demonstrate his control. But if she told Rex, he'd try to find Thad and make things worse.

"Hailey, talk to me. What happened? Why has this guy filed assault charges against you?"

"That's none of your business."

"It damn well is. You've been lying to me."

"I…I don't owe you any explanations."

"Maybe not. But I'm trying to help you." His eyes blazed with anger. "I saw the way you watched over your shoulder in town, as if you thought someone might jump out at you any minute." He slid a hand along the back of the seat as if to reach for her, then hesitated, flexing his fingers. "That's the reason you decided not to go to McDaver's office with me, isn't it? You were afraid he'd recognize your name from a police bulletin?"

She dragged her gaze from his and stared out the window. Frost dotted the glass, icicles clinging to the limbs of the trees. She'd thought she'd escaped Thad, but from the librarian's description, he was already here. And if Rex knew about the bulletin, the sheriff would probably see it, too. Then he'd arrest her and send her back with Thad.

"I can handle it," she said in a low voice, although she had no idea how. But Rex had already saved her life once. And she didn't want to add to his problems.

"That's just it, Hailey. I don't think you can handle it."

"It's my past, Rex, just leave it alone."

A sardonic chuckle escaped him. "Your past is going to catch up with you. Then what happens? You might go to jail—"

"I don't think he really wants me in jail," she admitted. But he did want her. And he'd make her suffer when he found her.

"But he wants you back."

"I don't intend for that to happen."

He would try to force her, though. She saw the recognition dawn in Rex's eyes.

"You can file countercharges, issue a restraining order—"

"That usually makes things worse." Hailey knotted her hands. "Just drop it, Rex. Leave me alone."

His jaw went rigid, his eyes burning with anger and something else…hurt. "Is that what you really want?"

"Yes." She had a gun now; she could defend herself.

Jerking his arm from the seat, he started the engine, then tore down the drive, the SUV bouncing over ruts in the road caused by the snow and ice. Dark clouds rolled overhead, casting gray shadows over the road, while sleet pelted the windshield.

Hailey hugged her coat around her, cold in spite of the heat. She should be relieved. Apparently Rex had decided to listen to her and leave her alone.

It was exactly what she wanted. Wasn't it?

WHEN REX PARKED at Hailey's, his emotions ping-ponged back and forth between anger at Hailey for shutting him out and worry for her safety. Apparently the attraction he felt was one-sided.

She wanted him out of her life. Why? Because she was afraid of him?

She should be, considering he'd reopened the case. But he'd never forgive himself if something happened to her.

He turned to her, tension rippling between them in the close confines of the car. Although the heater had warmed the interior, an icy chill had settled between them. She reached for the door to escape, but he grabbed her hand and toyed with her fingers. "I don't want you to get hurt," he said in a gruff voice.

Her gaze swung to his, the emotions in her eyes mirroring his own.

"Is that so hard to believe, Hailey? That I'm capable of caring? Just because my father was convicted of murder doesn't make me an animal." Though he tried to fight it, rage and pain hardened his voice. No wonder she was running....

"It has nothing to do with you." Hailey's gaze dropped to their joined hands. "I don't want to cause you more trouble. You saved my life. That's more than any man has ever done for me."

So she had a low opinion of the male population. "Why do you hate men, Hailey? Was it your father?"

"I don't hate men." She thrust up her chin. "And I don't remember my father. The only thing I know about him is that he was a trucker. He dropped me off at an orphanage when I was four."

She'd been abandoned, that explained a lot. He wanted to know more, to haul her in his arms and promise her everything would be all right, that he'd never let anyone hurt her again. But he'd barely scratched the surface of this investigation. Things might even get more ugly.

A soft labored sigh escaped her. "You'd better go."

Hunger surged through him, accompanied by a deep-seated need to touch her. To prove he wasn't the bitter, dangerous man she must think him to be. To let her know he wouldn't abandon her as her old man had done.

He raised a finger, traced the edge of her jaw gently, pausing at the corner of her mouth. His own watered for a taste. "I won't hurt you, Hailey."

She closed her eyes, turmoil written on her face. "Please, Rex."

"Why did this man file assault charges? Who is he?"

Her breath hissed out in the quiet, then she opened her eyes and stared into his. "His name is Thad Jordan. He's an attorney. He didn't like it when I ended our relationship."

His thumb slid beneath her chin, tilted it up, reading between the lines. "He put the bruises on your neck?"

She nodded, her lower lip trembling.

"Then it was self-defense. Why don't you go to the police and clear yourself?"

"You, of all people, know that the legal system isn't always fair, Rex. Thad has friends," she said in a stronger voice. "Influential friends in high places. They'd never believe me."

He studied her, comprehension dawning. Small towns. Judges and lawyers who owed each other favors. A factor that had gone against his own father.

"I won't let him get you, Hailey." He pulled her into his arms. She stiffened, fighting his embrace, but he stroked her back until she relaxed against him and snuggled into his chest. He savored the delicious contact. Grateful to win this minuscule fraction of trust, he silently vowed to protect her with his life. As soon as he absolved his father, he'd find Jordan, and make sure he never bothered another woman again.

And if Jordan hurt Hailey, he'd kill the bastard with his bare hands.

REX BUSIED HIMSELF changing the locks and adding padlocks to the door, then set about repairing the roof. After storing the gun in her bedroom, Hailey finished cleaning the downstairs and unloading her books. But as she placed each beloved treasure on the shelf, she thought about the way she documented stories on each antique she purchased so she could pass it on to potential buyers. Those stories made the piece more special, sometimes even more valuable. Yet did a person's past really define him?

Rex's past had certainly shaped him. And her own…her encounters with her foster parents had definitely taught her that forming attachments was fruitless. The first time she'd really liked one of the homes and been torn from it, she'd cried for days, withdrawing into a shell. The social worker had sent her to a child psychologist who'd claimed her anxiety was normal considering the circumstances. But Hailey had had to protect herself, so she'd never allowed herself to get attached to any of the other families.

And when the doctors had encouraged her to uncover

the blank spots in her past, she'd balked. She hadn't wanted to remember. Because there was something dark in her past, something evil. Something that terrified her.

And when Rex had commented he didn't want her to get hurt, she'd had a panicky feeling. She'd wanted him to care. But she'd also been afraid. And she'd been willing to send him away to protect him. Could she possibly tear down the barriers she'd built around herself long enough to let him inside her heart?

Especially with Rex, a man bent on revenge?

No. She couldn't chance losing someone she cared about again.

Finished with the shelving, she went upstairs to clean the children's rooms. Although her emotions were mixed—she felt compelled to honor the family's memory by preserving the rooms as they had been.

Her nerves on edge, she glanced inside the little girl's room and froze. The snow globe sat on the maple dresser, a red ribbon lying beside it, a silver comb and brush next to it.

The tune "White Christmas" echoed in the recesses of her mind, the air swirling around her with the dusty image of a little towheaded girl perched on the velvety stool, her mother behind her lovingly braiding her long blond hair...

THE DOWNSTAIRS DOOR swung open and heavy footsteps thundered inside, a man's harsh voice rising up the staircase.

"He's home," the woman whispered.

The little girl's smile faded. She gripped the silver brush and ribbon and started to cry.

"Shh, it's all right. Go and hide."

She nodded silently. She had to follow her mother's

instructions or she'd be in big trouble. Her father was mean. But why did he hate her?

Because she was a girl, not a boy. He wanted a son....

The footsteps grew louder. Boom. Boom. Boom. "Where are you?" he shouted.

"Go." Her mother whisked her down from the stool, hands shaking, her voice shrill. "And don't make a sound until I come for you."

Her throat clogged with tears as she clutched the silver brush and ribbon to her chest. She didn't want to hide.

She wanted her daddy to stay away and let her mommy finish braiding her hair. She tried so hard to be good so he wouldn't hate her. Maybe if her mommy fixed her hair all pretty, he'd be happy....

"Hurry." Her mother patted her behind, and she slipped into the closet. Hunching low, she found the secret door and crawled behind it. Hugging the ribbon and brush to her, she scooted as far against the wall as she could, praying there weren't any spiders or bugs inside. The walls closed around her, nearly suffocating her, and she buried her mouth in her hands to keep from sobbing out loud. It was so dark. She hated the dark.

Don't make a sound.

Her heart pounding, she felt along the floor of the small storage area until her fingers connected with red yarn. Her favorite dolly, Annie. She hugged the doll to her, then slid her fingers on the floor again until she found the blanket and one of her mother's silk scarves that she kept inside. It smelled like her mother. She squeezed it beside her face, then wrapped the blanket around Annie.

Hunching her knees up to her chest, she shut the door, and hugged the items to her, rocking herself back and forth, silently humming "White Christmas" as she waited for the night to pass. How long would it be before her father went to bed?

Before her mother could come to her….

First, he had to have his evening drinks. That yucky brown liquor that smelled awful. Then her mommy had to listen to him talk. Sometimes he complained about work, about the house, especially if it wasn't clean enough. And sometimes he got mad at Mommy. He said she smiled too much at the other men in town. But Mommy was good….

Mommy would come back for her and let her out.

Until then, she had to be invisible. It was a game she made up to pass the time. To help her forget that she had to stay in the cold, dark closet. That she had to be quiet and couldn't cry…

THE HOUSE WAS SO QUIET when Rex entered, he thought Hailey might have left. But he checked the driveway, and her car was still parked in the exact spot where it had been all day.

Where was she?

Had she finally ventured into the attic to explore its contents? From her earlier reaction, he doubted it. What was it about the attic that terrified her so, anyway?

An odd odor permeated the room, like some kind of aftershave, a musky scent that reminded him of a cologne an older man might wear. An older man with money.

Pausing by the stove, he glanced around to see if anything was amiss, but found nothing. Maybe Hailey had gone upstairs to take a nap.

Remembering their earlier conversation about her former boyfriend, he eased through the kitchen to the foyer. A quick check of the downstairs and he found it empty. His body tensed as he inched his way up the steps. "Hailey?

Nothing.

Alarm shredded his composure, and he picked up his pace. "Hailey?"

Still nothing.

Attuned to every sound and movement in the darkness, he climbed the steps. Outside, the wind howled and the sleet intensified, pounding the roof with its force. Thankfully, he'd patched the hole before the clouds had unleashed their wrath. A dim light flickered off, then on, then off again in the master bedroom. He slowly walked toward it, pushed open the door but found it empty. "Hailey, are you in here?"

The sound of the wind slapping branches against the window panes sent him looking outside. But he didn't see anyone lurking in the bushes.

His pulse racing faster, he stepped inside the hall and checked the attic. The door was locked from the outside.

He approached the boy's room with caution. The room was dark, shrouded in shadows from the half-pulled drapes.

"Hailey?"

No answer. Where the hell was she? Had that bastard Jordan gotten to her while he was on the roof? But how could he? Rex hadn't seen or heard any cars on the mountain.

What if the man had been hiding inside when they returned?

He pivoted toward the other child's room. Darkness cloaked the inside, the silence in the room alarming. Suddenly an odd sound splintered the quiet.

A tiny keening sound that was so small it was almost nonexistent. What the hell... Was there a sick animal in the house? Had an injured bird or another wild animal somehow crawled inside?

The crying sound grated through the darkness again, and the hairs on the back of his neck prickled as he entered.

Hailey?

His heart skipped a beat, his imagination soaring. The curtains fluttered beneath the heat from the ducts, the rumbling of the ancient furnace adding to his anxiety. He spotted the snow globe on the dresser, the crystal sphere shining in the stark blackness of the night.

His gaze shot to the closet. It was dark, too, and the room was empty. But the keening sound ebbed low and eerily close.

He pushed open the door and peered inside. The closet held a few odd objects, an old dresser, a box overflowing with toys, which had surprisingly not been destroyed or donated to charity.

"Hailey?"

The keening sound stopped, the sudden quiet jarring. But the cry had come from behind the closet.

But where?

He eased into the cramped space, then felt along the wall. A small indentation indicated there might be a storage area hidden behind it. He pushed the wood and a panel slid open. A small door led to a storage area behind the closet.

Stooping on his knees, he crawled forward, his heart stopping as he scanned the interior. Hailey was huddled against the wall, her head burrowing into her knees as she rocked back and forth in the darkness…

HAILEY HAD CURLED within herself, fighting off the monsters the only way she knew how. By blocking them out. By drifting off to an imaginary world where there were bright colors and rainbows and princes who swept in and saved little girls from the dragons.

But there weren't any real princes. And when the dragon roared at her with his fiery breath, she had to fight him herself.

Suddenly his hands were on her, reaching for her, pulling her from her safe hiding spot. She kicked and screamed out, dropping Annie while she battled him off. But his hands were so strong. The fear caught in her throat, and she tried to stifle her cry, but a strangled sob tore from deep inside her. She hated to be a baby. Hated to cry. Hated to let him win, because he liked it when she was afraid.

"Hailey, honey, stop it, it's me, Rex."

She pushed at his chest, but he gripped her arms so tightly she couldn't move. She wouldn't look at him, Couldn't stand to see those mean eyes.

"Hailey, listen, it's Rex. Come back to me, baby."

The deep voice that spoke to her sounded odd. Gruff, but softer than her daddy's.

He lifted her chin, stroked her cheek, wiping away tears. Then he was carrying her from the darkness to the light, wrapping her in the blanket, pressing Annie back into her arms, soothing her and tucking her hair behind her ear as he laid her on the soft pillows. "Look at me, honey, it's Rex. I'm not going to hurt you."

His soothing voice penetrated the fog of fear enveloping her. Slowly, she squinted, reality returning. Disoriented, she glanced around the room and realized he'd dragged her from the suffocating darkness and had carried her to the big plush bed. The bed that was soft and warm and covered in satin.

"Hailey, are you all right now?"

She swallowed, haunting memories warring with reality. What had happened? Where was she? "I… What are you doing?"

"You were hiding in the little girl's closet, crying." He dragged a hand over his beard stubble, the sound raspy in the night. "Why did you go in there? How did you know about the crawl space?"

She shook her head, her mind clouded with the terror that had gripped her. "I...don't know. I...was hiding."

His eyebrows puckered. "From what? Did you see someone in the house?"

She tried to sit up, but he urged her back onto the bed, plumping pillows behind her head. "I don't know. I went into the little girl's room, then I saw this silver brush set and ribbon..." She broke off, confused, searching his face. "Then I saw her, the little girl that lived here. She had long blond hair and her mother was braiding it, but her father came home." Now the image was so vivid, it was as if she had been there. But she had to have been dreaming. Or had she seen a ghost?

"What happened when he came in?"

"The mother was frightened. She told the little girl to hide, to be quiet, that she'd come back for her later."

"And she went into the closet?"

Hailey nodded, finally looking into his eyes. "Do you think I saw the child's ghost?"

His frown told her no. But what other explanation could there be? Unless she'd been imagining or remembering something from her past.

Something that had happened at one of her foster homes? Something she'd chosen to forget because it had been too terrifying?

THE WOMAN HAD TO BE TAKEN CARE OF. And so did Falcon's son.

First he'd found those damn bones. Then he'd dug the shirt from the storage bin in the shed. The rag had had blood on it. *His* blood.

How could he have forgotten about it? That one item could destroy him.

He cursed. And now Falcon was asking questions all over town. Confronting them all. Trying to dig up secrets that had been buried so long they should have turned to dust by now, just like slivers of those old bones.

He slipped through the woods toward Falcon Ridge, his hatred for the Falcons as bitter as the winter storm. When Falcon left the Hatchet House tonight, he'd be waiting in the shadows.

A screeching sound erupted, and he threaded his way toward the sound. It was those damn birds Falcon kept. The boy was just as weird as his father.

He lifted the covering over the cage. The bird stared back at him with beady eyes, his talons extended in defense. He reached for the thick gloves Falcon used, then opened the cage.

He knew what he was doing. The bird didn't have a chance.

And neither did his master.

Chapter Twelve

Rex had no idea what had happened with Hailey, but she'd been in an almost trancelike state when he'd found her, her terror so real tremors racked her body. Her eyes were glassy, too, as if she was in shock.

Something had happened to trigger her fear. Something so frightening that she'd resorted to a childlike state that had damn near scared the bejesus out of him. "Hailey?"

She flattened her hands in front of her, staring at them, her breathing finally settling into a more normal rhythm. But her face was still pale and her eyes glazed.

"How did you know about the storage space in the closet?"

She frowned, digging her nails into the blanket. "I don't know. I don't remember going in." Her voice caught. "The voice told me to hide, and to be quiet."

The voice? Jeez. What was she, schizophrenic? "Have you ever heard voices before?"

She shook her head, her hair falling over one eye. He slowly tucked it behind her ear.

"It was the mother's voice," she whispered. "She was afraid for the little girl. She wanted to protect her."

"Hailey, was the little girl you?"

Her eyes widened. "I...I don't think so." She slid the

doll from the blanket and looked at it, examining the yarn hair, the patched clothing. "I'm not sure, though. It might have been." She shook her head, looking disoriented again. "I think it was the little girl who lived here. I felt as if I'd floated outside my body, as if I was in the room watching her."

"Have you seen these things before?"

"No." A worried expression creased her face as she stared up at him. "Do you think I'm crazy? Or that I might have seen the child's ghost? Maybe the mother appeared and is trying to show me what happened years ago."

Outside, the wind rattled the panes, while he struggled with a reply. "I think your imagination might be getting out of hand."

"But the voice was so real." She pulled at his hand. "I heard the father's boots pounding…he was coming up the steps."

"You probably heard me walking up the steps. I was looking for you."

"No." Her eyes implored him to believe her. "I realize it sounds crazy, but it happened. The mother warned the little girl, and she ran to hide because she was afraid of her father."

Sensing her agitation rising, he stroked her arm to calm her. "Maybe you were remembering something that happened to you in your childhood." He hesitated. It was the only logical explanation. "You said your father abandoned you when you were four."

"Yes." She rubbed the doll's fingers between her own, biting down on her lower lip.

"You weren't adopted?"

She shook her head, her mouth tightening.

"Did you live in a foster home?"

She angled her face toward the pillow and nodded. "Several."

His chest squeezed. At least he'd had his mom and his brothers. Hailey had obviously been all alone. "Was one of your foster parents abusive?"

A flicker of her eyes gave him his answer. He should have known. Her wariness toward men. Her reluctance to let him touch her. The reason she'd run from this control-freak attorney.

Fury knotting his stomach, he reminded himself to tread with caution. "I think you're remembering one of your foster homes," he said gently, as if talking to one of the hawks he rescued from the wild. "And because of what happened to the Lyles, you projected them into your memory."

She averted her gaze, her expression troubled, confused. "I…I suppose that makes sense."

"Tell me about the man who abused you."

Her expression turned guarded. "I don't want to talk about him. It's in the past."

But it still haunted her wherever she went. It was obviously a painful, traumatic time in her life, a time that had affected her so deeply she'd repressed memories. And meeting that attorney who'd tried to control her, who'd hurt her, must have launched her memories to the present.

That and the violence associated with the house.

Guilt suffused him. And now here she was thrust into another dangerous situation because he'd reopened his father's case.

"Hailey, I've said this before, but I think you should leave town for a while."

"No." Her voice rose in pitch. "Please, I know you probably think I'm crazy, but I'm fine. I've been running all my life, Rex. I'm not running anymore."

"Then I'm going to stay here with you." The panic that flashed onto her face rekindled his vow not to force a relationship with her. But he refused to leave her alone. Not when she was so vulnerable. "I'm staying, at least until the security system can be installed."

"Do you think the man who killed the Lyles is still around, that he's in town?"

So she did believe his father might be innocent. All his life he'd felt condemned because of his past, but now hope sprang up that things might change. "I don't know, but if he is, he's probably aware we've been asking questions." He squeezed her hand between his, grateful when she didn't shy away. "And if he's not, there's still the chance that Jordan has found you."

Fear darkened her eyes again. He hated seeing it, but it was better for her to be alert than to let her guard down. If the attorney was close by, he was probably biding his time, waiting until she was alone to surprise her. And then what would he do?

Just how dangerous was this guy Jordan?

"DID YOU TAKE CARE OF FALCON, Wormer?"

"I'm working on it. So far, his parole hearing has been postponed, and he's pretty shaken up." The man's shortened, wheezing breath filled the line. Wormer was a heart attack waiting to happen.

"Are you with the girl?" Wally Wormer finally asked.

"I've got my eye on her. I'll have her back soon enough." But first he had games to play. Punishments to dole out.

He wanted her to sweat. To wonder how close he was. To feel his breath on her neck and anticipate him coming for her.

Jordan disconnected the line, then drummed his fingers on the polished desk inside Falcon's study. What kind of guy lived in a place that looked like a damn monastery?

Jordan's hands fisted inside his black leather gloves, the scents of wood and stone swirling around him, inciting his anger.

And why had shy, Little Miss Perfect Hailey ditched him, then hooked up with a creepy fellow like Falcon?

The sheer thought of another man touching her brought bile to his throat. Falcon was at that house Hailey had bought now. What was he doing? Had he stripped her barriers and talked her into sleeping with him? Or had she played her coy games with him, too?

Eager to get back and watch her, he slipped through the corridors of Falcon's house, amazed at the labyrinth of rooms in the massive stone structure. When he'd exhausted all the rooms and found nothing of interest, he hurried toward the basement. Jordan had done his research. Falcon supposedly had a detective agency with his brothers complete with high-tech computer technology. It must be downstairs.

He had to make sure Falcon didn't find anything to incriminate him. But if he went searching for information on Hailey, he'd discover she wasn't the woman she'd led them all to believe. A hearty chuckle resounded from his chest.

Then Falcon wouldn't be so anxious to climb into her bed.

In fact, if his plan worked, Falcon would turn her over to him and never look back.

He removed the diamond wedding band from his pocket, smiling at the stones glittering in the dark cavern of a room. Then he'd put this wedding ring on Hailey's finger where it belonged, and she would be his forever.

HAILEY CLUTCHED the blanket and doll, still unable to relinquish her hold on them as she stared up at Rex. She didn't want to reveal the gritty details of her unhappy home life to Rex. She'd endured whispers and pity stares all her life and couldn't tolerate receiving the same looks from him.

But what *did* she want?

His arms around her again. His voice crooning comforting words. His hands bringing her senses to life and obliterating the panic that had seized her muscles and limbs in that closet. The closet that had served as her sanctuary and her prison.

What was happening to her in this house anyway?

She'd always had nightmares, but they usually dogged her at night, in the twilight hours of sleep, not in the daytime. She'd never actually *seen* visions or heard voices before….

Rex didn't believe in ghosts, but she couldn't discount the possibility—hadn't other people who'd been in the house seen and heard them? She had a book downstairs on true-to-life citings of ghosts across the country, where parapsychologists had actually documented their findings through thermal photography.

"Hailey, tell me more about this guy Jordan."

An image of Thad throwing himself on her car flashed back, blood trailing down his cheek. "He's a corporate attorney," she said. "He works for a big firm in Denver, handles multimillion-dollar accounts."

"How did you two meet?"

Hailey fumbled with the doll's hair. "Forget it, Rex, he's not your problem."

"He is if he wants to hurt you."

Her eyes met his, the raw emotions in his touching her as if his fingers had caressed her bare skin. Did he really care about her?

"He came in to the auction house with a client to bid

on some artwork." She shrugged. "We dated a few times. Mostly corporate dinners, fund-raiser things he was involved with."

"He wanted to impress you."

She nodded. She'd thought the same thing. And at first, he had. Until she'd realized his generosity and charm were fake.

"Did he know about your past?"

She hesitated, again battling the choppy waters of her memory. "Not in detail, but when he asked me why I liked antiques, I explained that I found the stories surrounding them, their past, interesting. I suppose because I'd lost part of my own and didn't have any real home, no roots." She sighed, wondering if she was revealing too much about herself but wanting him to understand. The old furniture and items she collected weren't just things, they had a life behind them. "It fascinated me that families might hold on to an antique, a painting, a vase, or furniture and pass it down from one generation to another."

Only her family had thrown her away as if she was of no value.

His dark eyes were watching her so intently, a sliver of unease spread through her. Then he placed his hand over hers, and she stilled, studying his fingers. He had long, wide, masculine hands, hands that were strong and could protect or hurt. But she'd seen how gentle he was with the eagle and felt that same tenderness now.

In spite of his power and size, his animal-like nature, he wasn't like Thad. He didn't have to show off with money, extravagant cars or a prestigious position to be a man. He didn't have to control a woman, either, to prove his prowess.

She laced her fingers with his, her nipples tightening at the hunger flaring in his eyes. Suddenly she realized how vulnerable she was. They were lying on her bed, the two of them cocooned in the warmth of quiet conversation, gentle touches and a need that pulsed between them. A need that burned stronger every minute. Yet, he wasn't pushing her for anything.

Which made her want him more.

Hailey had craved safety her entire life, had searched for peace and tranquility, had avoided dangerous men. But even when she'd run from one pit of fire, she'd plunged headlong into another blaze.

Yet the kind of danger that fired the irises of Rex's eyes promised excitement, and a passion so enticing she couldn't resist. Tired of being alone, she responded to the hunger in his eyes with an answering one.

Her silent supplication should have been enough. But she didn't want to completely relinquish control. She ached to take what he offered, as well.

With a flick of her tongue across her lips, she teased him to come to her, then her fingers found the ends of his hair, and she played with the strands. His masculine scent intoxicated her, his raw passion inciting her courage.

He dropped his head forward as if waging a silent battle within himself. "Hailey?"

She traced her fingers along his jaw, the scraping of his five o'clock shadow a rough melody in the quiet. A hiss of his breath brushed her cheek as he leaned closer, so close she felt the tension rippling between them. The air in the room changed, became hot, electric, the temperature rising, as well.

He slid one hand to her jaw and cradled her cheek in his palm. "I don't want to hurt you," he murmured. "Tell me when to stop."

His gruff prelude to sex was a gentle reminder that she hadn't experienced the passion of intimacy before. But his sensitivity triggered emotions that teetered between admiration and love.

Shaken by the mere idea of love, she dismissed it readily, instead focusing on the tender way his thumb caressed her cheek as he lowered his head.

She leaned forward slightly, holding on to him as she threaded her fingers deeper into his thick black hair. Hair that felt like heaven on a man who had seen hell and come back, a man hardened by life yet still tender enough to respect her naiveté and the monumental step making love would mean.

Then thoughts fled as his lips melded with hers, slowly tasting, exploring, firing the flame of desire in her belly another degree. She leaned into him, opening herself to his hunger, savoring the delicious sensations as his tongue swept inside her mouth, stirring her own desires.

She moaned and met his tongue with tiny thrusts of her own, playing the game with instincts emboldened by his sensuality.

Then his hands slid lower. His lips formed a trail down her neck, sucking, biting, nipping at flesh sizzling from his touches while he massaged her back. When he slipped his hands beneath her breasts to cup them in his palms, her nipples tightened to rigid peaks.

A low moan reverberated from his chest as he teased one nipple with his finger while his mouth found the other, suckling her through her blouse. The buttons clicked open, the material falling away while his tongue scorched her bare skin. Then his fiery lips closed over one nipple through the thin fabric of her bra, and she groaned again, hot liquid flowing inside her. She arched toward him, practically pleading now to be closer. As if he understood her silent request, he unfastened her bra, let it drop to her waist, but instead of kissing her there, he raised his head and looked at her, questions again in his eyes.

"Rex, please," she whispered. "I don't want to be alone."

"You're not, baby," he whispered. Almost reverently, he paused to admire her naked breasts, the gleam of appreciation in his eyes heightening her hunger.

A throbbing took root between her legs, and her nipples ached with need. He licked his lips and dipped his head to taste the turgid peak, circling her fullness with his tongue until sensations skittered through her. Clutching his shoulders, she held on, feeling out of control, as if she might literally take off in flight any moment. Enjoying her torture, he moved from one breast to the other and slid one hand between her legs to caress her heat until she cried out in both pain and pleasure.

Erotic sensations rippled through her, and she wound her legs around his, yearning for more. He finally lifted his head, then stretched onto the bed above her, brushing her hair from her face as he gazed into her eyes.

"More," Hailey whispered. "Please Rex, don't stop now."

A smile warmed his dark eyes as she tore at his shirt, the snaps popping. Then her hands stroked his bare chest, exploring the rich play of sinewy muscle, brushing over a fine sheen of dark hair that trailed down a path to the waistband of his jeans. Jeans that held heaven for her desires, the answer to the hot ache within her.

He moved against her, the strength of his hard body fitting with the soft curve of her own until she cradled his sex between her legs. Even partially clothed, she felt the force of his desire, knew this man was potent and powerful. But instead of fear, excitement sprang to life.

Heat stirred again, the hunger increasing in intensity until she reached for his pants. But he caught her hands, held them still.

"You first."

His soft murmur was so erotic and tender, tears moistened her eyes.

He froze. "Hailey?"

"It's so wonderful," she said softly. "I didn't know."

Emotions flickered in his eyes, the moment suspended between them like an invisible barrier in time they had both just crossed. A line that now she'd stepped over, she wasn't sure she could ever go back.

But a shrill sound cut into the silence. A phone.

She glanced at the one on the nightstand, praying it wasn't another threat. Rex reached for his mobile phone, an apology in his eyes.

"Damn. It's my security agency." He connected the call, listening quietly, his expression changing from passion to worry. "I'll be right there."

Panic tightened her muscles. "What is it?"

"Someone broke into Falcon Ridge and started a fire," he mumbled. "I'm sorry, but I have to go."

"Dear God." Hailey reached for her blouse. "We'd better hurry."

"No, you're staying here." He grabbed her shoulders and captured her face between his hands, fear flashing momentarily in his eyes. But the fear was for her, not for himself, strumming an even deeper emotional chord within her. "Come down, though, lock all the doors, and make sure you don't open them for anyone but me. And keep that gun close by. Understand?"

She nodded, grabbed her robe from the end of the bed and pulled it on, then stood on wobbly legs. He gave her one last look of regret as they rushed down the steps. Passion still blazing in his eyes, he hesitated at the door, then smoothed the robe tighter over her naked breasts. Cupping them again, he dipped his head and kissed her. "I'll be back."

She whispered goodbye, locked the door, then rushed to the window and eased back the shade. His shoulders hunched against the wind and snow, he climbed into his Jeep and disappeared into the night.

Sleet and snow blurred the landscape. Shadows zipped along the forest, through the trees and fog. The cry of an animal in the wild sent a chill up her spine, followed by panic.

Who had broken into Rex's house? Were they still there, waiting on Rex to come back?

And if they were, what would they do to him?

REX'S HEART POUNDED as he sped up the icy road to Falcon Ridge. He prayed the stone walls of his childhood home would stand up against the fire, but living miles from town with roads nearly impassable half the year from snow and ice made it more difficult for the fire department to get through.

He heard the wail of the siren though as soon as he arrived and was thankful he'd installed the security system. They'd saved valuable time and, hopefully, his homestead.

The tires screeched as he braked to a stop and jumped out, wind and snow swirling in a white haze. He searched through the fog for smoke, and found it streaming from the door near the basement. His office!

Whoever had broken in wanted in his files. Rather, they'd wanted to destroy them.

Seconds later the firemen rushed through the house. The entryway was fine, but smoke billowed in the hallway near the basement door. He coughed, yanked a handkerchief from his pocket and covered his mouth and nose then followed to examine the main floor.

The firemen pushed him aside, dragging hoses in to douse the flames. Rex cursed as they worked, grateful the person responsible hadn't been able to breach his security system to get into his downstairs office. When the fire was contained, he raced to the front study and found it torn apart. Files littered the floor, drawers were open, and his computer had been trashed.

Furious, he searched the upstairs. His bedroom had been ransacked, too. Maybe he should call the sheriff. No. It would be fruitless to ask Cohen for help. He'd have to dust the place for fingerprints himself and conduct his own investigation. He stalked down the stairs and found the firemen putting out the last of the flames. The wood floor had suffered damage, and the fire had spread into the kitchen, eating up part of the flooring and walls there, as well.

A knot formed in his stomach when he noticed the back door ajar. The person who'd set the fire might still be around watching. Maybe he was hiding out in the backyard or at the edge of the woods.

His instincts surged to life as he explained to the fireman he wanted to check it out.

"See if you can find the source of the fire," he told the fire chief. "This was arson. I want evidence."

The fireman assured him he would, then conferred with his partner while Rex inched to the back door. The dark clouds in the sky added to the dismal gray of the night, the haze of snow blurring his vision. In the distance, between the trees, he thought he saw something move. A wild animal, or a man?

His gaze tracked the area, then skimmed the backyard. The covers from the hawk and eagle cages were gone.

So were the birds.

Emotions clouded his head as he stalked toward the edge of the woods. Fresh blood dotted the stark white ground, making a silent howl of fury well in his throat.

Assuming the birds were dead, he turned and

scanned the forest again, searching for the madman who'd killed them. Was it the man who'd come after Hailey? Or the same man who'd killed the Lyles?

If the shadow he'd seen in the woods was a man, he might be headed for Hailey's. Had the fire been a decoy to lure him away so the stalker could get to her?

HAILEY FINALLY DRAGGED HERSELF from the window and paced across the foyer, massaging the back of her neck where tension had knotted. How bad was the fire? Was Rex all right? Would he return safely to her?

The phone trilled, startling her, and she raced to it. But her hand trembled as she reached for the receiver. Who would be calling this time of night? What if it was Thad or the person who'd warned her to leave town?

Maybe it was Rex phoning to reassure her he was all right.

The harsh ring sliced the silence again, and she picked up the handset. "Hello."

"I'm watching you, Hailey." A man's heavy breathing punctuated the air. "I told you, you can never escape me. You're mine."

Hailey slammed down the phone, a cry escaping her. Then she heard a noise. She froze, clenching the stair rail. Her gun was upstairs in the bedroom. She had to get it. Another noise made her pause, though.

Footsteps in the attic.

Was it the ghost again, or the man who'd killed the Lyles? Or had Thad phoned from inside the house?

Chapter Thirteen

The screen door slapped shut, the gusty wind outside rattling the entire house. Hailey's stomach clenched. Should she run outside, try to reach her car? But what if the intruder was outside, waiting for her to do just that? He could be on the porch, lurking in the shadows, even inside the VW.... She wouldn't have a chance.

Outside the wind howled, shaking the walls. The floor above creaked again. She swallowed hard.

Was he upstairs? In the attic...?

The screen door slapped shut again, back and forth, back and forth. She stepped closer to the window and peered through the sheers, searching the shadows. But the weather had turned almost blizzardlike, the world a fog of white, obliterating her view. Her palms were sweating against the glass as she turned to scan the dark interior. The lights flickered off. On. Off again.

No.

A tremor raced through her as she rushed to the den for candles. She'd left the candelabra on the mantel where she'd found it that first day. But it was gone.

Panic surged to her throat.

The floor creaked again. He was on the stairs.

No. The sound was coming from the kitchen.

She had to get to the phone. Call Rex. Get help.

She fumbled through the darkness for the handset, knocked the lamp sideways and barely caught it before it crashed to the floor. A book she'd been reading earlier hit the wood floor with a thud. The handset slipped from its cradle, cracked against the table. She jerked it up and started to dial.

The phone was dead.

Her heart raced. Her cell phone… Upstairs in her bedroom with the gun. She had to get it. But what if he was up there?

She grabbed the fire poker and wielded it by her side as she inched to the hall. The clearing was empty, although the wind hurled the screen door against the house again, whistling through the frame.

Inhaling a deep breath, she ran up the stairs, her heart in her throat as she clung to the stair rail. The second floor was pitched in black, shadows leaping at her from the corners.

Just like when she was a little girl.

Déjà vu struck her, but she fought the memories. Then she froze at the sight of the little girl at the edge of her room….

The little girl had long blond hair and wore a pale pink nightgown that hung to her tiny, bare feet. Big frightened eyes stared up at Hailey through the darkness. She clutched the Annie doll to her chest with one small hand, the blanket hung from the other, touching the floor. Tears streaked her cheeks, but she didn't make a sound. She simply pointed to the attic, then began to rock herself back and forth as if to stop her own trembling. What was the little girl trying to tell her?

About the monster in the attic…

A crashing sound from below jerked her out of her stupor. Certain she'd seen a ghost, she launched herself forward into her room. The white swirl outside lit the interior slightly through the window, but a gray fog of despair overcame her. Then the whisper of her name floated through the shadows.

"Hailey…you can never escape me." Silence, then, "You're mine forever."

A sob welled in her throat as she glanced at her bed. On top of the satin comforter lay a ruby-red dress, a silk cocktail off-the-shoulder sheath, the one Thad had given her three months before. He'd asked her to wear it to a ball they'd attended in honor of his firm.

And then he'd surprised her with a ruby necklace. The one she'd thrown at him when she'd escaped him in the woods.

She stepped closer, knowing what she would find, paralyzing fear clutching at her. The necklace lay on top of the dress in a silver box. A small white card lay beside it, with the words, "I love you, Hailey," written in bold black ink in the center.

The handwriting was Thad's.

REX SPENT THE NEXT HALF HOUR dealing with the firemen, his agitation mounting over Hailey. He wanted to get back to her. But the fire marshal insisted they include Sheriff Cohen in the investigation and file a report through his office.

"Don't look like much damage." Cohen shifted on the balls of his feet as he examined the charred flooring in the hallway.

"Because of my security system," Rex said, disgusted with the man's lax attitude.

"We're done." The fire chief gestured toward the door. "I'll send you my report."

Rex nodded, then turned to Cohen as the fire truck descended the mountain.

Cohen smacked his gums. "I reckon someone wants you out of town, boy."

Rex glared at him. "You mean someone besides you?" He raised an eyebrow, a theory forming. "You keep telling me to leave town, to drop my dad's case. What are you hiding, Sheriff?"

A muscle ticked in Cohen's jaw. "Don't go accusing me of something like this, Falcon. You're messing with the wrong man if you think I'll put up with it."

"Is that what my father did? Mess with the wrong man?" He paused, then stepped forward. "I've heard some interesting things since I returned. Some people thought Lawrence Lyle was abusive. Said you'd even checked on the situation but never arrested Lyle."

"There wasn't any reason to," Cohen snapped.

"And some people said Mrs. Lyle might have had an affair. That Lindy Lou wasn't Lyle's child."

Cohen's jaw tightened another fraction.

"Maybe you had a thing going with her on the side. Maybe that little girl was yours, and you wanted Joyce Lyle to leave her husband for you. When she refused, you killed them all."

"That's the stupidest theory I've ever heard." He grunted. "I never had a thing for the Lyle woman. I always…"

He halted abruptly as if he'd admitted too much.

"Always what, Sheriff? Liked Ava Riderton?"

"My personal life is none of your damn business."

"The way I see it, Ava didn't want you, she wanted Lyle, so you decided to get revenge on him and seduce his wife. Lyle came home and found you. Since you're the sheriff, no one thought anything about you being at her house before. Hell, maybe you made up the bogus suggestion about abuse so you'd have a reason to see Lyle's wife." He hesitated. "But when Lyle caught you, he figured out the truth. He blew up, then things spiraled out of control." Rex crossed his arms across his chest. "So you rigged the evidence, then arrested my father and framed him before anyone could suspect you." Rex shrugged. "It was perfect. No one even questioned you."

"You got nerve, boy. You try to ruin my name, and I'll slap your ass in jail just like I did your father's, and throw away the key." Cohen's boots clicked on the floor as he strode outside.

Rex watched him go, his curiosity roused even more by Cohen's vehement denial of a relationship with Joyce Lyle. And now Cohen was headed back down the mountain. If Rex had gotten under Cohen's skin and guessed at the truth, what would he do now? He would have to pass Hailey's on the way back into town….

Hailey.

He had to make sure she was safe.

He dragged his coat back on, closed up the house, turned on the security alarm and headed to his Jeep, battling the blizzard. His cell phone rang as he turned the ignition. Anxious to see Hailey now, he answered while he thrust the vehicle into gear and maneuvered down the mountain. The tires churned out snow and ice, the gears grinding. "Yeah?"

"It's Brack. I just wanted to see if you have anything new. Mom's going nuts being cooped up."

"I have a couple of theories. Someone broke into Falcon Ridge tonight, tried to get to the basement to my files."

"You okay, man?"

"Yeah, I wasn't home." He'd been kissing Hailey instead, about to make love to her. God, it seemed like years ago. "Thank goodness I installed that security system. Anyway, damn bastard set fire to the house."

"How bad is the damage?"

"Minimal," Rex said. "But I had to deal with Cohen again. I can see why Dad hated him." He relayed his theory.

"Interesting," Brack said. "If Cohen was responsible, that would explain why he railroaded Dad so quickly." He paused. "Do you think McDaver knew and covered for him?"

"I don't know. McDaver acts like he's hiding something, too." He paused. "Have you met with Carl Pursley yet?"

"Not yet. But I'm on my way."

"Keep me updated." Rex dodged a pothole, the Jeep bouncing and sending chopped ice flying. "And tell Mom to hang in there. We're getting closer."

He hung up, his mind spinning over the theory he had discussed with his brother. He was still missing something; he just didn't know what it was.

Suddenly a bullet zinged through the windshield, cracking the glass. Dammit. He dived to avoid it, swinging the SUV sideways, but he hit the edge of the ditch and nose-dived straight into it. His seat belt snapped, jerking him back against the seat, the impact flinging his head forward. Then another shot pierced the window. The bullet grazed his cheek and spewed glass fragments in his face.

He ducked just in time to avoid another.

HAILEY'S BODY QUAKED. Thad had been inside the house. Inside her bedroom.

Was he still inside?

Her heart racing, she dropped the fire poker and reached for her purse to retrieve her phone, but a hand closed over hers, the fingers long and tapered. And cold. Icy cold.

"It's nice to see you, Hailey. I've missed you."

The room suddenly closed around her. Thad's suffocating breath brushed her neck, the vileness of his touch the last time they'd been together rushing back. She saw the flare of vindictiveness in his eyes as he'd thrown himself on the hood of her car. He was here to follow through on his promises.

"You knew I'd come for you, didn't you?" He brushed the ends of her hair from her neck. "I like you better as a blonde," he said in a low voice. "But we'll fix that later."

"Thad…" Hailey struggled for courage. "I told you it was over between us. Please don't do this."

"Don't do what? Love you?" He threaded his fingers deeper in her layered tresses. "I can't help myself, Hailey. I've never wanted anyone the way I want you."

"You only want me because I said no to you."

The gentleness forgotten, he gripped her arms so hard her legs buckled. Then he spun her around to face him, his fingers tightening into her skin. "And I promised you I'd find you." A slow smile curved his mouth, the gash beneath his eyes illuminated in the dim light filtering through the window.

"Why are you doing this?" She gave him a beseeching look. "You don't need me, you can have your choice of women in Denver." Her voice broke, but she cleared her throat, determined to rationalize with him. "I saw the way they fawned all over you at parties. You're successful, handsome, charming. All those society girls loved you."

"Everyone but you." Bitterness laced his voice.

"We were wrong for each other," she whispered. "Don't you see that? It's not you, it's me. I…I'm not ready to be with anyone."

"I thought that at first, too," he said. "I even felt sorry for you." Sinister laughter followed. "What a fool.

I had compassion for the poor little orphan girl who'd never been loved. I was going to save you."

"I…I'm sorry, Thad," Hailey whispered. "I didn't mean to hurt you, but I just can't be with anyone right now."

"Then why did you spend the night with that man, Falcon?"

"I…I don't know what you're talking about. I haven't slept with him."

"Don't lie to me, Hailey." He shook her so hard her teeth rattled, then lifted a hand to her cheek. "He scraped your skin with his beard. I can smell where he touched you."

Hailey's stomach roiled. How could she rationalize with a man who wasn't rational? "I swear, Thad, I didn't sleep with Rex."

"It doesn't matter now." He traced a path down her cheek to her neckline. "I'll forgive you, Hailey. We'll forget about him, and you can be my wife. I'll give you a good life, so much better than you'd have here in this hellhole in the mountains." He gestured around the room. "This haunted house is nothing compared to the home I'll build for you. It'll be a mansion…."

She closed her eyes, trying to remain calm and think while he droned on and on about the glorious life they'd share. Should she try to run from him again? Would Rex return soon, in time to help her? Or had Thad done something to him?

"You hurt me, too," she whispered, fighting panic. "You tried to force me to be with you, Thad, I can't forgive that."

He released her, and she tottered backward. Reaching out to steady herself, she prayed he'd calm down, and she could talk some sense into him. But he reached for the red silk dress, picked it up and dangled the garment in front of her. "I'm sorry, Hailey, truly sorry for that night. I'd had too much to drink, the pressure, it was too much." His gaze turned remorseful, his eyes imploring. Then the charming smile returned full force, as if the pain of that night had been erased by his words. "Now put on the dress for me, sweetheart." He slipped it into her hands. "We'll start all over tonight. Pretend it's our first date."

She clenched the dress in her fingers, the cold silk a reminder of his icy fingers on her skin. He had long since lost rational thought. Now he had gone mad.

"Thad—"

He pressed a finger to her lips. "Do it now, Hailey. I'll prove to you that I can be gentle, that I love you, that you never have to be afraid of me again."

But she was afraid. Her insides were a quivering mass.

He must have read the fear in her eyes. The apologetic look returned, his tone softer when he spoke. "Go ahead, my love. We'll dance the night away in each other's arms."

She had to stall for time. Pray Rex would return.

Rex, whose hands had touched her earlier and nearly brought her to heaven. So different from the emotions this man's touch evoked.

Growing impatient, he reached for her, slid his hands to the edge of her robe and pulled it apart. She was nearly naked beneath, her breasts bared in the dim light. A sick feeling stole over her, her stomach convulsing.

"I want to touch you." His eyes were glued to her body. "But I want you to trust me, Hailey. I can be patient."

Her lip quivered, the momentary reprieve rasping with tension as she nodded. Then, obediently she slid the dress over her shoulders, letting the fabric glide down her breasts and over her hips. The robe fell to the floor. He knelt, and tossed it aside.

Then he stood, picked up the necklace, released the catch and gestured for her to turn around. His fingers were stone-cold as they brushed her neck to fasten it. A whimper bubbled in her throat as she glanced down at the ruby. The blood-red pendant dangled between her breasts, a symbol that she belonged to him. Then he eased her around to face him, and cupped her cheek in his palm. Although his touch felt gentle this time, his leering smile sickened her.

"You are so beautiful, Hailey. And you're mine. Don't ever forget that, love."

Dusk splintered the shadowy room, the scent of his expensive aftershave swirling around her. Then he held out his arms, pulled her next to him and flipped on a CD. Classical music floated through the speakers as he began to dance, moving effortlessly into the rhythm of the waltz. He spun her around and around, gliding across the floor, humming the tune to her as she followed his pace. Something hard pressed into her ribs as he held her tighter, then his jacket fell open and she saw the gun he had tucked in his waist. She remembered the shooter who'd been in the woods that day she'd run into Rex. He'd thought it was a hunter, but now she wondered....

Would he use the weapon on her if she tried to escape?

REX DODGED ANOTHER BULLET as he jumped from his SUV. It zinged near his head, and pinged off the rocky incline. Stooping low, he darted around the other side of his car, hiding behind it as he unbanked his own weapon. He scanned the darkness for the shooter, searching the embankment and the neighboring bushes.

The glint of something shiny flashed into his vision, then another bullet soared toward him. He fired into the brush. Weeds rustled. A shadow moved. He darted toward the rear of the car, peering over the edge. The man fired again, then vaulted into the forest. Rex bolted up from the ground and raced for the woods, slipping between the trees to shield himself. A dark coat flapped, then disappeared behind a cluster of trees. The wind howled and bit at his cheeks, and he swiped a hand at the blood trickling down his jaw. He charged through the thicket, kicking and pushing aside weeds and limbs until he reached a clearing. Suddenly, an engine roared to life, and tires squealed. Dammit.

Rex plunged into the opening and fired again, aiming for the tires. But the dark sedan sped away in a cloud of smoke, ice and snow hissing behind it. Rex sprinted onto the road and fired again, but the bullet fell into dead air, the car disappearing into the murky fog.

Reeling with fury and adrenaline, he stared at the emptiness for several seconds, catching his breath, contemplating what had just happened. His mind had been on Hailey, not on his surroundings so this guy had completely ambushed him.

It wouldn't happen again.

Except he still had to make certain Hailey was all right. The fire, the shooter…someone had come after him. Hopefully, Hailey was safe.

Still, his stomach knotted as he jogged back toward his Jeep. Hunching his shoulders inside his coat, he slid his gun back to his waistband, but he kept his eyes peeled for danger as he melded into the woods and raced back to the ditch.

The blizzard raged around him, the intensity heightening his tension as he climbed inside and called Hailey. The phone was silent, though, as if the line had been cut.

Panic tightened his lungs as he tried to start the Jeep's engine. It sputtered, but finally roared back to life. The wheels dug and churned in the snow. He jumped out, grabbed the shovel from the trunk and dug around the tires to free it from the sludge.

Finally, he climbed back inside and tried again. It took him ten more minutes to get the Jeep out of the ditch. His body was cold and aching, his nerves strung tight by the time he reached Hailey's. Most of the lights were off, the silhouette of the Victorian house barely visible in the fog of snow.

Was Hailey all right?

Was she waiting up for him, naked and stretched out on the bed, ready to continue their lovemaking? Man, that would be nice.

Hope fought through the haze of fear, but when he knocked on the front door and jiggled it, it didn't budge. Then he glanced down. Muddy footprints marred the porch near the window. Not bootprints like Cohen would leave, but dress shoes. Jordan.

His gut tightened. Something was wrong.

He knocked again, then paused to listen. The drumming of music played through the cracks in the window. He pulled his gun, leaped over the porch railing and circled around to the back.

He had to take the man by surprise if he was going to save Hailey.

"IT'S TIME TO GO NOW, HAILEY."

Hailey willed herself to remain calm, to play along with Thad and wait for the right time. Then she'd make a run for it. "You said we'd take it slow. If you want my trust, let's plan a date. We can go to dinner in town." She hesitated, beseeching him with her eyes. "We'll start all over, just like you suggested."

He slowed the dance, holding her tightly in his arms, a twinkle in his merciless eyes. "Ahh, that sounds nice." But his lips parted in a no. "But if I leave you here, you'll change your mind. And I can't live without you, Hailey."

She swallowed hard. "Thad…you can't expect me to leave—"

"I expect you to please me, to make me happy."

"What about my happiness? If you care about me the way you say, you'll give me time. You won't force me to go tonight."

"You simply don't know what's good for you," he said. "Neither did my mother, but my father taught her."

So, he'd grown up in a home with a tyrant for a father. It was ingrained in him to be the same.

He clutched her elbow and twirled her toward the door. "Put on some shoes and get your coat, Hailey."

"But…I need to pack."

He shook his head no, his expression impatient. "I'll buy you whatever you need when we leave. You can choose an entirely new wardrobe."

She didn't want new clothes, she wanted love. But Thad was incapable of loving anyone but himself, his fame, his money and power.

"I'll need toiletries," she said, stalling.

He gritted his teeth. "We'll get those, too. Now come on." He shoved her to the bed, reached for a pair of black pumps on the floor and put them on her feet. Then he grabbed her elbow again and yanked her down the hall to the steps.

"Thad, please, you don't want to do this."

"Stop fighting me, Hailey."

She balked, dug her heels in and tried to pull away. If she made it to her room, she could lock the door. Get the shotgun. Use her cell phone. Call for help.

His fingers tightened, though, and she swung her fist out to hit him, but he caught her arms and shook her. "Don't make me hurt you." His eyes flashed in warning. "I don't want to, but I will."

"You'll hurt me if you force me to go with you."

Anger reddened his face, then he pushed her down the steps. She struggled against him, but he held on to both arms, then dragged her toward the front door and opened it. A gust of wind burst through the opening, flinging snow and ice inside, the incessant howl drowning out her cries.

Again, she fought, bracing herself against his weight, but he shoved her so hard she stumbled forward. Her knees hit the porch floor as she fell, but she caught herself with her hands.

He cursed, then yanked her up and hauled her down the steps. The cold sliced through the dress, an icy chill enveloping her. If he got her in the car, she'd never escape.

"Stop it now, or I'll shoot."

It took a second before the voice registered.

Rex. He was somewhere behind them.

Thad halted, holding her with one hand while he drew his gun with the other. A menacing look darkened his face as he pivoted and aimed. She screamed, searching for Rex. Thad fired.

Where was Rex? Was he hit?

Thad pushed her again, and she jerked at a tree limb, tore it loose and swiped it at his legs. He released a violent oath, shoved her backward until she fell into the snow. Another shot rang out. Rex firing at Thad.

Thad cursed, and bolted toward the woods, then fired again. Rex ducked behind the porch rail, and she scrambled behind the woodpile.

Thad fired again, and Rex sailed over the railing

with the agility of a bird in attack, then chased him into the woods. Seconds later, more gunshots rang out. Then the pounding of bone and flesh punctuated the air.

She held her breath, her body taut with fear. Finally a shadow appeared from the edge of the woods. Who was coming toward her?

Thad or Rex?

Chapter Fourteen

Rex's hands had tightened around Jordan's throat, his instinct to kill an urge within him. But just as he'd heard the gurgle of the man's throat his senses returned, and he slammed the butt of his gun against Jordan's head.

He couldn't turn into the murderer everyone claimed his father to be, or completely succumb to his instincts or he'd become an animal himself.

Even if Jordan had deserved to die.

The blood roared in his ears as he grabbed Jordan's gun and staggered through the trees. Blood trickled down his cheek, his arm was on fire from being grazed with a bullet and his bones ached, but he was more worried about Hailey than himself. Where was she?

And what had Jordan done to her before he'd arrived?

Nausea cramped his stomach as he walked closer to the house, fear nearly paralyzing him. "Hailey?"

The house was shrouded in darkness, a macabre feeling surrounding it.

"Hailey?"

She slowly rose from behind the woodpile, her eyes wide with terror. "Rex?"

"It's all right." Although he tried to remain calm, the tension rattled in his voice.

"Thad?"

Anger sharpened his words this time. "He'll live."

A sigh of relief escaped her, her gaze skating over him. Then she suddenly flung herself in his arms. He caught her, pressed her into his embrace, and wrapped his arms around her, the warmth of her body reassuring him that she was alive. But her tears and the tremors in her body scared the hell out of him.

He clung to her, immobilized by his feelings. At that moment, her life, her happiness, meant more to him than anything in the world, even more than freeing his father. He hadn't refrained from murdering Jordan so the locals wouldn't call him a killer, but out of respect and need for Hailey.

He had never allowed himself to need anyone before. And he had no idea what to do with the realization now. But he couldn't let her go or allow anyone else to hurt her. She was his now.

He'd die before he'd let Jordan ever touch her again.

He gently released her, ran to the woodshed for rope, then dragged Jordan to the porch and tied him to the post. Jordan barely came to, then faded off again. Rex coaxed Hailey up the stairs and inside, out of the blizzard and into the warmth of the house, cradling her close and rocking her back and forth in his arms until her tears subsided. She clung to him, her face burrowed against his chest, her breathing finally calming.

"I'm going to call the sheriff. You have to press charges this time, Hailey."

She nodded.

"I'll stand by you, testify against him. Even if he does have connections, you can't let him get away with attacking you."

"I know." She glanced down at the dress. "I'm going to change while you call." Her voice sounded weak, but also full of conviction, then she disappeared up the steps.

A knot of anxiety tightened his chest as he contemplated what they were up against. First of all, he had to call Cohen, a man who already hated him. And he didn't know a soul in town who'd volunteer as a character witness for him. And what about the Denver police? Were they in Jordan's pocket?

Would they believe him—the son of the convicted Hatchet Murderer?

HAILEY BARELY HELD HERSELF together while the sheriff questioned her. Thad finally rallied to consciousness, his irrational rantings solidifying her statement about his obsession, although he completely blamed Hailey for his actions, claiming she'd led him on. Thankfully, Rex stood quietly by, a pillar of strength, while she endured the inquisition.

"You definitely want to press charges?" the sheriff asked as they stepped onto the front porch.

Hailey nodded. She was walking out on a tightrope and she knew it. Once abusers had been charged, they usually returned afterward to their victims and made things worse. And Thad had a reputation to protect. But he had almost killed Rex....

Rex placed a comforting hand on her shoulder, squeezing gently, telegraphing a silent message that he would be there to protect her if that happened.

"She used me," Thad yelled as Cohen pushed him into the squad car. "Then she assaulted me in Denver. I filed charges against her. I came here to take her back to face them."

"You're obsessed with her," Rex said between clenched teeth. "You tried to force yourself on her in Denver, then she defended herself. And when she left town, you fabricated charges against her to scare her." He poked Jordan's chest. "Then you followed her here and attacked her. You even ransacked and set fire to my house to lure me away from her so you could kidnap her."

"That's a lie." Thad gasped. "I never started a fire—"

"Then we won't find your fingerprints in my house?" Rex asked.

Thad's eyes cut away, his eye twitching.

The sheriff cleared his throat. "Were you inside Falcon's house?"

Thad rubbed his forehead. "I…I simply wanted to find out who you were, but I didn't set fire to the house."

"I don't believe you," Rex said.

"We'll straighten this out at the station." Sheriff Cohen gave Hailey a skeptical look as if he was inclined to believe Thad, but the bruises on her arms and neck belied his denial of physical violence.

"You'll find out she's been lying to you," Thad bellowed. "She's not who she says she is. She wanted me for my money—"

Hailey shivered, grateful the sheriff closed the car door, blocking out Thad's accusations.

"You both need to come to the office to make formal statements," Cohen said.

Hailey hesitated, then nodded and climbed in the car with Rex. He covered her hand with his, his touch soothing. "Don't back down, Hailey."

"I won't. It ends here."

"You're doing the right thing," Rex said gently.

The next two hours at the police station were grueling. When Cohen discovered the charges against Hailey were real, he threatened to detain her. But the fire at Rex's, along with Hailey's injuries and the gunfire, made him reconsider.

"Drop the charges against me, Thad," Hailey implored softly, "and I won't file charges for attempted rape, just assault."

"Drop all of them," Thad snapped. "And come back with me, Hailey."

She shook her head. "I'm never coming back, Thad. Accept that it's over between us, and go back to Denver where you belong."

"You belong with me," Thad said stubbornly.

"No, I don't and you know it. I'd never fit into your world." She gave him a pleading look. "And you don't really want me to spend the night in jail, do you?"

For a brief second, the kind, charming man she'd first met appeared. He shook his head.

The sheriff grunted. "Are you dropping the charges, Jordan?"

"Yes," Thad muttered.

Sheriff Cohen jangled the keys to the jail, then reached for Thad's arm to escort him to the cell. Bitter hatred returned to Thad's eyes.

Cohen glanced back at Hailey and Rex. "Stay in town in case I need you for more questioning." He shot Hailey a warning look. "And if I find out you're lying, I'll arrest you and extradite you to Denver myself."

Hailey hugged her arms around her waist, hating that she'd dragged Rex into her drama. But he simply gave the sheriff a clipped nod, and led her back to the car, curving his arm around her to protect her from the wind as they ran through the blizzard.

Barring the blustery winds and churning tires, the ride back to her house was silent. Rex parked, killed the engine, then turned to her. "Come on, let's go back inside. You're freezing."

"Rex, I'm sorry—"

"Don't."

The gruffness of his short reply stopped her. Then he captured her face in his hands. "This wasn't your fault, Hailey. And I'm not sorry I'm involved."

She stared into his eyes and saw the truth. If his father was half the man he was, he didn't deserve to be in jail. After all, if the rumors she'd heard were true, that Lawrence Lyle had been abusive, maybe Rex's father had simply intervened to defend the woman or avenge her death the way Rex had just defended her against Thad. But if so, why wouldn't he have pleaded self-defense?

Rex rubbed his hands up and down her arms, the chill she'd felt since she'd spotted that red dress on her bed dissipating slowly. "Pack some things," he said in a low voice. "We'll go back to Falcon Ridge for the night."

She opened her mouth to argue, then stifled it. She didn't want to spend the night in her house alone, not with the memory of Thad forcing her to dress for him and dancing her around as if the waltz were a prelude to sex.

Sex that she hadn't wanted with Thad. Sex that would have been tawdry and ugly.

Nothing like the tender touches and passionate kisses Rex had given her earlier, kisses that tempted her to melt into his arms.

She hurried into her room, grabbed an overnight bag, tossed in a gown and some toiletries and hurried back to Rex. She had no idea what would happen now, but just being near him made her feel safe. She intended to savor the feeling. And she'd take whatever Rex had to offer, even if it was only his comforting arms for the night.

THE THOUGHT OF HAILEY spending the night in the Hatchet House was out of the question. The idea of Jordan touching her again, of him *having* her, fired a burning rage within him.

He'd wanted to kill the man with his bare hands. To rip out his throat and tear him apart limb by limb so he could never bother her again.

And Jordan would be back once he was released. The obsession had been profound, the intent clear, the evil in his eyes a promise. But Rex would be prepared next time. And next time, he would show no mercy.

He had to keep Hailey safe. And the only way to do that was to have her by his side.

She had been terrorized, though, manhandled, abused, just as the birds of prey that he found injured in the woods. Tonight was about comforting her, not his own smoldering desire to hold her, or to wash away the other man's vile touch with his own lovemaking.

When they reached Falcon Ridge, he rushed to the passenger side to help Hailey. He took her bag, then they slogged through the swirling snow, battling the wind as they climbed the steps. The look of vulnerability on Hailey's face as they stepped inside his cavern of a home squeezed deep emotions inside Rex. When she saw the damage to his house, she wavered, but he assured her it wasn't her fault.

He was beginning to care too much about this woman. So much that he wondered if she could accept the dark side of the Falcon men—their need to venture into the wild, to commune with the animals and the creatures of the forest for hours at a time.

"Why don't you take a hot bath and warm up. I'll make some coffee.

She nodded. "Thanks. I think I will."

He gestured toward the steps. "You remember the way?"

"Yes."

He watched her climb the stairs, then set the security system, stepping over the charred ashes and remains of the fire. They were the least of his problems.

Hailey was all that mattered, so he made coffee and carried the pot along with cups and a bottle of Baileys, rum and whipped cream up the stairs. Then he mixed a generous splash of each into the cups. When Hailey emerged from the bath, she wore a thick terry-cloth robe and was barefoot. Her hair lay in wet strands around her shoulders, the glistening moisture dotting her throat and neck making his desire spring to life. She looked so vulnerable, yet so sexy he ached to hold her.

"I spiked the coffee a little. I thought we could both use something stronger."

She smiled and accepted the cup, took a swallow, then licked her lips. The faint white of whipped cream lingered on her mouth, churning his hunger. But not for the coffee.

"This is delicious. Where did you learn to make it?"

"My mother. It's her favorite."

"What's she like, Rex?"

"Delicate like you," he said with a chuckle. "And tough, too. I guess she had to be to raise three boys. Especially…" He let the sentence trail off, avoiding reminders of his past. Not tonight. Tonight he wanted to just be with Hailey and forget.

But Hailey caught his train of thought. "Especially when she had to raise you on her own."

Her eyes met his then, and she moved forward, sipping the coffee again. He nodded and drank his own, not bothering to reply.

"I'm sorry. I understand what it's like to be alone, Rex." She paused. "I've been alone all my life."

He hesitated, then swallowed when she pressed a hand against his cheek. "Hailey, you're vulnerable right now."

"We both are, Rex. For heaven's sake, someone set fire to your house tonight."

"The damage is minimal, but someone shot at me on the way to your place."

"You think it was Thad?"

"It couldn't have been, not if he was at your house." She chewed her bottom lip. "But you didn't tell the sheriff."

"What good would it do? For all I know, he's the one who fired at me." He offered a small smile. "We must be getting close, Hailey. I'll find out the truth."

"I hope so, Rex." She sipped her coffee, then curled up beside him. "You saved my life. I don't know how to repay you, but if I can help you free your father, I will."

He gripped her wrist, wanting things to be clear between them. "Hailey, you don't owe me anything—"

"Shh." She dipped a finger into the whipped cream, then pressed it to his lip. He tasted the liqueur and coffee, and saw desire flare in her molten eyes. "This isn't about thanking you, Rex." Her chest rose with each breath, making her breasts swell beneath his gaze. "I want to be with you."

He squared his shoulders, fighting his own basic instinct, but his body responded anyway. "You've just been through a terrible ordeal, it wouldn't be right for me to take advantage of you."

"Don't you want me, Rex?"

God, yes. He'd wanted her from the moment he'd met her. From the second he'd looked into those reddish-brown eyes. "Yes, I want you, Hailey. I want you so bad I can hardly stand it. But tonight isn't about me. It's about making you feel safe."

"I feel safe with you," Hailey whispered. "And I want to be loved by you, at least tonight." A blush softened her cheeks as she pressed her breasts closer. She was so near he inhaled the sweet scent of her body wash, and felt the heat of her body inflame his own. An image of her lying back in the bubble bath came to him, her naked skin glistening with moisture, her nipples taut with need, her legs splayed for his taking.

"No past," she whispered. "No promises. No ghosts. Just the two of us."

Temptation, lust, hunger, all converged within him. He felt as if he were about to step off some invisible precipice and there would be no one to catch him when he fell. But his need was too strong, the heady sensations spiraling through him too potent to deny. He had to take the plunge off the ledge into the unknown.

So, he placed his cup on the nightstand, pulled Hailey into his arms and melded his lips with hers, the beating of his racing heart echoing in his mind.

HAILEY SANK INTO REX'S ARMS, the power of her need reflected in his eyes as he claimed her mouth. She had never felt so wanted, so desired, so loved.

It's not love, it's simply sex, a tiny voice inside her head whispered.

Yet another voice argued. The powerful emotions running rampant through her couldn't be anything but love.

Then her thoughts fled as his hands explored the outline of her body, the magic of his fingertips stirring sensations that brought her to the brink of ecstasy within seconds. He sipped her lips, his tongue combing her mouth, stoking the fire erupting within her as his fingers trailed down her neck and over her breasts. He cupped them in his palms, stroking and cradling her as his tongue plunged deeper into the recesses of her mouth. She moaned and threaded her hands into his hair, urging him closer, begging for the pleasure that his masculine body offered.

Then he slipped the robe from her shoulders and stared at her, his eyes painting a trail down her naked body that sent erotic tingles through her.

"You're so beautiful, Hailey." Heat inflamed his eyes as he shucked his shirt and tossed it to the floor. His pants and boxers came next, until he stood naked before her, a glorious sight of male flesh that made her swallow in excitement and shiver with the urge to couple with him. Hard muscular planes outlined his chest and arms and thighs, a thin layer of dark hair brushed his upper torso and dipped down toward his pulsing sex.

She wanted him inside her.

The hunger in his eyes was fierce, his meaning bold and clear as he hauled her to him, yet tenderness underscored his strength. Then he pressed her naked flesh to his, the passion between them explosive as they tumbled onto the bed. His hands roamed everywhere, seeking, yearning, touching, teasing, sliding over her breasts, circling her nipples until they formed tight peaks that he drew into his mouth and feasted upon. She groaned and clung to him, tangling her legs with his. His erection throbbed against her leg, the strength of his need igniting liquid heat in her belly. She arched her hips toward him, wanting more, craving him with the depths of her soul.

He denied her.

Instead, he licked at the tips of her breasts again, then played them between his fingers while he sank lower onto her, dropping kisses and tongue flicks along her belly until he spread her legs and crawled between them, tasting her honeyed folds.

She cried out for him to stop, that she couldn't withstand the torture, but he showed no mercy. His mouth worked to cover her, to inhale her heady scent as he dipped further into her. Sensation after sensation spiraled through her. The intimacy of the act sent tremors through her, the erotic thrill shattering into an explosive array of colors and emotions.

"Rex…"

He rose above her, slid a condom on, then kneed her legs apart and fit himself at the tip of her womanhood, gently stroking and easing his length into her until she could stand it no longer.

"Please, Rex, I want all of you."

"I don't want to hurt you…"

She cradled his face in her hands. "You won't."

His raw, passionate look sent her crumbling in his arms, yet she still sensed him hanging on to his control. The temptation to torture him rose, so she let her legs fall apart in a wanton show, then flicked his nipple with her tongue. He groaned, his jaw tight as he pushed himself farther into her tight sheath.

Sensing he liked her play, she encouraged him, pulling him tighter and deeper within her until he lost himself to the moment and began to rock inside her.

"Hailey…"

"Please, Rex, I need you."

Her soft admission must have broken his will, because he groaned and thrust hard and fast toward her center, lifting her legs and burying himself in her so deeply she cried out from the pain and pleasure. He looked into her eyes, the call of the wild reflected in his irises as he pulled out, then thrust into her heat again, over and over, harder, faster, deeper, until they were one, riding the waves into the churning waters together.

And when he climaxed, she saw in his eyes the primal mating call, the emotions tangling in her own mind. Then his whispered guttural release spilled into her, and she soared into the heavens again, the words *I love you* teetering on the edge of her tongue.

AN OVERWHELMING SENSE of pleasure and panic overcame Rex, the intensity of his feelings mind-boggling. His body jerked in response, his orgasm still rocking through him as he rolled to his side and swept Hailey tighter into his arms.

He wanted her again.

In fact, he didn't know if he'd ever be sated.

Fear bolted through him at the mere idea. Rex Falcon needed no one but himself, the wilderness and his brothers. The thought of needing Hailey on a permanent basis…it would destroy him.

But an image of Jordan's hands on her rushed unbidden to him, and a shudder seized him, making him draw her even tighter against him.

Hailey had been a virgin. She'd given herself to him freely. She had wanted him, Rex Falcon, the bad-boy son of the Hatchet Murderer, the man who had more in common with the hawks than he did with other men.

He cupped her jaw, lifted her face and looked into her eyes. A sleepy smile lit the depths, the haze of pleasure adding a rosy glow to her cheeks. "Hailey…"

"That was wonderful." She snuggled deeper into his arms, her softly spoken words, her blind trust and tantalizing body arousing him again. She seemed to sense his need, and began to play her fingers along his chest, then lower and lower until her fingers caressed his sex….

Within seconds, he took her again, the two of them coming together in a frenzy, as if the first time had only whetted both of their appetites for one another. And when he entered her and she cried out in oblivion, he moaned his pleasure into her mouth and flew to heaven with her.

Still reeling with emotions, he cradled her spoon-style against him, and they fell into a deep blissful sleep. But in his dreams, he heard her screaming.

He had turned into one of the hawks and was circling downward, flying in a low spiral, the mass of his wing-span beating the air as he soared toward his prey. The whites of her eyes nearly blinded him, and he realized that he had zeroed in on Hailey, that he had turned into an animal, and that he was going to destroy her with his talons.

Another scream pierced the air as he dove toward her.

He jerked awake, shaking with the force of his emotions, then stared at Hailey's sleeping form, reality slowly returning. Hailey wasn't screaming in terror but lying in his arms.

The sound was the telephone ringing.

Scrubbing a hand over his face, he slowly extricated himself from her warm body, sat up and reached for the handset. When he saw it was his brother's number, he groaned, picked it up and headed to the window. "Rex."

"It's Brack."

He glanced back at Hailey, already missing her warmth. "What's up?"

"I'm almost to Pursley's."

"Good."

"Anything happening there?"

He explained about the run-in with Thad Jordan, puzzling at his brother's long silence when he finished.

"Listen, Rex," Brack finally said. "Deke called me. He did some checking around about the Hitchcock woman. That guy Jordan is a big dog in Denver."

"I know that, he's also a bastard. If I hadn't been there to stop him tonight, he'd have kidnapped her and done God knows what else."

"That may be true, but how much do you really know about this Hitchcock woman?"

Rex gripped the phone tighter and glanced back at her naked shoulder above the sheet. He knew she was lonely, that she'd had a troubled past, that her skin was the softest damn skin he'd ever touched...

"Rex," Brack cut into his thoughts. "This woman isn't as innocent as you think."

Rex tensed. "What do you mean?"

"Jordan pressed charges—she assaulted him in Denver."

"She told me all about that—"

"Did she admit he caught her snooping in his office? That she warmed up to him to gain access to one of his client's files?"

Rex gripped the phone tighter. He didn't believe it. "Why the hell would she do that?"

"She's some kind of nut that likes freaky, gory murder cases. She even writes short stories about them."

What? She'd never mentioned writing. Although he had noticed her odd collection of books.

"First, she cozies up to the family to question them," Brack continued. "Once she even posed as a psychic to try to get people to talk. Had the family believing she had abilities and everything."

Just like the ghost of the little girl she claimed she'd seen? "What?"

"Don't you get it? She knew about you before she came to the Hatchet House, Rex. She researched the old house and the murder, then came there to write a story on our family. She even tried to get an interview with Dad at the jail, but he refused."

Hailey had tried to get an interview with his father? Had she really been using him?

"She wanted our father's story, probably found out

you'd returned to Falcon Ridge, and decided to seduce you to get information."

I want you, Rex.

No. She hadn't been lying.

Still, a knot of anger balled in Rex's throat, an old memory surfacing. When he was twelve, a woman had shown up at his door claiming to be a lawyer wanting to help his father. Rex had believed her and confided details about the horrible ordeal, everything from finding the bloody bodies to the arrest to his mother's depression following his father's incarceration. The next day the story had been printed in the paper, a photo of him and his brothers the day of the arrest below the caption.

And Hailey had been looking at his picture in the library…

Dammit.

Denial streaked through him. Hailey wasn't a reporter. But she had admitted that she wanted to find out about the hatchet murders. He remembered her reaction to the attic, the way she'd hidden in the closet—she'd seemed terrified, but had she been acting?

"I'll e-mail you the files," Brack said. "Just take a look at them yourself."

Rex muttered that he would, then strode downstairs and went to his computer. Seconds later, the denial turned to outrage as he read the report. He had been the worst kind of fool, had let another woman play on his weak side, and he'd fallen right into her trap. Not only had she pretended she didn't know who he was, but according to the report, Hailey was a compulsive liar, had been in and out of psychiatric treatment centers since she was four and had claimed more than once that she'd been attacked by a male, then later backed off when she'd been offered a settlement.

COLD AND FOG BLURRED the windshield as he parked the old Pontiac beneath a cluster of trees near Pursley's estate.

His fingers were numb from clenching the steering wheel, so he shook them until the feeling returned, then removed the photo of the Lyle murders from his pocket. Blood…there had been so much of it, coating his hands, the bodies, the floor…

The cheating Lyle woman had gotten what she deserved. The man, the little boy had been other casualties. And the girl—well… She'd seen everything. Would have recognized him, and they would have taken him away and locked him up forever.

He had only done what needed to be done.

So, who was this woman living in the house now? And how had she known about the closet? Was she some kind of damn psychic?

Did she also know that the closet had a passage that led to the attic?

Wind whistled through the window, ice crystals creating patterns on the glass. He had to talk to Pursley. Pursley had tried to clear Falcon, had snooped enough into the Lyle family's secrets to have guessed at the truth. Or at least part of it.

Now, he was a loose cannon waiting to go off. In his middle age, would he find his conscience?

The bitter wind clawed his face as he hunched inside the tattered coat, climbed out of the car, and crept through the bushes toward Pursley's house. Now Falcon was back asking questions, it would only be a matter of time until he questioned the lawyer who'd defended his father. And if Falcon discovered that Pursley had held back, that he'd had his own reasons for wanting Falcon in jail, Pursley might spill his guts.

A hearty chuckle escaped him.

Spill his guts...hell, he'd take care of that. He'd spill them for the man before he had a chance to talk to anyone.

Chapter Fifteen

Hailey rolled over in bed, expecting to feel Rex's hard, warm body against hers. But the space beside her was empty, the indentation of where he'd lain still hot from his flesh. The pillow smelled of his masculinity, the heady scent of their lovemaking permeating the room. Immediately, she felt alone, an ache burning in her. She wanted Rex again. Wanted him to know that coming together with him had been special.

But why had he left the bed? Because he didn't want her to cling to him? Was he afraid she'd expect some kind of declaration just because he was her first lover?

Who are you kidding, Hailey? You want him to be your only lover.

She reached for his shirt and pulled it on, fastening the buttons as she rose. The snowstorm raged outside, but the house was warm. Still, the bruises on her arms reminded her of the reason she'd come to Rex's. So she could be safe.

Because Thad had followed her.

Shaking off the memory, she padded through the bedroom, then down the stairs. A light was burning in the study, so she slipped inside, eager to convince Rex to return to bed. His back was to her, his head bent in earnest concentration as he studied the screen.

She moved closer, a chill in the room suddenly engulfing her. She missed him, wanted him to hold her again, to make love to her once more until the demons that had plagued her nightmares all her life disappeared forever.

But she couldn't pressure him. She had to accept what he offered.

Her heartbeat fluttered as she placed her hand on his shoulder. He tensed, the muscles in his shoulders bunching.

"I woke up and you were gone," she said in a low voice. "I missed you."

He slowly pivoted in the desk chair and looked up at her. Instead of passion, an angry glint darkened his brown irises and his jaw went rigid. "Really?"

She smiled. "Yes. It was cold in bed without you."

Instead of reaching for her as she wanted, he crossed his arms, his eyebrow raised intimidatingly.

The hair on her neck bristled. Something was wrong. When they'd fallen asleep, he'd been content, happy, sated. Now, he seemed distant, angry, the walls back in place. "What's wrong, Rex?"

He gestured toward the screen. "You lied to me, Hailey."

She frowned and glanced at the computer, shocked to see her name at the top of the page. It was a report from a private investigator. Betrayal rifled through her as she realized the implications. "You checked up on me?"

His silence answered her question.

"I don't understand—"

"No, *I* don't understand, Hailey. You told me that Jordan attacked you because you broke off your relationship—"

"That's right. You saw for yourself that he's crazy." Hysteria rose in her voice. He had to believe her. "He bought that red dress and made me wear it. He was going to force me to go with him."

"Because you assaulted him in Denver."

"No...I explained how that happened."

"You cozied up to him to sneak into his files," Rex said, "and you warmed up to me so you could find out about my father. It's all there in the report. You have this fetish about murder mysteries, and you use people to get the scoop, write the stories and sell them."

"What?" Hailey backed away, shock reeling through her. "I don't know what you're talking about."

Rex stood, his body as unyielding as stone. "You knew about the hatchet murders before you moved here, you knew I'd come back, that I was Randolph Falcon's son and you played me for a fool. "

"That's not true." The air in Hailey's chest constricted. "I swear, Rex." She searched his face, had to make him believe her. "The Realtor told me the house was haunted, and I was drawn to it. I don't know why—it was almost like I'd been here before. And maybe I have had a freakish interest in murder stories, but I didn't know who you were. You just showed up that day—"

"And played right into your hands." His look of disgust sent a sharp pain through her. "And then you acted as if you were afraid of the attic, talked about having nightmares, even pretended someone was chasing you through the woods to get my attention." He cursed. "For all I know, you probably planted that article and threatening note on the attic door to illicit my sympathy."

"Someone was chasing me," Hailey screeched. "It might have been Thad or the killer. I don't know who, but you saw how obsessed Thad was—"

"I saw what you wanted me to see." Rex held up a hand. "I'm not playing your game anymore, Hailey." He yanked a copy of the report from the printer and shoved it into her hands. "You read this and tell me what to believe."

His heels clicked as he strode toward the door. Reeling with emotions, she skimmed the paper, horror growing inside her. Lies. The report was full of them.

But where had it come from? Who had sent this to Rex?

Someone who didn't want them to be together. Someone who intended to hurt her.

That someone had succeeded.

Even worse, Rex believed the lies.

She glanced down at the shirt she'd pulled on, *his* shirt, the scent of his body still clinging to it, to her skin, where they had made love. But now he despised her.

Pain numbed her. Why had she opened herself up, allowed herself to care about someone again? Hadn't she learned that she was alone long ago, that caring only meant getting hurt, that no one had wanted her years ago, and no one wanted her now....

REX TRIED TO PUT Hailey's pleading eyes out of his mind as he drove to the prison to visit his father.

His first instinct had been to believe every word she'd said. After all, Jordan was a bastard. He'd assaulted Hailey, then he'd tried to kill Rex when he'd stopped him. Although Jordan claimed he was only trying to make Hailey return to Denver to face the charges he'd filed against her....

But Hailey had told the truth about Jordan being violent. Had she lied about the other things, or had she been honest with him all along? Had he been too quick to jump to conclusions? But if she hadn't lied, how the hell had that information shown up in the report?

Thad Jordan. The man had connections. All it would

take to alter someone's personal records was a little computer knowledge….

Troubled by the thought, he phoned his brother. "Where did you get that report on Hailey Hitchcock?"

Deke cleared his throat. "I checked with some of the other P.I.s in Denver. This one came back to me within seconds."

"Check it out," Rex said. "Make sure it's legitimate."

"What's up?"

"Something's bothering me." Rex scratched his chin. "Jordan has connections. What if he fabricated the report?"

"Are you sure you're not looking for a reason to believe this woman?"

Rex hesitated. Deke had a point. But Hailey's bewitching eyes haunted him. The hurt he'd seen flash in the depths when he'd accused her of using him had seemed so real. And she had been a virgin, the connection he'd felt so strong, almost hypnotic….

He had to know the truth. "Just verify the report for me. I'm on my way to talk to Dad."

"Good. Maybe we'll finally get somewhere."

"I don't intend to leave until he admits who threatened him."

Deke agreed, then Rex hung up, battling anxiety again over leaving Hailey home alone. What if something happened while he was gone?

His gut squeezed. Even if she had lied to him, he didn't want her harmed….

But she had distracted him too long. And the only way to keep her safe was to find the real killer.

Determined to focus on the case, he parked at the prison, went through security and found himself in the visiting area talking through the prison phone. A Plexiglas window separated him from his dad, but the stoic expression on his father's face told him more separated them than the thin wall of glass. A fresh bruise darkened the skin above his father's downcast eyes, and cigarette burns scarred his arms. What other injuries was he hiding?

"I told you to drop this," his father said in a husky voice.

Rex's throat tightened with anger. "What the hell's going on, Dad?"

"Nothing. But the case is too old. I'll finish my time—"

"That's bull, and we both know it." Rex fisted one hand in front of him while his other gripped the phone. "Someone got to you and I want to know who."

His father's gaze fell to his hands which he flexed, then cracked his knuckles, a habit Rex remembered from childhood. "I just want you boys and your mother to be safe. Dredging up the past will only cause more trouble."

"It's too late, Dad. We've all been hurt by what happened, and we're not dropping this until we find out the truth. The only way we'll ever be okay is to get you out of here."

Emotions flickered in his father's face before he masked them. "Rex, please. It's not worth putting your mother in danger."

"That's her decision. She wants us to investigate. Besides, Deke and Brack are grown up now—we'll protect her. And we're on to something, Dad, I can feel it. So, let's get down to business." Determined not to waste time, he continued, "Now, tell me everything you remember about the Lyles and the day they were murdered."

His father cleared his throat, then seemed to relent and spoke in a hushed tone. "I had spent the day tending the garden as usual. Although I'd seen the little boy outside playing in the yard, Joyce Lyle had been inside all day."

"She didn't go out with him?"

"No, she told me that she could see the yard from the nursery window where she stayed with Lindy Lou."

"And you didn't see the little girl?"

"No." He paused, his mouth twitching sideways with worry.

"Did they have any visitors? Had you seen anyone lurking around, watching the house? Anyone show up to do odd jobs, a repairman maybe?"

He shook his head "No one but the neighbor's little girl, Elsie Timmons. I saw her running through the woods chasing her cat."

"The neighbor's little girl?" Rex thought back to the files. "I don't remember anything about her in the report."

"I didn't think about mentioning it when they arrested me. But I had seen her at the house a few times before. She used to sneak in and play with Lindy Lou when Lawrence wasn't around."

"She wasn't there when the murders occurred?"

"Not that I know of." He rubbed his hands over his knuckles, a distant expression clouding his eyes. "But it's possible."

Some detail niggled at the back of Rex's mind, but he couldn't put his finger on it. "What happened to her?"

"Her father ran off with her around the same time as the murders. The Timmons couple weren't getting along. Deanna had filed for a divorce. She thought her husband took the child to Canada to live."

"And the sheriff didn't look at Timmons as a suspect?"

Rex's father grunted. "No, he had me. Why look further?"

The imbecile. "What about other visitors? Did the sheriff visit the Lyles' house earlier that day?"

"Not that I know of. Why?"

"Some people say Lyle was abusive. Ava Riderton hinted that Lindy Lou might not have been Lyle's child, so I wondered who the father was."

His father's gaze met Rex's. "Son, I never slept with Joyce Lyle."

"I never thought you did, Dad. But what if Lindy Lou wasn't Lyle's? What if the sheriff or someone in town fathered her and came to visit?"

"You think Lyle knew the little girl wasn't his?"

"Maybe. Or maybe he found out that day, and caught the other man at his house."

"But why would anyone kill the entire family?"

Rex shrugged. "Maybe they got in a fight and things snowballed out of control. Or hell, maybe Mrs. Lyle wanted the girl's father to admit he had a child. Maybe she even wanted him to take her away from her husband." He hesitated, trying to fit the pieces of the puzzle together. "Let's say she wanted to marry this other man, but he didn't want the truth to come out. Lindy Lou was autistic. Perhaps the dad didn't want to own up to having an impaired child. Or hell, he could have been married or involved with someone else. Or he might have been important in town…"

His father jumped on his train of thought. "He wanted to protect his reputation."

"Exactly. Who in town had the most to lose if an affair or an illegitimate child was revealed?"

"I can think of several. The mayor for one. But he was married, getting on in years even then. I doubt he'd have had the guts to kill the whole family." His father clawed his hands through his hair. "Sheriff Cohen was new in office then, too. He was cocky, had high aspirations. And the district attorney who prosecuted me had talked about politics." The light returned to his eyes. "They were both pretty quick to hammer the nail in my coffin."

"What about your lawyer?"

"He tried to get me off," Rex's father said, "but I always thought he could have offered a better defense."

"What do you mean?"

"He didn't give the jury any other possible suspects."

"And neither did the sheriff or the prosecutor." Rex rapped his hands on the table. "Cohen has been pressuring me to drop the investigation."

"He wanted to make a name for himself," Rex's father said. "And my case did it."

"Yeah, and it's odd, too, that Pursley lost your case, yet he fared well afterward," Rex said. "Seems he came into some money shortly after you went to jail. Has a big estate outside of town, further north. Brack's on his way to talk to him now."

A long tense silence stretched between them. Finally, his father rubbed his forehead. "I wish I had something more concrete to tell you. But I didn't socialize, so I didn't know much about the people in town."

Rex could relate. He wasn't very social himself. And his father's tendency to avoid people had been a bone of contention between his father and mother. Rex was certain his father hadn't changed in jail. If anything, he'd probably grown more reclusive.

Would his parents reconcile once his father was free or had they changed too much?

"We have two good suspects, the sheriff and McDaver. Three or four if we count Pursley and Timmons," Rex said.

"I also found a bloody shirt in the woodshed at the Lyle house. I'm waiting on DNA results." Rex explained about finding the bones. "If they don't belong to the Lyle girl, they might be the neighbor's child."

His father's face turned haunted again. "God, what a mess."

Rex's stomach tightened, as well. "If you think of anything else, Dad, anyone you might have seen with Joyce Lyle, call me."

His father stood, his eyes level with Rex's. "Take care of your mother and brothers, son. I'm depending on you."

The weight of those words settled on Rex's shoulder once again, just as they had when he was ten years old. Only this time he didn't go running into the woods. This time he squared his shoulders, embracing the challenge. "I will, but you'll be free soon, and that's going to be your job, Dad."

The faint stirring of hope that flashed into his father's eyes would stay with him forever.

THE MEMORY OF Rex's accusations still burned through Hailey when she let herself back in her house. She fought against the force of the heavy breeze tugging at the door as she locked it, then flipped on a light switch. The light flickered on, then off, finally settling into a dim flicker that only added to her already frayed nerves. Shamelessly frightened of her own house, she locked the dead bolt, reminding herself that Thad was in jail.

But the Hatchet Murderer was not.

A moment of panic attacked her, and she thought of Rex. Safe, warm, protective, strong Rex. She wanted him to embrace her, to protect her from the demons.

No one can protect you now. You're all alone.

Because Rex believed she'd deceived him.

Like Thad, he'd turned on her so quickly... Why? Because he didn't want a long-term relationship? Because he really believed she was a liar, that she'd use someone's pain to earn money?

Shivering, she dragged herself up the stairs and sank into a hot bath, hoping to wash the reminders of how wantonly she'd given herself to Rex off her skin. But his angry words echoed in the recesses of her mind.

Furious at herself for opening her heart to him, she toweled off, dressed in fresh sweats and went down the steps. She rummaged through the oak desk again, wondering if she'd missed something when she'd searched it before, something that might help identify the killer or tell her more about the Lyles.

First, she found the photo of the house the Realtor had sent her. Hailey had felt an odd connection with Deanna Timmons. She'd been drawn by the Realtor's voice on the phone, almost as drawn to her as she had to the Victorian house.

Deanna Timmons had looked tired with age, as if the sadness she'd endured had robbed her of hope just as the bitter Colorado winters stole the warmth from the earth. She obviously still grieved for her missing daughter. When she'd shown Hailey the picture of Elsie, a tear had slipped down her cheek. Hailey had squeezed her hand, understanding the woman's loneliness and vowing that if she stayed around, they would become friends.

Then Hailey had experienced that odd flash—an image of the Lyle house painted blue with a white wrap-around porch and roses growing in a garden out back. From the upstairs bedroom windows, she could see the wild columbine dotting the mountainside. When she'd mentioned her vision of the house, a strange expression had overcome Deanna's face, as if Hailey had described the house as it had once been.

A screech from the kitchen suddenly shattered her thoughts, startling her back to the present. She peered through the murky interior, her gaze drifting to the hall where the Lyle bodies had been found. A morbid sense of doom sent her walking in that direction, the whisper of caution brushing her neck as strong as the incessant voice inside her head urging her to face her fears or be haunted by them forever. Joyce Lyle and her children's spirits were not at peace and never would be unless their murderer was caught. Deanna Timmons had told her that. Somehow, even though Hailey didn't believe in ghosts, she felt it was true.

Clouds of gray clogged her vision as she wove her way through the darkness, the glow from the kitchen clock slicing through the haze. The cuckoo clock suddenly seemed familiar, too, as if she'd seen it before and recognized its sound.

She zeroed in on the spot where the bodies had been discovered and gasped. Blood dotted the floor, the splatters against the wall and back door crimson. Then horror struck her. The blood was fresh.

A dead hawk lay on the floor, its head twisted at an odd angle, the blood trail seeping from its battered body. It was the hawk Rex had saved. She gripped the table edge, backing up against the pantry door, flashes of the Lyles' bloody bodies bursting through the dark, replacing the hawk. Trembling in shock, she crouched down against the door surface and hugged her knees, rocking herself back and forth, back and forth, the bloody images flashing one after another like a movie trailer.

He was there. He had a hatchet. He was screaming and chasing the mother. Then he swung the hatchet down.

She rocked herself harder, faster, disappearing within herself.

"Hide, sweetheart. Run and hide from Daddy."

Hailey watched with terror, a scream erupting in her throat. *"No, don't kill her!"*

"Hurry," the voice whispered again. "Run, get out of here! Save yourself!"

She covered her ears and forced her jelly legs to move, but she was shaking, and she felt sick to her stomach. She clutched her abdomen and swallowed, trying not to cough up the sickness. She had to get away. Run and hide. Save the woman and boy and little girl.

Or he would kill her, too.

She had to find the telephone. Call the sheriff. Maybe he would come and save them this time. Only he was mean, too, She'd seen him and her mother arguing. And he didn't like her, she'd heard him say her name in that ugly loud voice.

What should she do?

"Run, hide. Save yourself."

But she wanted to save the woman and her little girl and boy. She didn't want any of them to die….

REX HAD A NAGGING FEELING they were missing something important as he drove back home. His father's comment about the neighbor's little girl, Elsie, had struck a nerve. Elsie had played with Lindy Lou. She might have known the ins and outs of the house. She also might have witnessed the violence. If so, had her father really kidnapped her, or had something happened to her?

He cursed aloud but phoned the M.E. for a report on the bones he'd discovered.

"Sorry I don't have the results yet, but it should be soon. We're looking at dental records now."

"Try to hurry it up," Rex said "It's important."

"I'm trying. But you know DNA tests take time."

Rex gritted his teeth. "Try to rush it. And call me as soon as you know who those bones belong to."

"We all know the answer to that."

Rex mumbled an agreement, although he was beginning to wonder if they might be Elsie Timmons's instead of Lindy Lou's. He remained silent, though, hung up, then phoned Deke. "I'm on my way to talk to Deanna Timmons. Her husband and little girl disappeared around the same time as the hatchet murders."

"You think their disappearance is connected?"

"I don't know, but the timing of his disappearance is too coincidental. Besides, the sheriff didn't even investigate Timmons's disappearance." He massaged his temple where a headache pulsed. "Dad said Elsie Timmons used to play with Lindy Lou. If Elsie was in the woods that day, it's possible she saw the killer murder Lindy Lou and dump her into the river." He explained about finding the bones, his hunch that Mrs. Lyle had had an affair, that Lindy Lou might be illegitimate, and his suspicions about Andy Cohen and Bentley Mc-Daver. "What if Timmons was Lindy Lou's father?"

"I'll see what I can dig up on him," Deke said.

"Good, I'm going to find out if his wife has heard from him or the daughter since they left."

"Listen, Rex, I tried to verify that report on Hailey Hitchcock."

Rex's breath caught in his throat. "Yeah?"

"You might be right. The report originated from a detective named Wormer. He does a lot of work for Thad Jordan."

Hailey's face flashed into his mind. She'd looked so hurt when he'd accused her of using him. Dammit, Jordan had to be held accountable for the pain he'd caused her. And so did he; he owed her an apology….

"I also found something else interesting," Deke continued. "She was an orphan—"

"I know that."

"Yeah, but get this. It turns out the man who dropped her off at the orphanage found her near Tin City."

Rex froze, his hands tightening around the steering wheel.

"It might not be important, but it seemed coincidental to me."

Rex didn't like coincidences. "When did she show up at the orphanage?"

"A few days after the Lyles were murdered."

Hailey had said her father dropped her at the orphanage. Timmons had supposedly taken off with his daughter the same week. What if Hailey was Elsie Timmons? And what if Timmons was the killer? If his child had seen him commit the murders, she might have been traumatized. He might have dropped her at the orphanage to keep her from talking….

Other pieces floated back, connecting the dots in his mind. Hailey said the Hatchet House seemed familiar. She had known about the crawl space in the little girl's bedroom. She said it was as if she'd been watching the mother warn the little girl….

What if Hailey was the Timmons child, and the ghosts she claimed she'd seen were really memories?

HE STARED THROUGH THE CRACK in the door at the woman cowering against the closet door. He knew who she was now. He had finally figured it out.

She had come back to haunt him. And when she remembered, she would identify him. Then it would all be over.

Unless he stopped her first.

He saw an image of her as she'd been years ago. A small little girl with pigtails and bright dark eyes and that smile that she had only for her mother.

She'd been so afraid of him.

As she should have been.

She had resisted all his teachings, had created a wedge between him and his wife, so he had had to punish her. And then she'd seen too much that day, had witnessed his temper at its worst.

So he'd had to get rid of her. He had no choice. And he thought he had until now....

His hands itched inside the black leather gloves, his mouth watering as he remembered the blood that had splattered the floor near her feet twenty years ago. The scent had stayed with him through the years, the screams taunting him in his sleep, the reality of what he'd done forcing him to live in isolation. That was all her fault, too.

It was time to finish it. Time to take her to the attic. Time to say goodbye to her one more time.

And this time it would be forever.

Chapter Sixteen

"Mrs. Timmons, I hate to disturb you, but I need to talk to you."

Deanna Timmons clutched the cameo around her neck and stared at Rex with the wariness he'd come to expect from the people of Tin City. Their distrust of him still rankled.

"I know who you are. I heard you were back trying to clear your daddy."

Rex nodded. "He's innocent, ma'am. May I come in?"

Her gaze flickered over him as if to search for weapons, then as if the grief in her life had driven her past the point of caring, she nodded and led him to a small parlor that had been cleaned so the wood polish shone beneath the bright lights. Antiques filled the room, along with knickknacks—ceramic cats, frogs and a series of snow globes that reminded him of Christmas.

And of the one Hailey had found in the Lyle house.

He cleared his throat, trying to think of a lead-in for his questions. "You have a lovely home."

"Thank you. It…it's all I have."

A moment of compassion hit him. He noted the framed photographs of a baby on the wall, another of a toddler, then a four-year-old with blond hair and brown eyes. Then the pictures had suddenly stopped just as this woman's life with her child had the day Elsie had disappeared.

His own photograph book was the same, the photos of his father ending when he was ten.

On the cherry desk he saw a copy of Deanna's real estate license. "You sold Hailey Hitchcock the H...Lyle house, didn't you?"

"Yes." She huddled on the edge of a Victorian love seat, knotting her hands. "I was surprised she wanted to buy it, but she was intrigued with the place."

"Yes, I've spoken with her." He stood in front of the fireplace. "There have been some odd incidences in the house. It appears that someone doesn't want Miss Hitchcock to stay."

She didn't react or appear fazed. "Some people say the house is haunted."

"Yes, well, I don't believe in spirits. Just human demons."

She almost smiled. "I believe in those, too."

He paused, choosing his wording carefully. "I've been investigating the murder of the Lyles and have heard some interesting information." He explained about finding the bones, thinking they belonged to Lindy Lou Lyle, and the possibility that Lawrence Lyle wasn't her father. She listened, her interest growing as he continued. "It's true you had a daughter who used to play with Lindy Lou?"

She nodded, her eyes watching him. "Yes. Elsie used to sneak over there to play sometimes," she admitted. "But it always worried me."

"Why didn't you feel comfortable with the girls' friendship?"

She hesitated, fidgeting with a thread on her slacks. "I don't know, the parents fought a lot." She raised her gaze and met his. "I saw the strain on Joyce's face. It was the same way I felt in my own marriage, trapped, as if I was fading into the woodwork."

Grateful for the opening, he asked, "You and your husband divorced?"

She nodded, plucking at the string again. "Ralph wasn't the nicest man. Although Lawrence Lyle seemed like a charmer, I saw the bad in him, too. He told my Elsie not to come around. I don't think he liked girls."

Rex frowned. "His daughter was autistic, right?"

"That's what they said. I never saw her much, only occasionally when I ran over looking for Elsie." A sad look darkened her eyes. "She'd just sit like she was in her own world."

"Mrs. Timmons, is it true that your husband took your daughter away?"

Fresh pain flashed into her eyes. "Yes. He did it to get back at me because I wouldn't let him see her alone. I was afraid he might…might take her away from me. And he did."

"How did your husband feel about Elsie playing with Lindy Lou?"

"He forbade it," she said. "He thought the Lyle girl was cursed."

"Have you heard from your husband or daughter since they left?"

"No, and not a day goes by that I don't pray she'll come back."

"Did you look for them or hire someone to find out where they'd gone?"

"I went through the police." She reached for a cigarette, shook it from the pack and lit up. "Fat lot of good that did me. Sheriff Cohen said Ralph was her daddy, he had rights."

Sounded like Cohen. "I thought Elsie might have tried to contact you through the years…."

"No, not a word or a letter, nothing. I hoped…" Her words trailed off, the sadness thick in her smoker's voice as she exhaled. "I've always wondered what she'd look like now, all grown up. If she'd even remember me."

Rex remained silent, his thoughts jumbled. He wanted to tell her that he thought Hailey was her daughter, that she was beautiful and strong and courageous, but he had to be certain first before he offered this woman false hope.

"I hate to ask you this, Mrs. Timmons, but it's important. Were your husband and Joyce Lyle friendly?"

She jerked her gaze to him. "You mean, did they have an affair?"

He gave a clipped nod, studying her reaction.

"It's possible." She shrugged, her hand trembling. "He had some other woman on the side, but I never found out who. To tell you the truth, I didn't want to know." Then the light seem to click on in her head. "Are you suggesting Ralph and Joyce had a child together, that Lindy Lou was his?"

"It's possible."

She inhaled another drag from the cigarette, then blew into the air. "That might explain why he didn't want Elsie around her. You think he killed that family to hide the truth?"

Rex shrugged. "It's one theory."

"He was selfish," she admitted quietly. "But to kill a woman and her kids…I don't know." She tapped the ashes on the ceramic tray on the table. Rex winced when he realized it was a clay one that had been made by a child. Deanna Timmons had kept it all these years waiting and hoping Elsie might return to her.

"Then again," she said, once more looking into his eyes. "He did steal my little girl from me and never looked back."

Rex nodded, moved by the depth of emotions in the woman's voice. He understood the deep anguish that ate at a soul over the years. Deanna had lost part of herself the day she'd lost her daughter just as he had the day his father had been arrested.

Hailey's face flashed into his mind. Had she come back to fill the void in their lives?

If Hailey was this woman's child, and she'd witnessed the Lyle murders, she was in terrible danger. And he had left her alone because of his own pride…

THERE WAS SO MUCH BLOOD. Blood on the mother's clothes, blood on her face, on her neck, on her hands. Blood splattered the walls, blood soaked the man's clothes. It oozed from his chest and spewed onto his shirt.

She clutched her stomach. She wanted to scream and throw up at the same time. But he saw her. He had big mean eyes. The curl of his lip said he was going to get her. Punish her.

And this time he wouldn't stop with locking her in the closet. Or the attic. This time, he'd kill her and make her look all bloody like the others.

She had to run and hide. She'd go to her room, climb into the attic. Bar it from the inside so he couldn't get her. The old trunk was up there. If she could turn it over and push it against the wood frame, he'd never break it down. But she wasn't that strong.

And he had the hatchet…

Her legs wobbled as she clawed her way through the hall. Her fingers were coated in blood.

He was coming closer.

Maybe she should run outside. Hide in the woods. Yes, she could run fast. Fast like the wind.

And maybe the man who cut the roses would be outside. He'd help her.

A cry floated up, erupting from her throat. She pawed her way up to the front door, jiggled the knob. No! It was stuck, wouldn't open. She checked the keyhole for the key, but it was gone. His footsteps thundered closer. Then his hand clamped onto her arm like a bear claw.

She screamed and kicked out like an animal. She had to fight, get away, get help. But he slapped her across the cheek so hard she saw stars. Colors blinded her, then faded into darkness as fear took hold.

He jerked her harder, shoving her up the stairs.

"No, let me go!" She thought she screamed out loud but she wasn't sure. Her heart was pounding so hard she could hear it. His voice boomed like thunder. She clamped her hands over her ears again to drown it out.

He yanked her harder, then pushed her down. She fell onto the floor. Crawled forward. Her knees scraped the wood. Or was she outside? She didn't know anymore. She was so dizzy.

Then he knocked her in the head again, and she blacked out.

A minute later, her head spun as she struggled to open her eyes. He was carrying her. Opening the attic door. Climbing the steps. Then he tossed her inside.

She hit the floor and rolled. Her knee jabbed something hard, and her head connected with the edge of the old trunk. She clawed her way to a sitting position, but it was so dark. Then the door clicked shut. The lock screeched. His footsteps pounded down the stairs. He was whistling. Whistling that happy tune that turned her stomach.

She curled herself into a ball, pressing her eyes closed to stop the tears. If he'd left her here, he wasn't going to kill her. He'd be back, though. Just like always.

Back to punish her some more.

Where was the snow globe? The music. She wanted to hear the song. But he'd taken it away from her last week.

Panic burned her throat, but she swallowed, working up the moisture in her mouth so she could hum the tune. But her mouth felt like cotton. Then an odd odor sifted through the door. Like the leaves burning when her daddy set them on fire.

She must be outside.

No, she was on the floor in the attic. A wooden splinter jabbed her palm as she slid toward the door. A thin stream of smoke curled through the bottom.

Oh, no! He'd set the house on fire. She yanked at the knob. It was locked from the outside.

There was no way to get out.

She coughed, inhaling smoke. She was going to die this time. And no one would ever know she was up here.

She jumped up and raced to the window. She had to break it. She scrambled for something to hit the glass, but the only thing she could find was an old hairbrush. Her heart racing, she beat at the window to break it. More smoke filled the room, thicker now. She glanced outside, down at the snow-covered ground. He was looking up at her with those mean eyes.

Memories floated back. For a while she had drifted outside her body. But now she had climbed back inside. And she wasn't watching the man kill the mommy.

She was the little girl this time.

Through the haze of smoke, the monster's face flashed like a camera. No! It couldn't be her daddy. Her daddy was dead. She'd seen the blood. Seen the whites of his eyes. He hadn't been breathing.

But it was him. He was alive.

And he was going to stand by and watch her die…

REX DIDN'T WANT HAILEY TO DIE. Not because of his father or him. And if Timmons figured out who she was, he'd come after her. Maybe he already had….

His heart racing, he sped down the highway, dialing Cohen as he maneuvered the icy roads. Although he didn't trust the man, he needed help.

"What the hell do you want?" Cohen asked.

"I have reason to believe Ralph Timmons killed the Lyle family and that he's back."

"Ralph Timmons? He left here years ago."

"Yes, he disappeared the same time as the murders occurred," Rex said in a curt tone. "Didn't you suspect that his disappearance might not a coincidence?"

"Family dispute," Cohen said with his typical small-minded attitude.

"Just put out an APB on him," Rex said.

"All right, but I still stay you're barking up the wrong tree."

"Because you know who killed the family?" Rex asked. "Or because you did it?"

Cohen released a string of expletives a mile long. Rex hung up to cut the sheriff off, not bothering to argue. If he discovered Cohen had purposely framed his father, he'd make sure he paid.

He was winding up the mountain to Hailey's, his nerves zinging a mile a minute, when his cell phone rang.

"Rex, it's Brack. I'm at Pursley's."

"You talked to him yet?"

A tense hesitation followed.

"Brack?"

"He's dead, Rex. Locals said he was shot in the back of the head with a .38."

Timmons? Or had his suspicions about Cohen been on target? What if Cohen was Lindy Lou's father, and Timmons's daughter had witnessed him murder the Lyles? He might have killed the Timmons's child, then Timmons himself. Timmons might even be buried in the woods....

Lord, his head was spinning with the possibilities, but something still didn't fit.

"Rex?"

"Yeah." He explained his theories to his brother, fighting the steering wheel to keep control as the tires spun on the icy asphalt. "I'm on my way to Hailey's. I'll call you when I get there."

Rex disconnected, his pulse hammering with panic. He remembered the hurt he'd seen in her eyes when he'd left, the hurt he'd put there. Then he saw her in his bed, the soft glow of the light bathing her naked body as she'd writhed in his arms.

He wanted to make love to her again, to erase all her pain, to feel her come apart in his arms and make her smile.

Guilt slammed into him, though, along with doubts. Would she want him again? Would she forgive him for believing the allegations against her? He'd jumped to conclusions that her ex-boyfriend had wanted him to believe. Was he any better than the people of Tin City who'd fallen hook, line and sinker for the first and easiest person to pin the Lyle murders on?

They had believed what Sheriff Cohen had told them, just as he'd believed the lies Jordan had fabricated about Hailey. Although they weren't all lies.

Hailey was troubled, alone, her memories obviously

distorted from the trauma she'd suffered. He saw her at age four, a tiny munchkin girl who trusted her parents. A kid who'd walked into a nightmare. He'd never recovered from seeing the bloody bodies after the fact; how had she handled witnessing the actual brutal murders? And what if her own father, Timmons, had killed the family, then attacked her....

Nausea rose in his belly, but he squashed it and stepped on the gas. Snow swirled in a fog around him, and the wind knocked his SUV back and forth on the curvy road, but he pressed the accelerator. Fear choked his throat as he turned into her drive and saw smoke curling from the rooftop. Dear God, the house was on fire!

Was Hailey inside?

The tires screeched as he threw the car into park. Snow and ice spewed from the wheels. He jumped out and ran to the front door. It was hot. So hot he didn't dare open it. His heart pounding, he ran to the window and peered through the glass. The fire blazed through the downstairs, eating the wooden floors and antiques, shooting flames up the staircase along the walls and ceilings. He stood back for a second to scan the exterior. If Hailey was inside, where would she be?

A red-tailed hawk suddenly batted its wings and swept across the chimney top in an arc. A flash of something caught his eye. He jerked his attention to the attic. Then he saw her. Her face was pressed against the window. She was trapped, banging on the glass, screaming for help.

He remembered the ladder he'd used to repair the shingles and ran to the other side. He jammed it against the side of the house and began to climb. He had to hurry and get her out before the flames reached the attic.

Before he lost her forever.

HAILEY FOUGHT AGAINST the painful memories bombarding her and banged harder on the glass. She had to find something stronger to break it. If she could get outside, she could climb down.

Wood sizzled and popped, the fire eating the planks. Flames shot through the bottom of the door. She scrounged for a cloth, then jerked off her sweater and stuffed it at the bottom of the door to ward off the smoke. But it seeped through the opening anyway, the flames hissing and clawing through the material.

Then something hit the window. She ran to it, half afraid her father was there again. Smoke and fog clogged the glass, and she squinted to make out what was happening.

"Hailey!"

Rex. He was here. He was going to save her.

He tried to jimmy the window but it wouldn't budge. "Stand back so I can break the glass!"

She ran to the corner and covered her head and face with her arms. Seconds later, glass shattered, spraying the inside of the room. Flames shot through the door opening, hissing at her feet. Rex reached inside the broken window.

"Come on, hurry!"

She broke into a cough, but grabbed his hand and crawled through the window frame. He braced her with his hands on her waist, then they slowly climbed across the roof. The ceiling felt hot to her feet, then boards in front of her splintered and fell into the well of flames. Hailey screamed and slipped, but he grabbed her, steadying her as they jumped over the crack. Then he crawled onto the ladder first, coaching her to follow.

She was still coughing when they landed on the ground, her hands and body shaking. Rex pulled her into his arms. "God, Hailey, I thought I'd lost you."

A shadow moved behind him. The monster returned.

Hailey screamed to warn Rex, but it was too late. He pivoted just as the man raised his gun.

Shock registered on Rex's face. "But y-you're dead."

The split second of hesitation gave her father just enough time to slam the weapon against Rex's head. Rex staggered, blood spurting from the gash on his temple. She reached for him, but her father grabbed her arm and fired the weapon at Rex. He collapsed, then she felt the pistol jammed against her side.

Hailey's heart shattered as he dragged her into the woods. Rex might be dead. And she was going to die, too.

And it was all her father's fault. Just as he'd killed the others.

If only she'd remembered sooner…

Memories of that horrible slaying rushed back as he hauled her deeper into the forest. She had seen him kill her parents. Seen her brother and mother fall, and her father.

No, it hadn't been her father.

Her uncle. Her father's twin, Lester. He had come to rescue them, to take them to live with him. But her father had stumbled in and caught them. He had blamed her, had attacked her. But her brother had fought to save her. So had her mother, and uncle.

Hailey had hidden in the pantry. She'd seen them fall into the bath of blood. Then he'd chased her into the woods. The same woods where she was going now.

But she had escaped back then. She'd run to the river. Had tripped and hit her head. Had crawled into a small fishing boat on the bank, and it had floated away. Away to safety. To her new life.

But now that life was about to be over.

He yanked her harder, the icy, spiny limbs tearing her

face as they ran through the woods. Her lungs ached, her legs throbbed, the cold seeping all the way to her bones.

Then he suddenly halted. She saw the grave where Rex had found the bones. Her father's leering smile fell on her, and she realized his intent. He was going to kill her and bury her there. Then he'd probably go back for Rex.

"You killed my family," she whispered. "You're evil."

"It was your fault," he snarled. "You should never have been born."

His words felt like a physical blow. Still, she struggled to get away, but he hit her so hard she collapsed onto the ground. She tried to recover, but she was so dizzy she was nearly blind. He quickly tied her hands then yanked the cord around her ankles, and shoved her down into the hole. She cried out in terror.

He was going to bury her alive.

Chapter Seventeen

Fiery pain burned through Rex's shoulder and head as he regained consciousness. What the hell had happened?

He tried to move, but pain knifed through him again. The sound of wood crackling jerked his attention to the house. Flames shot into the sky. The entire house was an orange fireball, the fire eating it as if it were nothing but kindling. The roof suddenly collapsed, splintering into pieces, sparks lighting up the dark sky.

Hailey? God, where was she? He'd rescued her from the house, then what? He rubbed the gash on his head. Then someone had hit him over the head and shot him. The man's face flashed back. Impossible. He'd had it all wrong. Lawrence Lyle was dead. He'd seen him with his own eyes twenty years ago. His picture had been in the paper.

But it had been Lyle's face staring back at him.

And now he had Hailey.

He gripped his upper chest to stem the ache, blood seeping from the wound. The world spun as he tried to lift his head, a dizzying frenzy of pain and fatigue clawing at him. He ground his teeth and struggled to reach his phone. He needed backup. His fingers shook as he punched in the sheriff's number.

"What is it now?" Cohen snapped.

"I've been shot. The killer has Hailey. Call the fire department and get over here now."

Panting to keep from passing out, he disconnected and struggled to stand. Every second counted. Whoever this man was, he looked like Lawrence Lyle, and he was dangerous.

What if he was too late? What if he'd lost Hailey before he had a chance to confess his love?

Utilizing every ounce of energy in his reserve, he forced himself to move his feet. Blinking to clear his vision, he removed his gun from the waistband of his jeans and trudged forward into the woods. Swiping at the blood trickling down his cheek, he searched the snow-packed ground for footprints, then followed their path. They had to lead to Hailey.

Every step was pure agony, every movement fraught with pain as he wove his way through the woods. Twigs snapped below his feet, the crunch of his boots in the snow echoing in the eerie quiet. The footsteps became more blurred as he went deeper into the woods, the bitter wind already covering the killer's tracks.

The sound of wings flapping above broke through the haze. He glanced up and saw a red-tailed hawk swoop lower, then raise its head and glide toward the north.

The area where he'd found the little girl's bones.

The killer was going to take Hailey there, bury her in the same place. A wave of pure rage engulfed him, making him dizzy again, but he grabbed a tree for support, inhaled sharply and forced himself forward. Another step. Another. He followed the path of the hawk, his instincts reassuring him his friend would steer him in the right direction.

A sound up ahead made him pause. A low sob followed. A cry. Hailey. Thank God she was alive. But he couldn't see her.

He peered around the tree, his heart throbbing. Hailey was down in the grave, and Lyle was shoveling dirt on top of her.

He was the worst kind of madman. Sick and vicious to the core.

Fury driving him from the trees, he had his weapon drawn and ready. "Freeze."

The man spun around, a stunned expression marring his face.

"You bastard. Who are you?"

"Lawrence Lyle, alive and well," the man said in a sinister voice.

"But how? You're dead…."

"My brother, Lester. Thought he was some kind of saint, that he'd come in and take my family away from me, but I showed him."

The missing pieces of the puzzle finally fell into place. The casual clothes, the lack of a wedding band. No one had even suspected that Lyle had a twin. "You killed him and the rest of your family," Rex said, clutching his shoulder to stem the blood flow. "Haven't you murdered enough people? You don't have to kill Hailey, too. Or should I call her Elsie?"

"Elsie?" A bitter laugh echoed from the man's chest. "She's not Elsie, she's Lindy Lou."

Shock hit Rex. Hailey was Lindy Lou Lyle? "That's impossible. Lindy Lou was autistic."

"Rumors." The man chuckled. "She used to rock herself back and forth when she got scared, go into this sullen shell. That's all it took for people to believe she had a mental disorder."

And he'd never let his wife bring her into town because she wasn't his real child. What a coldhearted bastard.

"Stop this insanity," Rex said. "You'll never get away with it."

"I have for twenty years." He waved the gun around. "And she has to die. She ruined my marriage. My entire life. I've had to hide in an old cabin the past few years, dependent on someone else to send me money."

Rex swayed. His body was slowly numbing from blood loss. He didn't have much longer. The ground twirled beneath his feet. The world faded in and out, turning black. But he had to keep Lyle talking, stall until Cohen arrived. He didn't want to kill Hailey's father in front of her.

"Who helped you?" Rex asked. "Who sent you money?"

"Carl Pursley," Lyle admitted. "Of course I had to share half my fortune with him to keep his mouth shut." Lyle aimed the gun at the grave.

No, he couldn't let him kill Hailey. Rex didn't hesitate. He fired, once, twice, three times, his arm jerking in response as Lyle's body bounced backward and collapsed onto the ground.

A low keening followed.

He coughed, feeling the gurgle of blood in his throat as he dragged himself forward. His heart stopped at the sight of Hailey lying in the hole, half covered with dirt and snow and debris, her eyes wide with terror. Rage took control, churning up every last vestige of strength and determination he had as he dropped to his knees. He shoved the dirt away with his bare hands, flinging it onto the trees, onto Lyle's body. A siren roared in the distance as he reached for her hands and pulled her up from the hole. He yanked the rag from her mouth, then untied the ropes binding her hands and feet. Hailey was shaking, going into shock. He folded her into his arms, then felt himself losing consciousness.

Hailey cried out his name, sobbing into his hair. He clung to her, tried to tell her that he loved her, but he was too weak to form the words. Then he drifted into the darkness.

THE AMBULANCE RIDE to the hospital lasted forever, but the long hours Hailey waited for news about Rex's surgery dragged by even slower. Every second she waited, she saw the blood gushing from his body and head, felt his strong body collapse against her. She was so afraid he was going to die. That she'd lose him forever.

And it was all because of her. Just as her mother and uncle and brother had died because of her.

Tears streaked her cheeks, the pain crushing her chest nearly unbearable. She'd lost her family years ago, had been in such shock that she'd completely repressed memories of her identity and what had happened. Even when she'd moved into the house and the memories had crept back in, she'd convinced herself she was watching the murders through someone else's eyes. Dissociation. She'd read about it, but hadn't realized she'd used it as a coping skill herself. Her family was gone. There was nothing to do now but mourn them.

But Rex had to live.

If he did, though, how could he ever forgive her for the past? Her father had completely destroyed his family's life.

Except Lawrence Lyle wasn't her father....

Then who was?

And what had happened to her friend, Elsie Timmons?

A shiver coursed through her as more memories returned. Elsie had snuck over to play with her. They'd shared dolls and made mud pies, and Elsie had found the crawl space from her room to the attic and visited her when she was locked inside. Elsie had been her only friend....

Sheriff Cohen stepped into the waiting room and handed her a cup of coffee. Retelling the gruesome scene to Cohen on the ride over had only ingrained the details deeper into her mind. Details she had buried for twenty years. Details that had become blurred in her nightmares and with her foster care experiences.

"Lyle's going to make it," the sheriff said in a low voice.

She still couldn't believe he'd survived. "Did he talk?"

The sheriff nodded. "Said the other man was his twin brother. He came to take your mother and brother and you away."

"My uncle...he was trying to save us," Hailey said, tears lacing her voice. "But everyone else died." Everyone but her. She had escaped. Why? Guilt welled inside her throat. They had lost their lives protecting her.

"Did he tell you who my real father is?"

"Pursley, the attorney who represented Falcon," Cohen said. "Your mother had met with him to file for a divorce, but then Lyle scared the fool out of him. Later, he bribed him not to talk."

And he'd kept silent and allowed the wrong man to go to prison. He obviously hadn't wanted her, either. She swiped at the tears on her cheeks, telling herself it shouldn't hurt that he hadn't wanted her. "Where is he now?"

Cohen hesitated. "Dead. Lyle panicked when you came back and was afraid Pursley would talk so he put a bullet in his head."

Hailey's lungs ached. How could she mourn for a man she'd never known, for one who hadn't wanted her in the first place? He'd thought she'd died with her mother and brother and uncle, yet he'd still accepted a bribe and let her father go free for murder….

That kind of man she didn't even want to know.

Not like Rex…Rex was strong and stubborn and fought for what was right, even if it had almost cost him his life.

"Falcon thought Ralph Timmons might be your father. We put out an APB on him, but nothing's turned up yet."

"What about Elsie?"

Cohen turned away, a muscle ticking in his jaw. "Still missing. Those bones…they weren't hers—they were over fifty years old."

Hailey sighed in relief. At least there was a chance Elsie was still alive, that Deanna would see her beloved daughter again.

A young nurse rushed in. "Excuse me, Miss, are you waiting for news on Mr. Falcon?"

Hailey nodded, the lump in her throat too thick to talk.

"He's out of surgery now. The bullet managed to miss his vital organs, so he should be all right."

"Can I see him?"

"Just for a minute. He's in ICU."

Hailey nodded, clenched her hands beside her and followed the nurse. The drone of tubes and other hospital machinery echoed in the background, the hush of nurses' voices adding to the tension.

"Brace yourself, Miss, he looks pale and has several tubes attached."

"I understand." Hailey stepped behind the curtain, her heart squeezing at the sight of the wide bandage across his shoulder and upper chest. A smaller bandage covered his forehead, the bruises on his body already purple. Tubes protruded from his chest, and oxygen tubes and an IV pole were connected to him.

She inched closer to the bed, tentatively slipping her hand over his. His felt cold to the touch, his breathing slightly labored. "Rex, I'm so sorry for all the pain I've caused you and your family."

He didn't move, but his hand tightened, closed around hers. Then his eyes fluttered open for a second, and he tried to shake his head. Pain colored his expression, drawing his mouth into a taut line.

"I didn't remember who I was when I came here," she said, her voice strained. She couldn't let him think that she'd planned this, that she'd used him as he'd once believed. "I guess I was drawn to the house because of the past, but I didn't remember…." Her voice broke as memories bombarded her. "I wish I had remembered sooner, though. I could have told someone, gotten your father released, and the police could have caught the real killer."

Hailey pressed a hand to her mouth, the tears overflowing in spite of her effort to stem them.

His eyes fluttered open slightly. "Hailey," he said in a pained whisper, "Sorry, so sorry I didn't believe you."

"Shh." She pressed her finger to his lips. "You have to rest…."

"Want you to know—"

"Miss?" The nurse poked her head around the curtain. "I'm afraid you'll have to leave now. Mr. Falcon's family is here, and they've requested to see him."

Hailey froze. Rex's family. They must hate her.

The nurse pushed the curtain aside, and two large, intimidating men who resembled Rex approached, a small dainty woman with dark hair and dark eyes between them. The closeness of the family was obvious, their anxiety palpable.

And she was responsible for putting that worry in their eyes.

Her heart breaking, she slipped her hand from Rex's and fled down the hall. She couldn't face his family, not now. Maybe never.

Feeling desolate, she ran past the nurses, past the waiting room and the sheriff, then outside into the night. She had no idea where she would go, only that she was all alone again, just as she always had been.

Just as she always would be.

FIVE DAYS LATER, Rex's shoulder and head hurt like hell. But it was his heart that felt as if it had been broken. Even though his mother and brothers swarmed all over him, doting on him, and insisting he do nothing but rest now that they were back at Falcon Ridge, he couldn't help but want Hailey by his side. He wanted to talk to her and hold her and make love to her. She must feel so alone….

But Hailey had not returned to the hospital to see him, and hadn't contacted him since he'd been released from the hospital. He was almost certain he'd apologized, that he'd admitted he was sorry for not believing her about Jordan. Or had he been so drugged he'd only dreamed his apology? Had he hurt her so badly she couldn't forgive him?

Feeling restless, he stared out the window through the trees where her house had once sat. Now, all that remained were ashes and embers. The impact of the ruined home looked stark against the snowy white. How did Hailey feel about losing her home, the place where her family was murdered? Would she want to rebuild it?

Now he knew her identity, the episodes in the house seemed so clear. The nightmares that had plagued her, the ghosts in the house, had been real memories that had haunted her. Memories she'd obviously repressed as a traumatized child.

How was she coping with the truth? Worse, not only had she lost her family and witnessed the horror of their murders, but Cohen had told him that Pursley was her father. He apparently hadn't wanted Hailey, either.

What was she going to do now? He'd tried to find her, had asked his brothers to look for her. Had she left Tin City completely? Didn't she want to see him?

If so, why hadn't she come back to see him or phoned to at least let him know where she was?

Not that he blamed her if she had left the town or him. When he'd seen Lyle burying her alive, his rage had consumed him. He'd turned into a pure animal.

Had that animal part of him frightened her away forever?

"You should be lying down." His mother bustled in carrying a tray of coffee and cookies as if he were a child that needed tending. He forced a smile, then leaned forward, the dull pain from his wound rippling down his arm.

"See, you're hurting, son."

But the pain came from missing Hailey. Jeez, he'd never ached for a woman the way he did for her, never thought he needed one just to survive. When he'd woken and found her gone, he'd damn near thought he'd die.

The front door screeched open, and Rex tensed, hoping it was Hailey. But his brother Deke appeared at Rex's office door, Brack behind him. Then his father stepped from the shadows, his face cleanly shaven, his eyes wary as he entered the room.

Rex's lungs constricted at the look on his mother's face. He had listened to her cry every night for months after they'd arrested his father and hadn't been able to help her. He'd even been afraid that eventually she'd move on to find someone else. And sometimes, God help him, he'd even wanted her to, just so she could have someone to ease the loneliness that she lived with day and night. But the love and joy shining in her eyes confirmed that she'd never given up on her husband, that his father, like a few of the birds of prey, had mated for life.

Just as Rex believed he had.

Only he'd been too damn scared to admit it to Hailey. And now he might have lost her.

"Randolph." The softly spoken word held such feeling that his father's wide jaw strained for control.

"God, I've missed you," he whispered in a harsh voice. Then he strode into the room toward her, framed her face in his hands and kissed her.

Deke and Brack hooted and pounded each other on the back. Rex gripped the chair arm to stand, clutching at his bandaged chest. His brothers hurried to help him, but he waved them off, slowly sliding one foot forward until he reached his dad. Then the five of them clung together in a family circle that Rex would remember the rest of his life.

THE LAST FEW DAYS HAD BEEN some of the longest of Hailey's life. When she'd left the hospital, she'd been in a daze, suffering from shock from the ordeal with Lawrence Lyle, from learning the identity of her real father, from praying that Rex would be all right. But she'd finally wound up at one of the bed-and-breakfasts in town.

She'd collapsed in bed and slept the first twenty-four hours. Dreams and nightmares of her past had encroached on her sleep, though, the haunting reminder of all she'd lost and the horror of her family's murder as fresh in her mind as if it had happened the day before.

But occasionally a happy memory rose through the pain. Images flashed back in the darkness—her mother pushing her on the swing out back. Her older brother teasing her and pulling her hair. The three of them sharing a picnic in the woods, feeding the birds, sliding down the hill on handmade sleighs her brother fashioned from cardboard boxes.

And then there was her friend Elsie. Elsie had been brave, had slipped away from her parents to play with her. Had sung silly songs with her, had brought her the snow globe….

Hailey had gone to see Elsie's mother, relayed her remorse over Elsie's disappearance. She'd also given her hope that maybe one day she'd come back as Hailey had done. Maybe Rex or one of his brothers could find her….

She'd been staying with Deanna ever since, working up the nerve to see Rex, to ask him.

To tell him she loved him and beg him and his family for forgiveness.

The doorbell rang and she nearly jumped out of her skin. When she opened the door and found Rex on the other side, hope sprang through the darkness. For a long minute, they simply stood staring at one another, tension mounting. Finally Rex cleared his throat.

"Hailey, can we talk?"

She nodded, her heart in her throat.

"Come with me."

Unable to deny him anything, she let him drive her to his house. Seconds later, they walked around his gardens together. His eyes darkened as they raked over her. Part wariness, part Falcon man, part hunger.

Did he see her as an injured bird, a project, or did he love her?

Looking oddly uncomfortable, he turned and walked

to the window and removed one of the dream catchers from the overhang. She followed him, once again her gaze drawn to the intricate craftsmanship.

"I want you to have this," he said, gesturing toward the dream catcher she'd admired the first time she'd visited Falcon Ridge. "To chase away all your nightmares. To help you believe that dreams can come true." He searched her face. "Do you have dreams, Hailey?"

A tear pressed against her eyelid. She was stepping out on a limb, but she had to move forward, one way or the other. "I dream about being with you."

"God, sweetheart," he said in a ragged voice. "I've been dreaming of you, too." His eyes flickered with emotions, then he feathered her hair from her face. "I'm so sorry I didn't stand up for you, that I believed those stupid files. Jordan fabricated them all. I was afraid...."

"It wasn't your fault," Hailey whispered.

"I should have listened to my heart, Hailey. Instead I was scared, too busy throwing up walls, protecting myself."

"You were only a boy when you lost your father, Rex. I can understood your bitterness. And I see why you blame me...."

"I don't blame you. For God's sake, Hailey, you were only four, practically a baby, when your family was killed." He stroked her cheek with the pad of his thumb. "When I think of what you went through, what might have happened to you...."

"It's over now," she said softly, blinking back the moisture in her eyes. "And I'm the one who's sorry, Rex...I was afraid your family...that you'd hate me for what happened to your dad. If I'd remembered earlier, I could have testified, gotten your father released..." Her voice broke, the heartache still simmering below the surface. "I could have saved you so much pain and suffering."

"At least I had my brothers and mother." He cupped her face in his hands. "You were so small and alone. I'm surprised you even survived." He cleared his throat, his voice gruff. "And you remembered when you were ready."

"But then I got involved with Thad. I kept asking myself why I'd date someone who was so much like my father—"

He pressed a finger over her lips. "It doesn't matter."

"It does to me." She kissed his finger, then gazed into his eyes. "But I finally realized that's why I chose Thad, because he was like my dad. I was repeating the cycle."

"You broke it, though," Rex said. "It took courage to do that, Hailey." He threaded his fingers into her hair. "I love you, but I have to know that you're not afraid of me. I turned into an animal when I saw Lyle burying you alive, but you have to know that I'd never hurt you. Never."

"I do know that," Hailey whispered, seeing the insecurities in his eyes. "I saw the way you handle the birds, Rex." She flattened her palm against his cheek, her heart swelling with affection. "You're a healer, a rescuer. I love that about you."

He cleared his throat. "God, Hailey. I want you so much it hurts." Hunger flickered in his eyes, then he lowered his mouth and kissed her.

Hailey's heart raced as she fell into his arms. His lips moved over hers, claiming her with the passion and hunger that radiated from him with every touch. "I love you."

She returned the kiss with the same fervor, protesting that he was going to hurt himself when he picked her up and carried her deep into the woods. There, he spread his coat and they lay on the jacket in the cold. They cuddled and talked about living at Falcon Ridge, about planting a garden where her old house had once been or perhaps rebuilding the Victorian manor, and renting her a small space in town for her antiques business. Those decisions could wait. But their need for each other couldn't.

So they made love once again, the physical bond as they joined their bodies in the wilderness only cementing the loving bond of their hearts together.

Above them, the red-tailed hawk soared, gliding gracefully across the sky, its beauty a reflection of the peace and happiness she'd found with Rex. She had run away from Tin City years ago, run from the horrors of her past, from the dark memories that had plagued her, from the childhood she hadn't wanted to remember. But she had been drawn to return anyway.

And with Rex's love, she'd had the courage to slay the dragons that had chased her away and the ones that had brought her back. Here, she'd not only found peace and forgiveness, but true love—a love that had erased the dark shadows from both their souls and would keep them soaring into flight together, forever.

Beware…there will be another gothic romance next month from the ECLIPSE *series, with* Spellbound *by Rebecca York.*

Turn the page for a preview of this thrilling story…

Spellbound
by
Rebecca York

The moment she asked the way to Belle Vista, Morgan Kirkland knew she was in trouble.

The gas station attendant stiffened, and the good ol' boys who had been lounging on a bench next to the soda machine came to attention.

"Belle Vista? Why do you need to know the way to that place?" the guy in the greasy overalls demanded.

She wanted to tell him in a steel-edged voice that her reasons were none of his business. But since the Light Street Detective Agency had sent her here on an undercover assignment, she gave him a tentative smile.

The patch on his right front pocket said his name was Bubba. She'd read all about him in the notes her client, Andre Gascon, had sent to Baltimore. Bubba Arnette was a high school dropout who pumped gas during the day. When the sun went down, he illegally trapped alligators in the bayou.

Trying to sound friendly, she spouted her cover story. "Mr. Gascon has hired me to catalog the books in his library with a view to possibly selling off some of the collection."

"Oh, yeah? You a librarian?" he challenged, staring

at her with the smug eyes of a man who thinks that any guy is the superior of any female.

She looked up at him through the car window, picturing what he saw: a very nonthreatening individual; a woman with straight, chin-length blond hair, blue eyes and a slender frame draped in a conservative beige skirt and a persimmon-colored blouse.

What he couldn't see was the martial arts training, the marksmanship badges, the woman who had abandoned caution along with cream in her coffee.

Really, she'd like to meet this guy in a dark alley and teach him some manners.

She took in a breath of the hot, humid air and let it out before answering, "Yes, I'm a librarian." She might not have a degree in the field, but she'd just been through an intensive crash course. The consultants from Baltimore's famous Pratt Library had pronounced her fit to decide whether to go with the Dewey Decimal System or Library of Congress cataloging.

"Well, you don't want to work for a secretive bastard like Gascon. He's bad news," the local expert allowed.

"In what way?"

"You want to get murdered, you drive right up to his estate, *chère.*"

Morgan gave him a wide-eyed look. In a shaky voice, she asked, "Murdered?"

"Guys end up in the bayou out by his place. Face-down in the muck. Clawed by a jaguar," he answered, a nasty ring to his voice. Apparently he was enjoying telling horror stories to the little librarian.

"There's a jaguar in the swamp?" she asked in a quavering tone, pretending he'd had the desired effect, wishing she were free to wipe the smug smile off his weaselly face.

One of the good ol' boys, a guy in his fifties with thinning hair combed across his bald pate and an inner-tube belly hiding his belt, pushed himself off the bench and ambled over to join the conversation.

"Bubba here is just giving you some friendly advice." He fixed her with a piercing look. "My cousin Willie shoulda listened to him. Leastways if he didn't want to croak hisself."

"Thank you all for the warnings," she answered. "But Mr. Gascon has already given me a retainer. I need the money, and I'm not about to return it."

"Suit yourself, *chère*," Rubber Belly said. Probably he was Bob Mansard, cousin of Willie Mansard, who had indeed ended up clawed to death in the swamp. Until his demise, Willie had been one of the troublemakers in town. Bob seemed to be ripped from the same cloth.

Gascon had told her about the local men and about the cat legend. He'd characterized the guys in humorous terms. She'd gotten the "rubber belly" description from him. But he'd never joked about the big cat. He'd said the murderer was a man—a man wearing claws. And he had hired her to find out who it was.

researching the cure

The facts you need to know:

- **One woman in nine** in the United Kingdom will develop breast cancer during her lifetime.

- Each year **40,700** women are newly diagnosed with breast cancer and around **12,800** women will die from the disease. However, survival rates are improving, with on average 77 per cent of women still alive five years later.

- **Men can also suffer from breast cancer**, although currently they make up less than one per cent of all new cases of the disease.

Britain has one of the highest breast cancer death rates in the world. Breast Cancer Campaign wants to understand why and do something about it. Statistics cannot begin to describe the impact that breast cancer has on the lives of those women who are affected by it and on their families and friends.

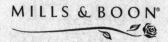

▼ SILHOUETTE®
INTRIGUE™

FULL EXPOSURE by Debra Webb

Colby Agency: Internal Affairs

Cole Dane's investigation revealed the unimaginable – Angel Parker had been leaking information about the agency. But the more time he spent with her, the more he came to believe in her innocence, and to realise their attraction could prove fatal.

PATERNITY UNKNOWN by Jean Barrett

Top Secret Babies

A year after their passionate night together, Ethan Brand was back to find Lauren McCrea, the woman he couldn't forget. When Lauren's daughter was kidnapped, Ethan began a desperate search. But would he forgive Lauren when he learned the child was his?

BRIDAL RECONNAISSANCE by Lisa Childs

Dead Bolt

When Evan Quade tracked down his amnesiac wife, Amanda, he got the shock of his life – she'd given birth to his son. Now she was determined to face the threat of a madman's revenge alone. But Evan couldn't abandon his family…

SPELLBOUND by Rebecca York

Eclipse

Someone was trying to frame Andre Gascon for murder, so he turned to the Light Street Detective Agency for help. But PI Morgan Kirkland realised she would have to unearth enigmatic Andre's secrets, before they became the next victims…

All these thrilling books are on sale from 21st October 2005

Available at most branches of WHSmith, Tesco, ASDA, Borders, Eason, Sainsbury's and most bookshops

Visit our website at www.silhouette.co.uk

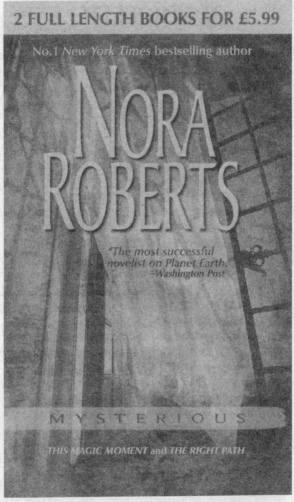

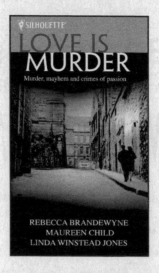

2 FREE

BOOKS AND A SURPRISE GIFT!

We would like to take this opportunity to thank you for reading this Silhouette® book by offering you the chance to take TWO more specially selected titles from the Intrigue™ series absolutely FREE! We're also making this offer to introduce you to the benefits of the Reader Service™—

- ★ **FREE home delivery**
- ★ **FREE gifts and competitions**
- ★ **FREE monthly Newsletter**
- ★ **Exclusive Reader Service offers**
- ★ **Books available before they're in the shops**

Accepting these FREE books and gift places you under no obligation to buy, you may cancel at any time, even after receiving your free shipment. Simply complete your details below and return the entire page to the address below. You don't even need a stamp!

YES! Please send me 2 free Intrigue books and a surprise gift. I understand that unless you hear from me, I will receive 4 superb new titles every month for just £3.05 each, postage and packing free. I am under no obligation to purchase any books and may cancel my subscription at any time. The free books and gift will be mine to keep in any case.

15ZED

Ms/Mrs/Miss/Mr ....Initials ....

BLOCK CAPITALS PLEASE

Surname ....

Address ....

....

....Postcode..

Send this whole page to:
UK: FREEPOST CN81, Croydon, CR9 3WZ